A COUNTRY APART

When Niki reached for the handle on the passenger door, Cary leaned across, stopping her. "I had fun tonight. Did you?"

"Yes."

That one word spoke volumes. He dared to hope. "What are we going to do about us?"

"There is no us."

She was sending mixed messages again. Inside the club, they'd danced as one. Frustrated, Cary exploded. "What's the problem? I'm not good enough? Or are you just determined to ignore the chemistry between us?"

"So what if we do connect?"

What did it take to get through to her? He tried again. "Is it every day you find someone who turns you on physically and mentally? Is it that easy to find a compatible mate? Someone who likes your son and he likes her back?"

He had no right to pursue this. No hold on her. Maybe if he told her what he did for a living, that would make the difference.

She turned back to him, her voice low. "What would be the point of our embarking on a relationship? I live in San Francisco, and I have to start thinking about getting back." *And dealing with the threats again.*

"Sounds like a good excuse. Make geography an issue. Is it that you're scared of becoming too attached? Emotionally dependent on me?"

"Maybe."

Cary folded her into his arms. Her entire body quivered. "Don't be scared," he said. "Get rid of the stone wall around your heart and give me passage."

Before she could utter another word, he kissed her . . .

BOOK YOUR PLACE ON OUR WEBSITE AND MAKE THE ARABESQUE ROMANCE CONNECTION!

We've created a customized website just for our very special Arabesque readers, where you can get the inside scoop on everything that's going on with Arabesque romance novels.

When you come online, you'll have the exciting opportunity to:

- View covers of upcoming books

- Learn about our future publishing schedule (listed by publication month and author)

- Find out when your favorite authors will be visiting a city near you

- Search for and order backlist books

- Check out author bios and background information

- Send e-mail to your favorite authors

- Join us in weekly chats with authors, readers and other guests

- Get writing guidelines

- AND MUCH MORE!

Visit our website at
http://www.arabesquebooks.com

A REASON TO LOVE

Marcia King-Gamble

ARABESQUE

BET BOOKS

BET Publications, LLC
www.bet.com
www.arabesquebooks.com

ACKNOWLEDGMENTS

I would like to thank some key people for making this book happen. My special thanks to Steve Williams and Karen Adair for their medical expertise. Thank you, fellow authors, Linda Anderson, Marilyn Jordan, and Debra St. Amand. You were, as always, a great help. Thank you, Buf, for helping me with an essential part of the plot and for reminding me why trust is so important. A great big thank-you to Chuck for putting up with me during this challenging time.

Chapter 1

"Get your butt on a plane, Niki," Kim Morgan shouted into the receiver. "That's an order, girl."

Even though Onika Hamilton felt as if the earth were crumbling under her feet and she were sinking fast, she managed a watery smile. The much married Kimberly Morgan-Smith-Goldberg-Daniels-Rosellini-Morgan was an original. They'd bonded from the moment they'd shared a suite at Mount Merrimack College with two other coeds, Lisa Williams and Charlie Canfield.

Even now, with their lives taking them in different directions, the four women remained close. Theirs was a friendship destined to last a lifetime. Now, twenty-one years later, with the whole country separating them, not much had changed. They were still best buds.

Niki ran a trembling hand across her forehead. She

could swing it, she supposed. She was overdue for a vacation, and San Francisco and New Jersey weren't that far apart. The four-and-a-half-hour flight would go quickly, giving her time to catch up on her reading. Kim's effervescent personality and call-them-as-she-saw-them attitude would have her laughing again. Her flamboyant girlfriend would be a refreshing change from the sterile hospital personalities whose conversations centered around prognoses and diagnoses. Kim's down-to-earth repartee would be salve for a beaten-down soul.

"So what do you say, girlfriend?" Kim's voice pulled her back to the present. "Call your travel agent. Get her to find a good fare. Come to New Jersey. Long Branch is crawling with tourists this summer, and, girl, the men are finer than fine. Business at Coffee Mates is percolating." Kim laughed at her weak joke. "Who knows, we might even find you a mate."

Despite not feeling particularly happy, Niki chuckled.

"Now that sounds more like the old Niki," Kim said. "Seriously, girl, I could use the company. There's a place on Monmouth Beach with our names on it. Break out the piña coladas and coconut oil, Kim and Niki are here." Kim cackled again.

"All right, all right. You've convinced me. I have two weeks coming. Shoot, I may even put in for an extended leave."

"An extended leave? Something's seriously wrong, girl. Better tell Auntie Kim about it."

Niki took a deep breath and reined in her emotions. If she could deliver the news in the same detached manner she'd been forced to earlier, maybe she'd make it through without crying. Still, it never got easier, no matter how often she did it. And in this particular case it shouldn't have happened.

"Niki?"

"I lost a patient today."

"Oh, Nik. That's awful. Would it help to talk?"

Counting on her professionalism to get her through, she took a couple of deep breaths and told the story—omitting the threats.

"Well, what do you think?" Arms wide, Kim twirled in the middle of her remodeled Victorian home.

"It's lovely, Kim. Definitely you." Niki set her bags down in the foyer before stepping into the spacious living room. She took her time looking around. Kim had filled every possible spot with an eclectic assortment of antiques, some quite valuable, from what Niki could tell.

"You'll be sleeping upstairs. Let's put your bags away and we'll go to Asbury Park and hit The Stone Pony."

Niki followed Kim up the winding mahogany stairway and into a bedroom that was out of Africa. A huge four-poster bed, complete with mosquito netting, dominated the room. Framed National Geographic covers hung on the walls. Niki trailed a finger across animal print wallpaper. Trust Kim to create a bedroom that was an exotic haven.

"In here's the bathroom," Kim said. "I'll be back in ten."

After Kim left, Niki walked around the room. A comfortable-looking divan draped in zebra skin sat off to the side. An antique secretary held jars of quills and cleverly rolled parchments. A quick visit to the bathroom revealed a huge claw-footed tub and an oversized wash basin with brass fixtures.

Slowly Niki began to relax. This was a far cry from her underfurnished town house on Nob Hill, with its white-on-white furniture and unending chrome. Kim's house, like its owner, was unique, warm, and welcoming.

Niki took a moment to splash water across her face, powder her freckles, then add a dash of lipstick. She settled her horn-rimmed glasses firmly in place, shook the pins from her hair, and debated whether to twist it back into its familiar knot. At the last minute she decided to leave it down. No one in Long Branch—or Asbury Park, for that matter—knew who Dr. Onika Hamilton was. Nor would they care.

"Ready?" Kim was back.

"Ready."

Kim eyed Niki coyly. "Love the hair. You should wear it down more often. Now open a couple of buttons on that blouse. Flaunt that cleavage."

Niki ignored Kim and ran a hand self-consciously through her auburn tresses. "The look's not too ingenue?"

"Hell, honey, what if it is? You and I are both over forty, but who would even guess? Black skin doesn't age. Course, yours is more like yellow. Still, black skin it is."

Seated in Kim's lipstick-red Saab, top down, they took the Ocean Avenue route into Asbury. It was well after eight, but twilight hadn't yet descended. Niki feasted her eyes on expensive homes, miles of sandy beach, and vast expanses of ocean. Feeling the tension leave her body, she drank in deep breaths of briny air and watched the wind ruffle Kim's braids. Previous visits to New Jersey hadn't prepared her for this. Her other trips had been limited to industrial towns like Newark and Elizabeth. By far, this was a different world. Kim pulled up across the street from an unimpressive building.

"We're here," she announced. She gestured to Niki's still tightly buttoned blouse. "Come on, give us access to Fort Knox."

Niki compromised by releasing one button. Side-stepping the idling traffic, they hustled across the street.

"Maybe we'll run into Bruce or his sax player, Clarence Clemens. They're supposed to be out tonight," Kim said in hushed tones. "Did I tell you The Stone Pony's where those guys got their start? Ummm, honey, that Clarence is one fine man."

"Isn't he up there in age?" Niki quipped.

"And so are we, honey. So are we. Anyone asks, we're twenty-nine, OK?"

Niki simply nodded and followed her friend into the dark interior.

All the music and smoke was making Cary Thomas's head pound. What had possessed him to accept this invitation? Curiosity, that's what, plus the possibility of becoming reacquainted with members of the E Street band.

Aaron, his buddy since nursery school and owner of a successful pharmacy, had mentioned Bruce might be playing tonight. That home boy had never forgotten his roots, and whenever he was in town, he stopped by to jam. In anticipation of seeing Bruce, Cary had left Brett at home with a baby-sitter. Now here he was sitting in a smoke-filled room, shooting the breeze with his embittered friend. If he heard one more complaint about mercenary women, he'd call it a night.

"Look what just walked in," Aaron said, his eyes focused on the entrance.

Cary followed the salivating man's gaze. A stately dark-skinned woman with a head of intricate braids bore down on them. She and her friend took the vacant table opposite. Her light-skinned companion seemed uncomfortable.

"Check out the size of those . . ." Aaron swallowed hard.

Cary cleared his throat. ". . . braids."

Aaron sucked his teeth. "You turn into a monk or something, Thomas? They're way over the age of consent."

"That might be the case. But women deserve to be treated with respect."

"Yeah, right."

Cary didn't trust himself to say another word. Aaron was a pig, and nothing would change that. He'd come to pick up women, while Cary was there to hear Bruce sing and get reacquainted with Clarence.

"Lighten up," Aaron said. "Just suck down the brewskies and ogle the women."

Cary focused his attention on the two women, who were busy giving orders to a hovering waitress. On second glance, he recognized the woman with braids. Kimberly Morgan, ex-Playboy bunny and owner of the dating service Coffee Mates, was one of his best customers. She paid her bills on time and never tried to get something for nothing.

Kim must have sensed him staring. She looked over, grinned, and waved. She'd always been the friendly type, just a bit too loud for his liking. Aaron immediately began preening. Typical male, his hormones had gone into overdrive.

"Hi." Kim pushed back her chair and started over. Erect, she was close to six feet and definitely regal in bearing. Aaron went for that type.

"Nice to see you." Cary took the hand she offered. "Are you pleased with the job my guys are doing?" His gaze shifted to her companion. "Cary Thomas," he shouted over the din.

The woman's smile wasn't exactly warm or welcoming. It reminded him of a cool ocean breeze, skimming across his skin and getting the goose bumps going. "Onika Hamilton," she said in clipped, modulated tones.

"Niki's visiting from out of town," Kim added. "And yes, I'm pleased. My yard's turning out just the way I want it."

Her companion was British. How intriguing. He even liked her name.

Cary introduced his friend. Kim acted as if Aaron was the only one who mattered. His buddy practically drooled all over himself.

"Can we buy you and your friend a drink?" Aaron quickly inserted.

"We've just ordered. Make room. We'll come over." Kim strutted away, leaving Aaron salivating.

Surreptitiously, Cary glanced at Kim's light-skinned companion. She had auburn hair and hid behind horn-rimmed glasses. Hard to hide classic good looks or the dusting of freckles liberally sprinkled across her nose. She sensed his scrutiny and self-consciously toyed with the one button she'd managed to leave open.

His reaction—or rather his attraction—surprised him. His taste usually ran to dark-skinned women, women who were clearly African-American.

Kim seemed to be having a difficult time convincing her companion to join them. Not good. He wanted to hear Niki's voice, see if she had something to say. Intelligent women were a turn-on.

At last Niki Hamilton rose, albeit reluctantly. Purse in hand, she followed on Kim's heels.

Shifting, the men made room. Aaron somehow managed to secure two chairs, and Cary found himself squished in next to Niki. More drinks were ordered all around.

On stage, the local group, though loud, had promise. Out on the dance floor, blue-collar types bumped hips with neighborhood Rumson yuppies, an eclectic customer base if ever there was one. But this was The Pony.

"So how come I haven't seen you here before?" Aaron said to Kim.

Not exactly original. My boy can do better than toss out that sorry line.

"You haven't been looking," Kim shot back.

"Ah, but I have. And I would have remembered."

Kim shook her braids and eyed him coyly. "I bet you say that to all the women."

"Not all the women. Just the finer ones."

Oh, God!

Niki, listening to the repartee, seemed clearly bored. Cary attempted to include her in the conversation. "How about you? You come here often?"

Now that was just plain lame.

"No. I'm from out of town."

There was that delightful British accent again, the one he could listen to forever.

"You're a visitor? Where from?"

"San Francisco."

"It's my favorite city." That was no lie.

"You've been there?" She seemed mildly astonished, even surprised that he traveled. Clearly she didn't think much of him.

"Many times." He could have told her he'd gotten his master's at Stanford, but he chose not to elaborate.

"Another round?" their waitress inquired.

Cary declined, choosing instead to nurse the lukewarm gin and tonic he'd originally ordered. The others, with the exception of Niki, who was still sipping her wine, placed their orders. He watched her finger the beeper clipped to the waist of her linen slacks. Why would anyone wear a beeper to The Pony? You could hardly hear your voice over the noise.

Kim and Aaron were deep in conversation. Apparently now the world revolved around them.

"What's with the beeper?" Cary asked.

Niki shrugged. "Lots of people wear them."

"Yes. Health-care professionals, drug dealers, airline employees." He ticked the list off on his fingers. "Just nod when I come to the right one."

"I'm none of those." She offered no further explanation.

"You're a computer technician? Working mom? Off-duty cop?"

Niki threw him an evasive smile. "You're way off base."

Trying to get her to open up, his answering smile was designed to be encouraging. "Help me out, then."

"Why is what I do so important to you?"

He reached across the table and removed the wine glass from her hand. "Relax. We're making small talk. It's called getting to know each other."

"Some would call it being nosy."

"You're brutal," Cary said, trying to make light of the put-down.

Niki flushed.

Careful to keep his expression bland, he sipped on his gin and tonic. Maybe Niki just didn't like men. Kim didn't seem to have that problem. She was yakking at Aaron a mile a minute, tossing back those long braids, flirting up a storm. Plainly he'd lost his touch.

The moment the words flew from her mouth, Niki regretted them. Asking her about her beeper wasn't exactly crossing the line. Pure force of habit had made her clip her pager on before leaving the house. Though she was unofficially off call, it remained an essential part of her wardrobe.

The white guy seated next to her seemed nice enough, and she had to admit he was good looking. She just wasn't in the mood for trivial conversation. Besides, volunteering what she did for a living would only lead to questions. Medicine wasn't a topic she wished to discuss—not tonight and not with him. Still, she could at least have been civil.

"You're awfully quiet." Kim's voice intruded.

Her friend's attention had been momentarily diverted from the olive-skinned man with the goatee, the one built like a quarterback who'd introduced himself as Aaron.

"I'm fine."

Niki caught Cary's searching glance, but refused to give him the time of day. What would be the point? She hadn't come to New Jersey looking for a man, especially this one. The crowd here seemed simple, hard-working folks, mostly blue and pink collar. Why encourage friendships that had no place to go? Besides, past experience had demonstrated men couldn't handle a relationship with her. She was too successful and too busy. They felt she didn't need them.

She sipped on her drink and ventured a look over the rim. Cary stared back at her. Smiling, he raised his glass in a quiet salute. He had lovely eyes—not exactly brown, more like whiskey. The tempo of the music picked up and she looked away. Still no sign of Bruce or the old E Street band.

"Want to dance?" Cary asked.

God, he never gave up. "Dance?"

"Usually that's what one does to music."

In spite of her vow not to encourage him, she chuckled.

"You should do that more often," Cary said.

"Did I hear you say dance?" Kim was already up, dragging Aaron with her. Together they headed for the floor.

Cary set down his glass and held out his hand. Niki surprised herself by taking it.

"Laughter's good for the soul," he said. "So is dancing."

Chapter 2

"Oh, no! Tell me she's not ..." Kim hugged the receiver, looked to the ceiling, and blinked. Even so, tears trickled down her cheeks.

Niki, guessing something was very wrong, moved in closer. Irrepressible Kim, crying? She placed a hand on the nape of Kim's neck and massaged gently. "You OK?"

"No, I'm not. Hold on a moment." She covered the mouthpiece with her palm and turned to Niki. "My sister's calling from Florida. My mother had a stroke."

"Oh, Kim. How is she? She's not ..."

"She's alive." Kim sniffed. "But one side's paralyzed and she has trouble speaking."

"With intensive therapy and some prayer she *will* make a full recovery. What hospital is she in? I have connections at the better ones. I'll call, if that helps."

Niki hoped Kim's mom, like so many seniors, hadn't subscribed to an HMO. Admittedly she was biased, but her experiences with managed care had left her soured. The supposed money saved wasn't money well spent. Things might be different in Florida, but she doubted it.

"Of course I'll come," she heard Kim say. "I'll just have to find someone to run Coffee Mates."

Niki tugged on the back of Kim's black silk shirt. "I'm here."

Kim again covered the mouthpiece and shot her a puzzled look. "I hate to leave you alone, but I have to do this. This is my mother we're talking about."

"I said *I'm* here, Kim. We've always watched each other's backs. I'll gladly watch yours now."

What Niki meant finally dawned on Kim. "*You* run Coffee Mates?" Her expression was priceless. "You're kidding." A chuckle broke through the torrent of tears.

"Hey, what's so funny? I work at a large hospital. I deal with humanity at its worst. If I can handle arrogant doctors who think they're God, I can run a dating service."

Kim kept laughing. "You'll find out it's not that easy. Some of my clients are extremely difficult. Others are downright bizarre."

"Similar to patients. Now what do I do? Chat the customers up a bit, get basic information, match one lonely heart up with another?"

Kim rolled her eyes. "If only it were that simple. I'm only agreeing because I'm desperate. Be sure to let me know how easy it is when I get back." She returned to the person on the other end. "I'll be on the next flight to Miami. Have someone pick me up at the airport. Don't forget to feed Scarlet," she said to Niki in parting.

"Don't worry. Your cat won't starve."

After Kim left, Niki perused the list of instructions she'd

left behind. In the time it took to get her clothing together, Kim had tried to explain the business. The way it worked, potential candidates filled out a detailed application, then were interviewed and later videotaped. Kim screened all candidates personally, and two part-time college students answered phones.

"It's my credibility on the line. I want to see the candidates myself and ask them questions. That way I can plow through the BS," Kim had explained.

"Is there that much misrepresentation?"

"You'll see." Her friend had nodded sagely.

Niki clicked her tongue. Kim so often exaggerated.

Kim snorted. "You're out of touch, honey. Too much time spent doctoring. These men call up telling you they're finer than sliced pumpernickel, and when you see them they're stale bread."

Trust Kim to provide the visuals. Niki turned her attention to the appointment book. Scarlet, the office cat, purred contentedly at her feet. Kim had said there would be walk-ins. With three face-to-face interviews scheduled, tomorrow promised to be busy. To add to that, she had to videotape prospects for a stockbroker claiming to be too busy to wine and dine losers.

His instructions were specific: *Get me only women who look good on my arm.* By that he meant leggy and with good hair. Since he was shelling out big bucks, Kim had implored Niki to keep her opinions to herself. Kids were starving in Angola, but money was being thrown away by jerks.

Although it was well past midnight, Niki didn't feel the slightest bit tired. She'd had years of practice functioning on coffee and very little sleep. Pediatricians were never off call, and Niki was one of those rare doctors who still made house calls. She'd told the hospital to beep her if any of her patients needed her. For something to do, she turned on the computer and began scrutinizing Kim's files.

One attorney was on the hunt for a woman with nice feet. Not just any old feet, mind you, but ones where the second toe was slightly longer than the first. A madman, she decided. As she scrolled down further, another photo and bio popped up. A full-figured woman with a wild mass of store-bought hair basked in a minuscule bikini. Her Mr. Right had to be lanky—over six feet and not a pound over one-fifty. Niki continued to scroll, becoming more and more convinced Kim's customers weren't playing with a full deck.

The jingling phone got her attention. At that late hour, she was tempted to let the machine pick up. It had to be Kim or someone from the hospital. No one else knew she was here, certainly not the person threatening her. Niki answered on the fifth ring.

"Kim?" a resonant male voice queried. "Carett Designs here. Sorry to call so late, but I thought I'd just leave a message on your machine. Several of my guys have the flu and I'm doing my best to keep my promises. Your flowers won't be there by nine, but they will be there."

The man hung up before she could tell him she wasn't Kim. Leaving Scarlet behind, Niki poured herself a glass of spring water, grabbed a pile of applications, and made her way upstairs.

Cary Thomas helped his men unload the last of the plants from his pickup truck. After removing his dirty gloves, he slapped them against his jeans, dislodging the last remnants of soil.

"Make sure those pots are lined up neatly and out of

the way," he instructed, heading for the gate leading to Kim's front yard.

It was almost midafternoon before he'd been able to break away and make Kim's delivery. The summer flu had most of his employees flat on their backs, and overnight he'd become both boss and landscaper. Good thing he didn't have a problem getting his hands dirty. His willingness to do most everything had gained him the respect of his employees. What was the old adage? An honest day's work kept one humble and in touch.

Cary had started off the day answering phones. Later he'd checked on the few remaining men who'd made it to work. He'd gone back and forth to stores and nurseries, picking up sod and buying yard art and assorted materials for a goldfish pond. One did what one had to do under the circumstances. He'd worked too hard to make Carett a success to let a few sick men ruin his credibility.

He pressed the buzzer on the side door and waited impatiently for an answer. A large brass sign announced Kim's business—COFFEE MATES. *What a crazy world we live in,* he thought. At thirty-eight, he couldn't imagine placing an ad or paying for someone's company. But Kimberly Morgan had made a successful living of matching people up, so why knock it? Her Victorian home on the river was testimony, as was her imported automobile.

Cary glanced at his watch and pressed the buzzer again. He could stick the invoice in her mailbox, he supposed, but he preferred to hand it to her in person. That way they could straighten out any discrepancies on the spot. Brett needed to be picked up from baseball practice, and he had to stop by the Klein place. His wealthy Deal clients needed their Oriental garden done in time for their son's bar mitzvah.

The door sprang open and Cary's mouth dropped. "Umm . . . I . . ."

"Yes?" Niki inquired.

"Well . . . uh . . ."

"Having a hard time with words?"

Tart. Spirited. The way he liked women. What an unexpected bonus to have Kim's houseguest greet him in person.

"I'm here to see Kim." Cary's breathing became shallow all of a sudden.

"She's not here. She got called away on an emergency." On second glance, Niki seemed harried, not at all her cool self.

Her accent sounded more clipped than he remembered. More British, too. Had he made that much of an impression on her? He hoped so.

"I wanted to tell her . . ."

"That you're signing up at Coffee Mates?" Her hazel eyes did another rapid inspection of him. Niki actually wrinkled her nose. He'd come up lacking.

Cary was so taken back by her assumption, he simply stared.

"You might as well come in," she said, grudgingly. "There's paperwork that needs to be completed."

What picture did he paint in his grimy blue jeans, soiled T-shirt, and battered hiking boots? Cary ran a hand through his wild mass of curls. Boy, he needed a haircut badly.

Folding the invoice, he placed it in his back pocket. Obviously Niki saw him as a potential client. Here was the perfect opportunity to get to know her better. Might as well play along.

Cary followed Niki into Kim's charming little waiting room filled with white wicker and hanging ferns. The smoky smell of vanilla candles scented the air. Seated on the ledge of a bay window, a big red cat gazed down on the manicured lawn. It was Cary's job to change the look of that lawn and transform it into a tamed jungle.

"Have a seat," Niki said, pointing to an antique settee. "Better dust off those denims before you do. I'll be with you in a moment." She plopped down at a computer and began typing. After several minutes she printed the document, retrieved it, and thrust a pen and clipboard at him.

"Now write legibly. I'll be happy to explain anything you don't understand."

He attached the paper to the board, glancing at it briefly. An application with some very prying questions. The phone rang. On the fifth ring, Niki jerked her heavy horn-rimmed glasses off and planted them on top of her head. "Someone better bloody well answer that," she shouted into the back room. The ringing ceased immediately. Focusing on him again, she offered as explanation, "College kids. Do you need help with that mess?"

This was going to be fun. "Sure. Walk me through it."

Plopping down beside him, yet careful not to make contact, she crossed one leg over the other. The faint smell of citrus shampoo tickled his nostrils. What was it about this woman that got to him? Was it her controlling manner or her glib attitude? What could have happened in her life to make her so tough? He loved her processed light brown hair and the dusting of freckles trailing across her nose. Her laughter, rare as it was, had been infectious the other night.

He'd hazard a guess she was biracial. Although he was two generations removed, it did take one to know one. Based on his own physical appearance, few ever guessed him to be the product of African-American parents. He looked whiter than white, and his summer tan did little to change that.

Cary's extremely light skin, wavy black hair, and high cheekbones had once been the bane of his existence. Now he used it to his advantage. Since people felt free to say things they wouldn't dare if they knew he was black, he felt equally free to put them in their place and turn down their business. He didn't need money that badly.

Niki cleared her throat. Cary realized he'd drifted off. She waited quietly. Her creamy skin was devoid of makeup; her startling hazel eyes held the slightest tinge of green. She was a very attractive woman without her glasses. Underneath that shapeless sundress was a body most women would envy. He'd held that body the other night. Now she acted as though she didn't remember.

Niki sidled even closer. Her face scrunched in concentration, she placed the prim-looking glasses back on her nose and scrutinized his application. He was tempted to reach over and pluck off the disfiguring spectacles.

"Let's start with the first question. Write your name. That should be simple." Niki handed him back the clipboard.

He wrote down his age, phone number, and some basic statistics. "We met the other night."

"Yes, I know," she said dismissively. "Now fill in your race." She pointed to the question.

He hid a smile and checked the African-American box. Ignoring her puzzled frown and surreptitious inspection of him, he continued to jot responses.

"What are you looking for in a woman?" Niki's finger pointed out yet another question.

What *was* he looking for in a woman? He hadn't given it much thought lately. The better part of eight years had been devoted to building a business and fighting for custody of Brett.

"Trophy? Helpmate? Companion? Fun?" Niki's words came at him like bullets.

"Intellect," he answered, writing it down.

"That's a new one."

"You don't think intelligence adds something to a woman's appeal?" He scanned her face, trying to read her thoughts. She refused to make eye contact.

"Could have fooled me. I thought it was bra size," she muttered.

"What was that?" Her cynicism hadn't been lost on him. His fingers circled her wrist. "You never let up, do you? What's happened to make you so jaded?"

She flushed, tugged her arm away, and again focused on the questions. "What about looks? Did you have a particular height, weight, or physical attribute in mind?"

"I'm here at Coffee Mates. Obviously I'm looking for a woman who shares my ethnic background. I'm more interested in what she has to offer intellectually than the surface stuff."

Her hazel eyes flickered over him briefly. He'd gotten her attention. Aroused her curiosity.

He continued, "I like smart women. Smart enough to know that having a personal life is more important than a high-profile career. I'm fine with a homemaker. If she comes with a couple of kids, all the better. She'll be more understanding of the time I commit to Brett."

"Who's Brett?"

He'd definitely gotten her attention now.

"Brett's my son," he said, standing and reaching for the wallet in his back pocket. He removed his son's picture and handed it over.

She scrutinized the photo before returning it. "Cute kid."

"Yes, he is. Of course, Dad's somewhat biased."

"And has every reason to be."

Under her hardened exterior lay a practiced diplomat. Niki even managed a smile. God, he wished she would smile more often. It totally transformed her features, making her look more attractive as well as vulnerable and human. While most people had a hard time believing the brown-skinned eight year old with the tight cap of curly hair was his, Niki hadn't even blinked.

Delivering bad news to already stressed parents had taught Niki to keep her expressions neutral and her voice even. Cary's ethnic background had come as a complete surprise—not that she didn't know blacks came in a range of colors, everything from Native American red to ebony.

Looking at the child's photo had reminded her of the patient she'd lost, the little Eldridge boy. Todd had been around Brett's age. There was no reason the child should have died except for the HMO's stalling. Managed care had ruled her treatment experimental, and so it had not been approved. All the second guessing on their part and all the fact gathering, phone calls, and letters on hers had taken time. Valuable time. The little boy had finally succumbed to cancer, leaving behind two brokenhearted parents who probably blamed her for not doing enough. After that, the threatening phone calls had begun.

Niki felt Cary's eyes on her. Time to pull herself together.

"How are you doing with your application?" she asked, trying to sound nonchalant. That awesome body and GQ face were beginning to get to her.

"I'm almost done."

He jotted another sentence and handed over the paper.

Niki felt the slightest twinge of guilt as she accepted his application. Out of bizarre curiosity, she'd doctored some of the questions. She spot-checked his answers, focusing on the ones about income and career. A laborer didn't make much. How could he possibly afford Kim's exorbitant fee? Thank God for MasterCard, she supposed.

Her eyebrows rose slightly when she saw the staggering amount he claimed to make. He'd even called himself a landscape designer. It ranked right up there with the garbage collector who considered himself a sanitation engineer. Earlier, when she'd looked out the window, he'd been hauling plants out of the back of a pickup truck. Some designer. Gardener didn't have the same cachet, obviously. Now she understood what Kim meant by misrepresentation.

Niki crossed over to the desk and retrieved a Coffee Mates card. "You'll need a picture to go with your application, and our next step is to get you on tape. Call me in a day or two and we can set up a time."

As he accepted the card, his fingers brushed hers. She was surprised by the static electricity sizzling between them. Quickly she withdrew her hand and stuffed it into her pocket. The flutter in her gut had to be this morning's breakfast repeating itself. Cary's whiskey-colored eyes scrutinized her, and she stared back.

No, Niki, this is not happening. You will not fall for another pretty boy, a charmer like your ex-husband. You will not let your guard down and allow another operator to worm his way into your life.

"I'll be in touch," Cary said. If you need me call me. You have my number."

"Likewise."

She watched his broad shoulders and dusty denim-clad behind as he went out the door. Gardener or not, his body was bound to make some woman happy.

Not her.

Chapter 3

"Dad, Dad, you'll never guess what happened!" Excited, Brett hopped from one foot to another. Cary pushed the salad he'd been blending aside and scooped the boy into his arms.

"OK, short stuff, what did you do, make center field?"

"No. Better than that. I'm the pitcher!"

"That's wonderful, Brett." Cary kissed his son's cheek before setting him down.

All things considered, he'd adjusted to the role of single parent relatively easily. Four years ago, Elsa, a woman he'd dated briefly, had come back to town, bringing the child with her. She'd told Cary he was the father and had expected him to support the boy. During her absence, Cary had discovered Elsa had slept with the entire town. But even that didn't matter. One look at Brett, and he'd fallen in love. Good thing the child had turned out to be his. The ensuing custody battle had been long and drawn out, but had ended in his favor.

Cary had suspected the boy was being neglected. Elsa clearly wasn't the maternal type. She loved to party and Brett had been handed off to a series of baby-sitters, one of whom had ended up abusing him. That had been the final straw.

"Dad, will you come to my first game?" Brett whined, ending Cary's reminiscing.

"I plan on being at every game," Cary said.

His son's face lit up like the proverbial beacon. "I love you, Dad. Now, what are we having for supper?"

Cary wiped his hands on a gingham towel. "Spaghetti and meatballs—but only if you eat your salad first."

Brett made a face. "Yuck! I hate salad. Couldn't we have burgers?"

"How do you think your favorite athletes became big and strong?"

"Sammy Sosa didn't eat greens."

"He did, too. Now go wash your hands."

The eight year old hurried to comply.

It was sometimes hard to believe that with everything Brett had been through, he'd remained even-tempered. While the child didn't look like him, he'd inherited his easygoing personality and affinity for sports. Elsa, although they didn't see her often, was proud of the way he'd turned out.

Still, he'd be fooling himself if he didn't recognize the boy needed a mother. Interaction with a woman would do wonders to smooth out his rough edges. Brett also needed someone to listen and soothe away his fears, someone who wasn't so busy building a business. Cary often wondered how the child explained the absence of his mother to his friends. Maybe Niki would find Brett a mother at Coffee Mates.

Thinking of the biracial beauty made his breath come in little spurts. It had been eons since he'd been this interested in a woman—not that Niki had given him the first word of encouragement. But her allure, their chemistry, defied logic.

After dishing out Brett's salad, he watched the boy toy with the lettuce on his plate. The child was what he lived for now. He'd devoted his time to making sure Brett was brought up right and wanted nothing. Some might call Brett spoiled, but considering his early years, whatever Cary did for him simply wasn't enough.

"Can I have my spaghetti now?" Brett asked.

The boy had actually managed to consume a decent amount of salad.

"Sure. How's the reading assignment coming?"

"I'm done."

Cary shot him a skeptical look. "You answered all the questions? After dinner we'll look it over together."

Brett squirmed. Cary picked up the half-eaten salad and replaced his son's dish with a bowl. He heaped on a sizable amount of spaghetti and meatballs and chose not to correct the child, who, ignoring utensils, slurped up spaghetti by the mouthful.

The phone rang. Cary's eyes drifted to the kitchen clock hanging on the far wall. Aaron rarely called during the week. He left Brett still stuffing food into his mouth and picked up the remote.

"Hello."

"Mr. Thomas?" an accented female voice inquired.

Cary frowned. Mr. Thomas was his father. "Who's this?"

"Onika Hamilton."

His heart thudded. "Hi, Niki. What can I do for you?"

"I started processing your application and realized the second page was missing. There are several questions I don't have answers for."

He didn't remember a second page. But if she said there was one, there must be one.

"I'll be happy to answer them now."

"I was hoping you would."

"Dad, I'm done," Brett interrupted. "If it's OK with you, I'm going to turn on my computer."

"Hold it for a minute, squirt."

Cary knew if he allowed that to happen, it would be the end of Brett's reading.

"You sound busy," Niki said.

"My son and I are finishing dinner. Any possibility of you calling me back in, say, an hour? Better yet, can you swing by? That way I can give you the photo I promised." The invitation popped out of nowhere. A forward move on his part, asking a woman who was basically a stranger over to his house.

A long, drawn out pause.

He held his breath. "Niki, are you there?"

"Yes, I'm here. How about we meet at The Wave Runner?"

The Wave Runner was a popular waterfront eatery. Kim must have mentioned it.

He was tempted to say yes, but he couldn't leave Brett. "I can't leave my son," he said. "It's almost bedtime and I don't have a sitter."

"Where do you live?" Niki asked, sounding put out.

"Five minutes from you. Off Ocean."

"Dad, I thought you were hanging up," Brett whispered in the background.

Cary covered the mouthpiece. "I am. I am." Returning

to the conversation, he reminded Niki his address was listed on the application and gave her directions.

What on earth was wrong with her? She'd called a man she'd met only a few days ago under some bogus pretense and then agreed to go to his home. Cary Thomas could be a murderer, for all she knew. Well, perhaps that was a little far-fetched. He did work for Kim. By virtue of that alone, he came highly recommended. Kim was not one to have anyone around she didn't trust or have confidence in.

After Cary'd left, Niki had perused his application. He was thirty-eight, four years younger than she. He'd listed himself as six-feet-three and two hundred ten pounds. *Two hundred ten pounds of solid muscle,* Niki silently added. In the short time it had taken to scrutinize the paper, her interest had been piqued. His hobbies were basketball and scuba diving. He volunteered at a crisis center and was involved in an adult literacy program. Given all that, she'd felt an overwhelming urge to know him better—hence the quickly typed up second page.

It had been a long time since a man had gotten her attention as this one had. Cary Thomas was different from the buttoned-down-oxford types she worked with, pomp-ous asses who thought they were something. He was more laid back and seemed happy with himself. True, the infor-mation on his application had thrown her off a bit, but even that was worth exploring.

Single parent, he'd written. What was that supposed to mean? Did that mean he was divorced? It was a rare man who raised a son alone. What if all his responses were fabricated? The inflated salary and creative occupation certainly were. What if there was a wife in the picture?

As Cary had instructed her to do, Niki made a right onto Brighton Avenue, then a quick left. She idled down the next few blocks, taking in the well-tended lawns and renovated saltboxes and Cape Cods. The central Jersey shore was truly a beautiful place, laid back and definitely different from San Francisco. She'd finally began to relax and unwind.

Niki parked in front of an updated bungalow, hopped out of her rented Jeep, and grabbed the clipboard with the made-up questions. A landscape designer should be able to afford more than this. *Not your business.* She trotted up the pathway leading to the cedar-shingled home and banged the brass knocker.

"I'll be right there," a male voice she assumed to be Cary's shouted.

Niki nervously smoothed her hair, tucked her crisp white shirt into black walking shorts, fingered the beeper at her waist, and gulped deep breaths of ocean air. Cool, collected, and brazen, she waited.

The door flew open. The same delightful child she'd seen in the photo stood in front of her. His father, maintaining a protective stance, kept his hands on the boy's shoulders.

"Come in," Cary said. "I hope my directions weren't too bad." He stood aside so she could get by.

"They were perfect."

"Dad, you didn't tell me she was pretty," the little boy piped up.

"She is, isn't she?"

Niki found herself blushing, something she rarely did. Instead of opting for contacts, she should have worn her glasses. They would have given her something to hide behind and would have made her feel more confident. She tended to discourage male attention. Making herself too pretty only led to trouble. Why encourage men like her ex?

"I'm Brett," Cary's son added. "You're?"

"Niki." She held out her hand.

The little boy took it, pumping vigorously. "Dad said you were coming by to drop something off."

"I am." Niki patted her purse. "I have it right here."

"Time to go to bed, Brett," Cary said, pointing to a passageway.

The child made a face. "Why can't I stay up and visit?"

"Don't give me lip. You have baseball camp tomorrow."

"Come on, Dad," Brett pleaded.

Cary continued to point in the direction of what Niki assumed were the bedrooms. Realizing he couldn't win, Brett said, "You will come see us again?" then headed off.

"I will. Good night."

After he'd left, Niki admired the tastefully decorated living room. Cream walls and robin's egg blue upholstery made it a warm and comfortable place to be. Two Queen Anne chairs were grouped in front of an unlit copper fireplace. A cool breeze blew through the open bay windows, ruffling the window treatments.

Niki, remembering the true reason she was here, reached into her purse and removed the hastily constructed addendum to the application. She waved the sheet of paper at Cary. "Where shall we do this?"

"In the kitchen. I left the photo you need on the table."

Niki followed him through an arched doorway and into a kitchen that must have been recently updated. It was obvious he'd spent a small fortune on the house. A stainless steel stove got her attention. An expensive purchase for a simple man. Some might even call it frivolous. Did he do his own cooking?

"She's a beauty, huh?" Cary stroked the surface of the stove lovingly.

"That she is. Do you cook?"

He seemed amused by the question. "Don't have a choice. If I don't cook, Brett and I don't eat."

"No housekeeper?"

"No housekeeper. I do it all myself."

Apparently no Mrs. Thomas and no current love. That explained why he'd registered at Coffee Mates.

Niki laid the legal-sized form on the table and smoothed it out. Removing a Mont Blanc pen from her bag, she handed it to him. His brows rose slightly as he checked out the pen.

"I need you to fill in your educational background, religion, that sort of thing," Niki instructed. "I also need you to indicate how you plan on paying for our service." She pointed the questions out to him. "Now this section of the application is a bit personal, but important. I need to know what your expectations are. Is sex acceptable on a first date? How would you react if the woman wanted to wait? What if she made the first move? Would you consider her aggressive? What about safe sex?"

Cary's expression said it all. Niki wished she had a camera.

She interjected quickly. "I don't want to pry into your personal business. My goal is to find you the ideal mate. What if I fixed you up with a conservative woman, and you're looking . . . well . . . you're looking for purely physical release?"

"So Coffee Mates covers all the bases." The corners of Cary's mouth twitched as he continued to peruse the paper.

What had she said that was so funny? She'd pushed the envelope a bit, but did he suspect the questions were fabricated? The imp in her had prompted her to ask him these personal things. It said a lot about a man if he expected sex on the first date. It said even more if he didn't believe in safe sex. But why should she care? It wasn't as if she were dating him.

Cary scribbled busily.

"How will you be handling payment?" Niki asked.

Cary stopped briefly to remove his wallet from his back pocket. He took out a gold card and slapped it on the table. "American Express."

Niki sensed her eyes must be bulging out of her head. Cary, a gold card holder. Who would have thought? He must be solvent. What was it the people at American Express said? Theirs was a charge card, not a credit card— meaning no extended payments.

"Visa . . . MasterCard are what we take," she stuttered. "You can also pay by check."

Cary slipped the American Express card back into his wallet and took out another. "Will this do?" He waved a Visa platinum card at her.

"That'll do."

He scribbled down the number, signed the appropriate place, and handed his photo and the application back.

"Would you like something to drink?" he asked, rising and crossing to the refrigerator.

"No thanks."

"Wine? I have a special bottle I've been saving."

"Nothing."

"Ice cream, then? Home made." He winked at her. "I'll be offended if you say no."

Niki nodded. He was obviously stalling, trying to delay her departure. She didn't want to insult Kim's client. She needed to keep him happy!

Hey, who was she fooling? She enjoyed the man's company. Having ice cream with him might give her time to analyze the bizarre chemistry between them.

She watched Cary open the freezer and remove a plastic container.

"Mint chocolate chip," he announced. "My own concoction."

"Looks tempting."

He scooped out a gigantic portion and set it down before her. After filling his own bowl, he took the seat opposite.

So much for her plans to diet. Niki shoveled spoonful after spoonful into her mouth. "Heavenly," she confirmed.

"Isn't it? I'll share my secret recipe with you." He winked again.

"I don't cook."

"We can change that."

What did *we* mean? Niki decided to let it go. She was going to sit here with him and discuss nothing more serious than ice cream. A big change from the crazy existence she lived in San Francisco—days filled with tending patients, scheduling operations, fighting with HMOs. Fielding threats.

Her personal life had gone to hell in a handbasket. She hadn't dated in months, unless she counted the brief affair with Oliver Stanton, and that disappointing night out with Glenn Jacoby, the hospital administrator. She never should have mixed business with pleasure. Both involvements had been mistakes. And so had been her brief marriage.

"So would you say I make it as a chef?" Cary asked, licking ice cream off his spoon.

"Yes, you do. Maybe you'll give me that recipe after all. Your ice cream's delicious."

"It's not as delicious as you."

The words were said so softly she couldn't have heard him right. Was he coming on to her?

"I have to get going," Niki said, shoving to her feet.

"So soon?"

"Our business is completed."

"Is it?" He smiled, revealing beautiful teeth, and those gorgeous light eyes held her captive. He had a head of thick hair most women would kill for. God, he was beginning to get to her.

She scooped up his completed application and photo and tucked it into her purse.

"I'll call you," he said, accompanying her to the door. "We have a date to set up."

"We . . . do?" Niki stuttered, hurrying off.

"Yes, we do," he called after her. "We have a video to make."

Chapter 4

"You killed my son," the woman's voice screamed.

"Mrs. Eldridge, Todd's death was . . ."

". . . murder! May you rot in hell!"

"I'll sue your ass for malpractice." Mr. Eldridge jabbed his finger inches away from her nose. His eyes were red rimmed from crying.

"Murderer . . . murderer . . . murderer," shrill voices chanted.

Niki's heart pounded in her chest and her eyes flew open. She eased into a sitting position and reached for the glass of water on the nightstand. The dreams were getting worse. While intellectually she knew she wasn't responsible for little Todd Eldridge's death, she felt she could have done more to save him. She'd tried. How she'd tried. Just as she'd tried to save the other two children.

Why were these recurring nightmares happening? The

Eldridges, though they might feel differently now, had never once accused her to her face of not doing enough. It was she who felt she could have done more—bucked the system, maybe. Fought the HMO tooth and nail and gone ahead with the treatment, even if she'd had to eat the cost herself. All this self-flagellation was a waste of time now. Todd Eldridge had hung on as best as he could until he'd given up. Now nothing and no one could bring him back.

Glancing at the clock radio made Niki realize it wasn't that late, just a little after midnight. She'd returned from Cary Thomas's wound up and confused, unable to figure out what about the man had gotten her hormones churning. She'd gone upstairs with a book, determined not to think about him, and had dozed off.

The phone rang. Niki's heart rate escalated. Who could be calling now? Kim had phoned earlier and left a message on the machine, saying she still wasn't ready to come home. Phillip, the doctor who was covering for her at the clinic, knew in an emergency to beep her. The anonymous calls, the threats had all occurred in San Francisco. Why, then, did she still feel such trepidation reaching for the phone?

"Hello?"

"Kim?"

"No. This is Niki."

A shrill scream on the other end. "What are you doing in Jersey, girl?"

She was suddenly wide awake and feeling a heck of a lot better. Even her heart rate had slowed. Before she could answer, a deep male voice Niki recognized as Devin Spencer's interjected, "When did you leave San Francisco, Doc? We've been trying to get hold of you."

Second to Kim, Charlie Canfield-Spencer and her husband, Devin, were her two most favorite people. Devin affectionately called her Doc. She was delighted to hear their voices and was pleased they'd tracked her down.

"Do you know what time it is?" Niki pretended to grouse.

"It's not that late—only a little after nine. Besides, what do you care? Half of the time you don't know whether it's day or night," Devin joked.

"You're on San Diego time, my friend. We're three hours ahead here," Niki reminded him

"Ooops. Got to pay more attention. '

"Should we hang up and call tomorrow?" Charlie interrupted, sounding contrite and just a tiny bit guilty. "Kim usually keeps strange hours. Actually, we were phoning to see if she'd heard from you."

"What's going on?" Niki asked. Although Charlie and Devin lived in San Diego, they always made a point of keeping in touch. One or the other took turns making the long drive. Niki cherished those rare weekends when they were together. It reminded her of freshman year at Mount Merrimack. Back then she'd been the exchange student from England, clearly out of her element. Kim and Lisa Williams had taken her under their wing, but Charlie and Devin had made her feel at home. Today, despite their success, they were still the most down-to-earth people she knew.

Niki heard the rustle of paper on the other end, and Charlie exclaimed, "This has got to be journalism at its worst. Wait until you hear this. The reporter should be sued."

Sensing bad news coming, Niki took another sip of water. "Read it to me."

"It's not very complimentary," Devin warned. "Someone's trying to do a hatchet job on you."

"I can handle it." She gulped more water.

"OK, here goes. It begins with the headline, 'Eldridge

boy's death being investigated.' " Devin then read the entire article.

It wasn't a very objective piece. Sure sounded like she'd upset the reporter. But sensationalism sold.

"How about you fax me a copy?" She gave Devin Kim's fax number.

"Consider it done. Don't let these idiots get you down, Doc. Your friends are behind you, and so are a number of other people. You've got a loyal following at that clinic where you volunteer."

"That makes me feel better."

"You should feel better. Your patients haven't been shy about expressing their views. They're loyal and vocal. Even that sorry article acknowledges how opposed you are to managed care. The advocacy groups are all on your side. You've challenged the HMO's rulings time and time again. Didn't you tell us you even butted heads with one of the high-muckety-mucks at the hospital?"

"Reaffirms my faith in people to know that I have support from some groups," Niki said. She paused then continued. "Bill Morris."

"Who's he?" Charlie inquired.

"The contracts administrator. The high-muckety-muck Devin referred too."

"He seems to have quite a bit to say. Is he friend or foe?" Devin asked.

"He's a friend, supposedly."

"With friends like that, who—I'd watch him."

The conversation changed to other things. By the time Niki hung up, they had her laughing.

She was determined not to let the piece get to her. Tomorrow, she decided, was another day. Tomorrow she would call Cary Thomas and set up a time to videotape. Tomorrow she would play.

* * *

Cary woke to find a leg thrown across his chest and Brett's head buried under his arm. The child must have had another nightmare.

"Time to get up, sleepyhead. You'll miss the bus." Cary poked Brett in the side. The little boy groaned and rolled over.

"Must I?" A muffled voice came from under the covers.

"Yes, you must. Pitchers have to practice every day if they want to keep their position on the team." Cary plucked the comforter off and tugged on his child's pajama-clad behind. "Move it. Shower time."

"OK, OK. I'm getting up." Rubbing his eyes, Brett scrambled off the bed and headed to his own bathroom to wash up.

After a quick shower, Cary shrugged on T-shirt and jeans. He had the sneaking suspicion that unless most of his men showed up, he would be playing landscaper again. In that case, he might as well dress the part. He stuffed a pair of denim shorts and a clean T-shirt into a gym bag and hurried to feed Brett breakfast.

"You're riding the bus today, squirt," Cary said, escorting Brett out. As they waited for the camp bus to show up, he asked, "Sure you don't mind not having chauffeur service?"

"I don't mind, Dad. All of my friends take the bus."

Seconds later, the bus filled with chattering children came to a rolling halt in front of them. Cary kissed his son's cheek and gave him a gentle shove. "Go get 'em, champ. I probably won't be home when you get back, but I've arranged for Mrs. Gonzales to be there. She'll feed you."

Brett looked a bit put out at the idea of being left with

a sitter. He quickly recovered when several of his friends screamed for him to get on board. He would be OK, Cary decided, turning away. He had to stop coddling Brett and allow him to grow up.

About midmorning, after fielding dozens of phone calls at Carett and confirming appointments, he decided to do some site inspections. With several men still out sick, Cary could only imagine how behind they were. The Klein goldfish pond was an urgent project that needed to be completed. To make the deadline, he'd have to pitch in. He was pleasantly surprised to find three men on the job and the pond nearly finished. The work would be completed well in advance of the Klein's bar mitzvah, making the Mrs. one happy lady.

Cary made a few more stops, helping out and offering advice where needed. On one job, when it became clear two of his men had slacked off, he read them the riot act and laid the sod himself. By then it was late afternoon and, except for a quickly nibbled sandwich, he hadn't taken a break.

He suddenly felt an overwhelming urge to see Niki again, to hear that proper British accent interrogate him. If he swung by Coffee Mates, he could always pretend he was checking up on the landscaping. Hell, he didn't need an excuse. He was now officially a client of Coffee Mates. He'd simply say he'd come by to make the videotape.

A cursory look at his attire confirmed that he wouldn't exactly present himself in the best possible light. What did it matter, anyway? He wasn't interested in meeting women. The one woman who'd captured his interest clearly felt he was beneath her. He couldn't wait to see her face when she found out what he really did.

When the temperature soared that afternoon, Cary had changed into the gym shorts he'd packed. Now his sweaty

T-shirt clung to his chest and had large rings under the arms. He sniffed himself. Thank God he didn't smell.

He parked the pickup truck in front of Kim's house and let himself into her backyard. No sign of men at work. Wandering to the side of the house, he found the potted plants right where he'd left them. So much for asking his men to get them out of the way. Not one scrap of work had been done. Of all clients to ignore, why did it have to be the one person who paid her bills on time? Cary began moving the pots himself.

"Well, it's about time," a woman's clipped tones snapped behind him.

He took his time finishing, dusted his hands on his thighs, and straightened up. "Are you speaking to me?"

"There's no one else around." Niki glared at him. "Where have you been?"

"Taking care of business."

She snorted. Today she wore a skirt that skimmed her knees and a close-fitting tank top. The beeper remained clipped to her waist. It was by far the most skin she'd shown. The heat must be getting to her.

"Kim called," she said, ignoring his last comment. "She wanted to know if you chaps made any progress. She just about pitched a fit when I told her you hadn't shown up."

Cary groaned inwardly. He would have hell to pay when Kim returned. "I'm sorry," he said, meaning it. "It won't happen again. I'll make sure someone's here when they're supposed to be." He leaned against a shady maple tree and folded his arms. "Did you tell Kim I'm one of her clients?"

"Should I have?"

"No. I'd prefer to tell her myself."

Without knowing it, Niki had bought him extra time. If he could keep up the charade, it would give him the chance to get to know her better. "When will Kim be back?" he inquired.

Niki shrugged. "Who knows? Her mother's not well and her sister can't take more time off work. I'm to cover for as long as I can."

"You're a good friend. How does that affect your job?"

Niki shuttered her eyes. Her entire body tensed. "What job?"

"Most everyone has a job."

"I'm unemployed," she said after a while, fingering the beeper at her waist.

"Unemployed? As in fired? Laid off? Or not looking?"

"None of the above."

Since he'd covered most of the bases, he deduced she might be one of those professional students who took the summer off.

"When can we make your video?" she asked, changing the topic.

"How about right now?"

"Now?" She made it sound like he'd lost his mind. She examined him briefly, critically, before boldly returning his stare. "You might want to tidy up a bit."

"That goes without saying. If you'll let me use your bathroom, I'll . . ."

"You'll shower and change clothes?"

"Is that what you'd like me to do?" he asked, moving in closer until he could see the dusting of freckles powdering her yellow skin and the wariness in those beautiful hazel eyes hidden behind the dreadful spectacles. "I'm not dressed appropriately?"

"It's not what *I* would like," she gritted out. "Most men want to appear their best. Look at you. You're dirty, sweaty, disreputable."

"Translation: I don't cut it with you." He got in her face.

Whooshing out a breath, she stepped back.

He continued, "Some women like men who work with their hands. Sweat usually means they earn an honest living." His fingers trailed along her cheek.

Niki moistened her lips and looked away.

"What type of man do you like?"

"It's not what I like," she snapped, slapping his hand away. "We're not talking about me. I'm just warning you. You're limiting your chances of meeting Ms. Right if you appear ill groomed and disreputable."

Cary ran his fingers through matted curls. "You mean I'm limiting my chances with you?"

"With me?" she sputtered, seemingly horrified by the possibility he would even think to pair them.

"Is the thought so repulsive?"

"I'm not in the running."

"You don't like men? Or is it just blue-collar ones who don't measure up?"

"Mr. Thomas, this conversation has gotten way too personal." Niki made a sharp U-turn and headed for the house.

"Cary," he corrected, falling into step with her. "Mr. Thomas is my father." When they got to the veranda, he said softly, "You know what I think, Niki? You're not as tough as you'd like the world to believe. And you're hardly immune to me."

"You're deluding yourself," she snapped, shooting him a look designed to freeze water. "The bathroom's to your left. Try using the cold water on your head. It may bring you to your senses. I'll see you back here shortly." She gestured to the reception area before dashing off.

"I just need to get my duffle bag out of the truck," Cary called after her.

"Don't be too long. I don't like to be kept waiting."

"Neither do I," he said, smiling brightly. "Neither do I."

Chapter 5

Glenn Jacoby snapped his briefcase closed and ran a hand over weary eyes. What a day it had been. Now all he wanted was to go home and forget San Francisco General and its problems existed. But even leaving the hospital would be a challenge. It meant sidestepping pesky reporters camped on the front lawn. That thought alone made his head throb. Who would ever have imagined one little boy's death could have attracted so much attention?

It wasn't as if San Francisco General didn't have its fair share of births and deaths. It was like any other hospital. Why, then, should this child's demise draw such media attention? It was unfortunate and sad that Todd Eldridge had passed away. But the child had been diagnosed with advanced lymphoma, and, despite what Dr. Onika Hamilton believed, nothing short of a miracle would have kept him alive.

Trust overly conscientious Niki Hamilton to recommend some newfangled and outrageously priced treatment. She had to have known no HMO would approve anything so experimental. But that hadn't stopped her. She'd charged ahead like a bull seeing red, taking on anything and everyone in her way, including Bill Morris, the contracts administrator. By doing so, she had made herself a powerful enemy.

It was her stubbornness, that aggressive nature, he'd initially found so attractive. For his entire five years at the hospital, he'd tried his best to get her attention. But except for the one night she'd agreed to go out with him, she seldom even gave him the time of day. He still didn't know how he'd blown it with her.

Glenn picked up his briefcase and prepared to leave. The phone rang. His first thought was not to answer it, but to put one foot in front of the other and head for the door. What if it was the call he'd been waiting for all day?

"Hello," he said, making his voice deeper.

"Good. You're still there." Bill Morris was on the other end, sounding unusually ruffled.

"What's up?"

"That damn Hamilton woman, that's what. Look, I'd rather not get into it over the phone. How about having a drink with me?"

Glenn considered it for a moment. Having a drink with Bill meant he'd be the one picking up the tab. "OK. We'll meet at Die Hards in, say, twenty minutes?"

"Half an hour's better. I have a couple of quick calls to make and I'll be there."

What Bill had to say must be of a highly sensitive nature. He'd known the man these past five years, and he'd never sounded this stressed. Who would have thought he would be so bent out of shape on account of one little boy's death?

Frankly, Glenn couldn't figure out why Bill was so uneasy. He and Bill had tenure with the hospital. If anyone would hang, it would be the good doctor herself. Any investigation would prove Dr. Niki Hamilton negligent. One of her colleagues had seen to that.

Niki could have opted for the recommended and traditional treatments. Instead she'd chosen to go the controversial route—gene therapy. She had to have known the Eldridges' health plan would never approve anything experimental. He felt badly she was under scrutiny now, her job possibly on the line. He actually had the greatest respect for Niki Hamilton. He might even love her. But love didn't pay the bills.

Niki focused the camcorder and prepared to zoom in. Cary had settled in comfortably on Kim's couch. He'd cleaned himself up and managed to look presentable. Not just presentable, but incredibly sexy. In the few brief moments he'd taken to use the bathroom, he'd lost the stained gym shorts and grubby T-shirt, replacing them with faded jeans and a clean jersey. It wasn't the type of outfit she would have chosen for making a debut on film. Still, it was considerably better than the getup he'd come in wearing.

Even his wild mass of curls had been tamed into a semblance of order. He'd obviously been out in the sun. His face and forearms were now an attractive shade of terra cotta, the same exact shade his legs had been in those cutoff denim shorts. His whiskey-colored eyes seemed to flash private messages at her. *Purely your imagination.*

"I'm going to count to five," Niki said, getting down to

business. "You need a catchy opening line, something that will get a prospective mate hooked from the outset. Don't forget to tell the ladies a little bit about yourself, what you're looking for in a woman. Are you sure you don't want to rehearse?"

Thank God, she could occupy herself with this. It gave her a reason not to think. Even now, Todd Eldridge's wan little face still haunted her. Why hadn't she ignored the HMO's recommendation and absorbed the cost of treatment herself? The child might still be alive today. *Stop beating yourself up, Niki.*

"Nah. I'll wing it," Cary said, bringing her back to the present. He jumped up and began pacing the length of the room, flashing her that killer smile of his. "Should I go for the serious, studious approach? Or should I be Mr. Happy-Go-Lucky? Maybe I'll play it safe and just be the all-around nice guy."

"Be yourself."

"Hmmmn. You think? How long is this going to take?"

"Ten, fifteen minutes, max. Our clients have a limited attention span."

Cary chuckled. "What you mean is if I don't capture their interest in the first few minutes, it's on to the next."

"You said it."

Kim had explained exactly that to her. This dating/mating business was a fickle one. People paid good money and didn't want to waste time.

Cary appeared to be getting himself together. All the while, his fingers stroked his chin. She wondered if he knew what he was getting into. Even in the few short days she'd been left running Coffee Mates, she'd concluded the majority of females were barracudas. They'd just as soon chew up a man, spit him out, and not give a damn in the process.

But that wasn't her problem. Cary Thomas had come to Coffee Mates looking to find someone. He'd paid Kim's exorbitant fee and was obviously on the hunt for a wife, probably someone to care for that sweet little boy she'd met. It was a figment of her imagination that he was coming on to her. He was only looking to make the right match. Even so, the thought of Cary and another woman left her feeling unsettled. But what interest could she possibly have in a laborer, or he in her?

"I'm ready," Cary called, folding himself back onto the couch and shooting her another one of those smiles that said, *I wouldn't mind bedding you.* A crazy thought. Obviously it had been way too long between partners. Cary was being friendly. No point in misreading his intentions.

Niki positioned the camcorder and zoomed in on his body before slowly panning to his face. He sat legs apart, elbows propped on his thighs. His curled fist had found a home under his chin. He flirted outrageously with the camera and even had the audacity to wink and blow her a kiss. She lowered the camera and glared at him.

"Save it for the women you're hoping to seduce," she snapped.

"My, we're bitchier than usual. Hungry?" Before she could answer he added, "When I haven't eaten, I'm grouchy. And I haven't eaten. Well, at least since lunch. How about you and I go to dinner after we take care of this business?"

"You and me?"

He was sending confusing signals. He'd come to Coffee Mates looking for a wife. Why was he asking her out?

"Are you saying you've eaten?"

"No. I'm saying I wasn't planning on doing so until much later."

"Then it's all settled. We'll go to The Wave Runner,"

he said. "The sooner we get this tape completed, the sooner we can eat."

The cat had climbed onto the back of the couch and now took a seat on Cary's shoulder.

Niki zoomed in on his face. "No, Scarlet. No. You can't do that," she shouted.

"Oh, leave her," he said.

"If you say so."

"Five, four, three, two, one. You're on," Niki called, trying to hide her amusement. Cary Thomas, the epitome of the manly man, with a cat on his shoulder.

"Hi, I'm Cary Thomas," Cary said, smiling into the lens and making her hands tremble and her stomach go into revolt. "I believe in getting down and dirty. I'm a landscape designer by trade and a single parent of an eight-year-old boy." He continued without missing a beat. "I believe in living life to the fullest. What is it some famous person once said?" he scrunched up his nose, recalling the memory. " 'Life isn't a dress rehearsal.'

"Basketball and scuba diving are hobbies of mine. In my spare time, I teach adults to read. What I really am is an old-fashioned guy looking to make a match with a reasonably attractive woman. Being articulate is a plus. I'm looking for someone content to be a wife and mother to my child. I'll be the breadwinner if you'll stay home and create a warm, supportive environment for me and my son."

How funny. Cary Thomas was looking for Susie Home-maker. He viewed strong career women as threats. If he only knew.

She'd thought he was different. How wrong she had been. He believed women should be barefoot and pregnant. Well, that might be a little strong. Niki focused on his closing.

"I don't care if you have a little meat on your bones. I don't care if you're not a college graduate. What I do care about is whether you have the capacity to love not just me, but my ready-made family."

Instinctively, Niki knew a certain type of woman would lap up what he had to say. Cary Thomas was charming, all right. And smooth. He was a gardener passing himself off as a landscape designer. Could she really blame him for attempting to elevate himself?

It suddenly didn't seem important what he was or was not. It did take a special man, one with a great deal of warmth, compassion, and patience, to teach adults to read. Anyone who advocated literacy had to have some depth.

"Did I do good?" Cary was up and off the couch, circling her. He came to a full stop inches from her face.

Sweat moistened her armpits and her throat went dry. "Yes, better than I expected."

"You obviously don't think much of me."

She remained silent.

"Shall we go eat?" he asked taking her elbow.

"Careful," she admonished, "the camcorder's still running." She didn't have a clue how to turn the silly thing off.

Cary, realizing her dilemma, came to her aid. He seemed to be doing a lot of that lately.

The pickup truck seemed out of place amidst the rented convertibles and imported automobiles parked in front of The Wave Runner. Cary, after circling the parking lot, finally slid into the spot a black Porsche vacated. He put the truck in park, hopped out, and went to help Niki down. As she exited the vehicle, he got a good view of legs that went on forever. *Easy, boy. No point in salivating like a rabid dog. You'll only scare her off.*

In order to make tonight happen, he'd found someone to fill in for him at the shelter where he taught adults to read. Inhaling the tangy smell of ocean, he escorted Niki across the lot and into the brick-red building. The tantalizing smell of seafood greeted them, and a handful of customers waited to be seated.

"Table for two?" A willowy blonde inquired when it was their turn.

"Yes, please. We'd like one by the window. Is there a wait?"

"About ten minutes. You can make yourself comfortable at the bar."

Off to the side, an exuberant crowd fortified themselves with happy-hour-priced drinks. Wall Street types who had just gotten off the ferry chatted with construction workers and traded stories with vacationing New Yorkers. Cary scanned the room, looking for his buddy, Aaron. No sign of him. Strange.

He spotted an empty table and quickly claimed it, ordering Chablis for Niki and Coors for himself. He could tell by the way men's heads turned that Niki had caught the eye of several regulars. Placing his elbows on the table, he leaned in, establishing his territory.

"So what do you think of the infamous Wave Runner?"

"It's got charm. It's not at all pretentious."

"Weekends in the summer it draws all of North Jersey plus the New Yorkers."

"I'll remember not to come here on a weekend," she said dryly.

"Thomas's table is ready," an amplified voice announced over the intercom. The ten minutes had flown by.

"That's us," Cary said, setting his almost empty bottle of beer down and holding out his hand. She surprised him by taking it.

They sat at a table for two overlooking the ocean. Although he'd lived on the central Jersey shore most of his life, it never ceased to amaze him how beautiful this part of the state was.

"Drinks?" a big-breasted waitress asked as she set down their menus and jolted him back to reality.

"I'll have another beer. How about you?" The latter was directed Niki's way.

She debated for a moment, then said, "Why not? Another glass of Chablis wouldn't hurt."

He studied her, noting she seemed less tense now that she'd had her first glass of wine. What was the real story? he wondered. She'd come to visit Kim, had ended up running a dating service—and managing it remarkably well, he might add—yet although she claimed to be unemployed, she still wore a beeper. It was as if she were on call, waiting for someone or something to summon her.

"Tell me about yourself," Cary said, breaking the silence.

"There isn't much to tell."

He reached across the table and covered her hand with his. "Come on, everybody has a story. Some are just more interesting than others."

"Mine is awfully boring, I'm afraid."

"Let me be the judge of that."

She told him about life in San Francisco and about her town house on Nob Hill.

"Snob Hill? Isn't that awfully expensive?"

"*Nob* Hill. Any place in San Francisco is expensive," she said smoothly.

Not as expensive as Nob Hill. "What did you do before you became unemployed?"

The question elicited a reaction. A squirm. A perceptible shifting in her seat. "I worked with kids," she said carefully.

"That could mean almost anything."

"It did."

The conversation was going nowhere fast. Cary decided it was time to try another tack. "How long have you known Kim?"

This time Niki managed a smile. They were on safer ground. "It seems like all my life. Actually, we went to the same college and were suitemates most of our time there."

"You've been in the States for quite a while, then." He could have kicked himself the moment the words slipped out. Would she think he was implying she was old? "I meant . . ."

"I know what you meant. And, yes, I've been in the States a while. I came as an exchange student and ended up staying. I found the United States agreed with me better than foggy old London. Thank God my father's a naturalized American citizen. It made it that much easier to get a visa."

"And your parents? Are they still in London?"

"No. They moved around. I was an army brat. My dad's last assignment took him to Germany. He completed his duty and stayed."

"Sounds like you're well traveled."

"I've gotten around."

Their waitress returned, pad in hand. "Folks, are you ready to order?" Neither had even glanced at the menu.

"Give us another couple of minutes," Cary said to the hovering woman.

"Sure thing. I'll be back."

After she'd moved off, Cary turned his attention back

to Niki. She was flipping through her menu, trying to decide. A beeping noise got his attention and that of everyone at the surrounding tables. Heads turned. Niki removed the pager clipped to her waist, looked at it, and was up like a shot.

"I'll need to find a phone," she said by way of explanation. "If I'm too long, go ahead and order."

Cary's eyes followed her swaying hips as she headed toward the phones. Niki Hamilton was one intriguing woman. If it was the last thing he did, he planned on solving the mystery surrounding her.

Chapter 6

There was a line at the pay phones. Niki could have kicked herself for not bringing her cell phone with her. She'd rationalized that she was on a pleasure jaunt to New Jersey and, determined to get away from it all, had left her cellular phone at home. Dumb move on her part.

Several minutes ticked by as she waited her turn. She tapped her foot impatiently and finally said to the guy on a long-winded call to his broker, "Are you close to winding down?"

He shot her a fierce look, but continued yakking. Lucky for her, the guy next to him signaled he was hanging up. She thanked him and slid into the spot he vacated. Bringing the beeper to eye level, she checked the digital message. Phillip Jordan, the doctor filling in for her at the clinic, had left a message.

Niki dialed. On the second ring Phillip picked up.

"I was beginning to think you weren't getting back to me," he said in his proper Caribbean fashion.

"What's going on?" Niki was now fully alert and in physician mode.

"Nothing to worry about, it's handled. I'm merely calling as a courtesy, to update you on one of your patients."

The air whooshed out of Niki's lungs. At least he wasn't calling to tell her another child had died. She could handle anything but that. While death was an occupational hazard in her profession, four patients in a row would definitely push her over the edge.

Turning her children over to him hadn't been easy. Though it was volunteer work, she'd become especially attached to these poor kids. That had made it so much harder to leave them. Little Angelique had a rare bone disease. Rosa, a four year old, had a propensity toward heart attacks. She'd weathered five of them during her short life. And baby Jamal had stopped breathing so often his parents practically stood vigil at his crib.

"All right, break the news to me," she said at last. "It must be serious if you're calling."

"It's serious, but not entirely hopeless. I thought you would want to know about Robyn Saunders's tests. The results came back today. She's HIV positive."

Niki took a beat or two to digest the news. The six month old's diagnosis did not come as a complete surprise. The mother was a drug addict who made a living selling her body. Now her innocent child was paying for her irresponsibility. On the positive side, an HIV diagnosis was no longer the death sentence it used to be, not with all the new medication out there. And at least little Robyn didn't have full-blown AIDS—not yet.

Niki listened as Phillip brought her up to date. He'd

worked beside her at San Francisco General the past three years and had volunteered at the clinic for two. She had the utmost respect for him. His philosophies were similar to hers and he treated his patients compassionately, dealing with them as human beings, not idiots. So what if he thought writing prescriptions would solve all of their problems?

By the time they were done talking, over fifteen minutes had elapsed. She'd left Cary alone all this time. How rude. Niki thanked Phillip for filling her in and ended the conversation.

Appetizers had been delivered to their table by the time she returned.

"I'm sorry," she apologized, "my phone call took longer than expected."

"Problem?" He pushed a dish filled with appetizers in her direction. "Hopefully not a crisis."

While deciding how to respond, she spooned shrimp and steamers onto her plate. She hadn't deliberately meant to deceive Cary; she just didn't feel it necessary to tell him what she really did. What difference would it make if he knew she was a doctor? She focused her attention on the man seated across from her and smiled brightly.

"Nothing major. I handled it. Smells delicious." She took a bite. "Tastes even better."

"That's one thing you're guaranteed here, superb cuisine. The Wave Runner's food's consistently good. That's why the restaurant draws such an eclectic crowd."

"Yes, I noticed that." Niki's eyes scanned the room, taking in burly blue-collar workers, tourists in brightly colored shirts with neon sunglasses hanging from cords around their necks, and couples obviously on a first date. Did this dinner with Cary classify as a first date?

A silly thought. Wine over matter, obviously. What if he

tried to kiss her when he dropped her off? The thought wasn't repulsive. They were consenting adults, and she wouldn't be opposed to one little kiss. With a body like that, Cary had to be a good kisser. *He's probably even better in bed,* her evil twin whispered.

Niki snapped back to the present as warmth suffused her face. She looked over in time to catch the amused glint in Cary's eyes.

"What's so funny?" she snapped.

"Watching you go pink in the face. Must be some pretty X-rated thoughts you're having."

He was beginning to read her. She'd better be careful.

"Why would you think that?" she said evenly, as heat settled in her cheeks. Her throat must be splotched with the tiny red patches she'd been cursed with since childhood.

"You're getting even pinker," Cary confirmed. "It started at the base of your throat and worked its way up. Even the tips of your ears are pink. Please tell me you're not having an allergic reaction."

Niki, not trusting herself to speak, shook her head.

"Then it's kind of cute. Blushing makes you more human. You're not at all like the proper Onika Hamilton I've had to deal with. Always in control."

Time to change the conversation. Niki cleared her throat. "How's Brett?"

Intense pride and tenderness flashed across Cary's face. She could swear he puffed out his chest. The boy was his heart, obviously.

"Wonderful. Actually, better than wonderful."

"And where is he this evening?"

Cary glanced at his watch. "Brett should be getting home about now," he said.

A Tag Heuer. A pretty pricy acquisition for a gardener. Something about Cary Thomas didn't add up.

"You left him alone?" The words just slipped out. She knew it came across as if she was judging him and he'd come up lacking.

"No. Mrs. Gonzales stays with Brett until I get home."

"And Mrs. Gonzales is—"

"A paid baby-sitter and very good friend. Have you decided what you want for an entrée?"

The conversation ended abruptly and diplomatically. Niki again feigned interest in the menu. Just how old was this Mrs. Gonzales? she wondered. What did it matter to her whether the woman was eighteen or eighty? Her job was to find Cary a mate. By virtue of the fact he had registered with Coffee Mates, it was safe to say Mrs. Gonzales was not in the running.

Drinks replenished, entrées ordered, Niki sipped on her wine. Glass number three was definitely hitting the spot, making her feel more confident and just a tiny bit flirtatious. Where would this whole dinner thing lead? Though her evil twin told her she was playing with fire, she smiled at Cary and leaned across the table.

"Can I ask you a question?" she began tentatively.

"Fire away."

"Are you biracial?"

Cary grinned wickedly. He didn't seem at all disturbed by the question. "What if I am?"

"You are quite light skinned. Some might even say white."

"Does that pose a problem between us?"

She eyed him over the rim of her wine glass. "There is no *us*. I'm only asking because I'm biracial. My mother's British, my dad African. I thought maybe we had something in common. Mixed kids sometimes have a difficult time growing up. It was far worse in London. I didn't fit into one group or another. What I did acquire was a strong sense of self."

"There is no *us*?" Cary repeated, raising an eyebrow.

Niki felt herself go pink again. She chose not to comment.

Cary continued. "Those experiences also taught you to be resilient and tough."

"How do you know?"

"Just an educated guess." He chugged his beer and set the bottle down.

"But you haven't answered my question," Niki said, her finger rimming the wine glass. She was feeling slightly giddy but wasn't about to let on.

"I'm black," he said matter-of-factly. "The biracial relationship happened two generations before. Both my brother and sister are quite dark skinned. No mistaking what they are."

"I have a healthy respect for genetics. Still, it must be difficult looking the way you do. No one would guess you were African-American unless you told them."

"Makes for an interesting life. My physical appearance has worked well for me. I get to see the nastier side of people come out. Hear how they really feel. It's saved me from making some big mistakes."

"Like?"

"I'll tell you over dinner."

Sure enough, their waitress hovered, balancing a tray of hot food.

"Everything smells heavenly," Niki commented after the woman had set down both surf and turfs and departed.

They dug into the succulent lobster and tender steak and ate in silence for a while. Eventually Niki picked up the conversation where it had left off.

"I'm anxious to hear these stories," she said.

For the next few minutes, Cary regaled her with tales of clients who had mistakenly used the N word around him and suffered the full effect of his wrath. He told her of those assuming he was white, feeling free to tell bigoted jokes. In each case, he'd pulled them up on the spot, not caring if he lost business in the process.

The clients he referred to were obviously his company's clients. As the time ticked by, Niki found herself enjoying his companionship more and more. She had to remind herself that theirs was strictly a business relationship. She also had to remind herself to stop drinking so much wine. Cary was not looking for a career woman to share his life, and she certainly wasn't looking for a gardener—even if that gardener happened to be educated, articulate, and amusing.

"Can I tempt you with dessert," Cary asked, "or maybe cappuccino?"

"Cappuccino," Niki said, patting her full stomach.

"Cappuccino it will be, then." He gestured for the waitress and gave their orders.

"When will my videotape be ready for viewing?" he asked, stirring a copious amount of brown sugar into his cup.

"As soon as I look at it. I'll do some editing, if necessary. Then I'll attempt to match you."

"By that you mean?" He took a careful sip from his cup.

"The computer links clients based on interests, likes and dislikes, income, that sort of thing. It even matches you based on the particular physical type you seek."

"Sounds pretty advanced."

"So Kim tells me."

"Have you heard from her recently? When will she be back?"

Niki shrugged. "Who knows? She phones periodically. Her mother's in stable condition, but there's still the issue of needing someone to care for her. Kim would never consider getting outside help. She thinks family should care for family."

"She's right. Blood is blood."

She acknowledged his comment with a nod of her head. "That might be the case, but there are times friends are a heck of a lot more supportive than relatives or a spouse."

She was thinking of many of her patients, those diagnosed with AIDS who'd been abandoned by their families. So often it was left up to the partner or a caring friend to provide emotional and financial support. She thought of one recent case, a young mother diagnosed with full-blown AIDS contracted through a blood transfusion. The husband, on hearing the news, had walked out, leaving her to mind three young children when she barely had the strength to care for herself. The parents, thinking the worst, had turned their backs on her. A friend had stepped in to care for the children and to lend emotional and financial support. And when she passed away, the friend paid for her burial.

Cary's voice came at her from a long way off. "Sounds like you've been badly burned by relatives." He smothered a yawn.

"Not relatives. I have a warm and supportive family. Am I keeping you up?"

"It's been a long day."

She remembered his job entailed back-breaking labor out in the hot sun, hauling shrubs and plants back and forth. How insensitive of her to linger over cappuccino. "Why don't I get the check?" she said.

He was already reaching for his wallet. "I asked you out. I'm paying."

"But you're my client."

"Not for long."

She shot him a puzzled look. "What was that?"

"Nothing important." He flagged down their waitress and signaled for the check.

The ride home went too quickly. Fortified by wine and good food, Niki felt her eyelids drooping. She jolted awake when Cary's rough palm stroked her cheek. "You're home, sleepyhead." He'd come around to her side of the truck to help her out.

She was suddenly aware of his subtle cologne and the body heat he radiated. When he held out his hand, she took it. Together they walked up the pathway toward the house. Although she was five-foot-seven, he made her feel petite and protected. This was sheer madness. They weren't on a date. The man was her client—no, Kim's client. She needed to remember that.

After climbing the steps of the wraparound veranda, Cary led them to the porch swing. He sat, bringing her down next to him, and placed an arm around her shoulders. Niki drank in the salty breeze from the ocean, closed her eyes, and let the cool night air tickle her skin. Cary's cologne wafted its way up her nostrils, befuddling her senses and making her realize how vulnerable she was. He turned her toward him and in one fluid movement took her into his arms. Plucking the glasses from her face, he placed them in the space beside them.

"You don't need these," he said, trailing a finger down the bridge of her nose. "They're simply a prop you hide behind."

"I—do," she sputtered.

Indeed she did. She didn't want men to notice her or view her as a sexual being. That's why she'd hidden behind the thick horn-rimmed glasses and frumpy clothes. Involving herself with a man meant opening herself up to hurt. She wouldn't make that mistake again. Not ever. She wouldn't make the mistake of supporting some underemployed man who would take her to the cleaners after things soured.

Cary put a stop to the inner dialogue. His kisses started at her eyelids and trailed down her cheeks. His hungry lips closed over hers, demanding, probing. The connection, though brief and fleeting, started a chain reaction. She tingled from her head to her toes. Wrapping her arms around his neck, she leaned in closer. This time he rewarded her with another tongue-probing kiss. She savored the cappuccino on his breath. A heady taste. A heady man. The wrong man.

"See," Cary said, coming up for air. "I knew it. There's another side to the cool and seemingly collected Niki Hamilton."

He kissed her again. This time the veranda tilted.

"I plan on discovering every inch of the real you," Cary said into her ear. "My guess is Niki Hamilton is a woman I'd like to know better."

"My guess is you may not like her when you get to know her."

"That's highly debatable." Cary silenced her with another earth-shattering kiss.

No man had ever made her feel like this. Wrong as Cary Thomas was, why not explore the possibilities and see where it went? Niki kissed him back with a passion even she hadn't known she possessed.

Chapter 7

"I've got several videotapes I want you to look at," Niki said. "When can you stop by?"

The sound of her British accent made Cary's heart pound. He shifted the receiver to a more comfortable position against his shoulder. "I can't get away right now. Maybe later."

He must not sound particularly enthused. Niki's call had come at a time when all his creativity had dried up. Though his fingers moved, nothing of worth appeared on the monitor. Nothing went on in his brain. He didn't want to see videotapes of women. He'd already found the one he wanted.

Cary tried his best to focus on the courtyard he was commissioned to design. It was a special project for the African-American Heritage Museum and gave him a unique opportunity to leave his mark. Why, then, would nothing come? Frustrated, he drummed his fingers against the desk. He heard Niki's crisp tones from far away.

"As you wish." She sounded cold and distant, not at all like last night. "Call me when you're free."

Sensing she was about to hang up, he shouted, "Hold it." Where on earth had the warm, caring woman who'd melted in his arms last night disappeared to?

"Problem?"

"I just wanted to apologize. l know I sound preoccupied. I'll try my best to stop by later and view those tapes."

"Apology accepted. Be sure to call me before you come, though. I may have other appointments."

Talk about not giving an inch. Cary purposely remained silent, waiting to see what she would say next.

"Actually I'm quite surprised to find you in," she said, sounding a little friendlier. "I dialed the work number on your application and figured I'd leave a message."

"You're disappointed to get me on the phone?"

Her long, drawn out pause could be interpreted either way. Last night wasn't to be mentioned, he supposed.

"Did I say that?"

"You implied it."

No point in prolonging a conversation that was going nowhere fast. Cary ended it quickly and returned to business. Try as he might, his heart just wasn't in it. He'd had a vision for this courtyard as a place of peace. He'd dreamed of fountains, brick walkways, and loads of nooks and crannies where people could hide. There would be paths where people could meander, shady trees where they would linger. Now if only he could make his vision reality.

Cary maneuvered his mouse, testing several ideas, moving garden benches and shrubbery from one vantage point to another. Still not exactly satisfied with the results, he saved the drafts for later when his mind was clearer.

A quick glance at his watch told him over an hour had flown by. Brett had baseball practice this evening, and trusty Mrs. Gonzales could be convinced to sit for him again. She always needed money.

Predictably, the sitter was agreeable. Cary made a few calls to the men still out sick. The majority said they would be at work the next day. After the last call, he got into his pickup truck and headed for Kim's place. He was excited and anxious to see Niki again. He couldn't remember the last time he'd enjoyed a woman's company this much or, for that matter, a kiss. Face to face, would Niki deny their mutual attraction?

Not that he was a monk, or even pretended to be, but the women he met were jaded. They were experts in the art of seduction, so practiced that lovemaking seemed programmed, their reactions faked. But not Niki Hamilton. She'd responded spontaneously to his kisses, giving him back everything he'd asked for and more. She'd kissed him like he was the only man who mattered. Like she couldn't get enough. She'd jump-started a part of his heart he'd thought dead.

Cary pulled up to the front of Kim's house and parked behind a black Mercedes. He made his way to the side door where Coffee Mates was located, and smiled in anticipation of seeing Niki again. After knocking, then knocking again, and getting no response, he opened the door and walked in. The same red cat he'd heard Niki refer to as Scarlet half dozed on the window seat. She opened an eye and meowed loudly.

"Hi, kitty," Cary said, crossing over to scratch her behind the ear. Scarlet purred and rolled over, all four paws in the air. He rubbed her belly before returning to the couch.

After a minute or so, a woman's loud voice floated in from the outer room.

"He's not for me. Bring on the next one." Cary hoped she wasn't referring to him.

Niki's British accent was clearly audible. He could tell she was trying to be agreeable.

"What about him? He's got a nice smile, a good job, and he's athletic."

"He might be a possibility," the woman responded. "But I was hoping for someone better looking."

Cary cringed. Women could be brutal.

He sat there a full twenty minutes, overhearing the woman's disparaging comments about each man she viewed: Nah. He doesn't make enough money. I don't like homeboys. He dresses funny.

God forbid if she'd selected him.

"Well, that's it," Niki said, sounding disgusted. "Why don't you sleep on it tonight? Call me tomorrow and tell me what you've decided."

Cary waited expectantly while tapping heels came his way. A woman with a short, almost mannish haircut sailed out. She was dressed in enough gold jewelry to give Cartier a run for its money. She gave him a quick once-over and promptly dismissed him. He knew that look. It was the look of an African-American woman who'd mistaken him for white. Automatically she'd eliminated him as a viable prospect. This time he was thankful.

"Good. I see you managed to make it here before I closed," Niki said, acknowledging his presence. "Since you didn't bother to call, you'll have to give me a few minutes."

"Not a problem." What else could he say?

The witchy client actually deigned to give him a second look. He could tell she was clearly puzzled. He didn't fit the Coffee Mates profile. Let her think what she would.

After the client left, Niki rolled her eyes. "God help the man who gets her."

"As long as it's not me."

"Would I do that to you?"

Cary stood and brushed imaginary lint off his jeans. "Would you?"

"Only if you were an especially bad boy." Niki tossed him an enigmatic smile. The ice was slowly thawing.

"Can we see those tapes you wanted me to view?" Cary followed her through an attractively decorated inner office. The homey atmosphere immediately put him at ease. "Where are your part-timers?"

"Gone. It's happy hour. No chance of holding them here this late."

Cary tsked. "Ah, to be young and free again."

"You're not exactly ancient." She gave him the once-over, then went completely pink.

Good, she was hardly immune to him. Maybe she even remembered how passionate their kisses had been.

"Didn't you sow wild oats in your youth?" Cary asked, pretending not to notice her blotched throat.

Niki raised an eyebrow. "Not me. I was a good girl. Most of my time was spent studying. I wanted to be a—anyway, I was too busy to party. Only Lisa Williams could get me out."

He ignored her slip of the tongue, choosing not to pursue it. "Who's Lisa Williams?"

"One of my old suitemates. An artsy type. Spent half of her life at the bar or student union."

"One of these days you'll have to tell me about your escapades. For me, growing up at the Jersey shore was loads of fun, summers in particular. I hung out at the popular watering holes and met tons of people."

"Mostly women, I'm sure," Niki said dryly.

"I met my share."

They entered a room with stark white walls that had been converted to a media room. It held a couch, coffee table, cabinet, and big-screen TV with built-in VCR. Niki gestured toward the camel-colored couch. "Make yourself comfortable." She knelt, began removing tapes from the cabinet, scrutinized labels, and set them down.

Cary plopped onto the sofa, his legs splayed out in front of him. He watched Niki peruse the tapes, slide one into the VCR, and hit the play button. She returned to perch on the arm of the couch next to him. It took all he had not to touch her.

The enchanting smell of her body lotion wafted toward him, titillating him. Cary's gaze slid to the legs she'd crossed one over the other, hiking her skirt up an indiscreet inch or so. She had lovely legs. Perfect legs. He blinked, shutting out the distractions, and fastened his eyes on the television screen. The image of a mocha-colored woman with an attractive blunt cut finally came into view. Cary forced himself to listen to what she had to say.

"Hi, I'm Kendra York." The woman flashed a toothy smile. "I own a small florist shop in Toms River. Flowers are my passion."

Her recitation sounded canned. In his business, it was difficult not to know everyone who sold flowers or plants. Even so, he didn't know her, and didn't plan on remedying that.

Kendra continued. "My ideal man works with his hands. He's the earthy type." She licked her lips. "Rugged and outdoorsy, that's how I like them. I'm a single parent and mother of three, ready to settle down. Having your own house would be a big plus. Buying me elegant champagne dinners and loads of gold jewelry is a sure way to my heart."

She'd lost him. He'd already tuned her out. That predatory look in her eye, coupled with her comments, had done it for him. Not that this Kendra person wasn't good-looking; she just wanted more than he was ready to give. He didn't find greed particularly appealing, either.

Niki uncrossed those fabulous legs and stood up, looking around—for the remote, he guessed. Failing to find it, she walked over to the equipment and pushed the power button, dissolving the image.

"So what do you think?" she asked, standing before him.

Cary shrugged. "She's not the one."

"Then on to the next."

This time the image of a buxom, dark-skinned woman with locks filled the screen. She came across as confident, educated, and articulate. *She* was simply looking to have fun. Had he not met Niki, he might have been interested.

"Well?" Niki waved her hand in front of his face. "Come back to me, Cary."

"A definite possibility."

"I sense some hesitancy."

"I know what I'm looking for. I'm just not sure she's it."

"What exactly are you looking for?" She stared at him.

He stared back. "Like you don't know."

The pink in her face had taken a dangerous turn for red. Niki swallowed hard.

Cary gave her time to gather her composure. He rose and swivelled his neck and shoulders back and forth. He'd spent much too much time hunched over a computer. It was beginning to take its toll. And he still hadn't come up with an original design.

"I don't know, but *you* do it seems." Niki had boxed him into a spot difficult to get out of. "Why are you wasting my time and your money if there's already someone you fancy?''

"Because the person I want is clearly ignoring my message. I'm not sure what else to do except to keep trying."

Niki turned the same shade as the friendly cat. Scarlet. Maybe he'd gotten through finally.

She spoke quickly. "I've saved the best for last. Up for viewing another tape?"

"Sure."

Cary returned to his seat and fastened his eyes on the flickering screen. When it had straightened itself out, he acknowledged this woman was stunning. Deandra had golden skin and a tight cap of wavy curls. Her light eyes sparkled when she spoke. She was high energy and talked quickly, a stockbroker looking for a man who still enjoyed smelling the roses. She liked leisurely walks at sundown and wasn't looking for loads of money. She had plenty of her own—that and enough love to share. The clincher was she would willingly give up her career to stay home and raise a family.

But was that what he really wanted? At one point he'd thought he did. But a woman who was her own person was even more appealing, someone who could keep and hold his interest. Someone able to stand up to him. Niki, from what he could see, was that person.

"Now tell me she isn't the one," Niki demanded, tapping an impatient foot.

"I don't know. She's lovely, but . . ."

"But she doesn't ring your chimes?"

If he said she did, would he get a reaction from her? Some sign she was interested? "She's seen my video?"

"Yes, she has. And she's very interested."

"OK. Set it up."

"Done deal."

Niki removed the tape from the VCR and plopped a bright pink label on it. Cary watched her carefully. Her skin was still flushed and her jerky hand movements indicated she was ruffled. He'd shaken her up at last.

Cary came to stand beside her. He placed a hand on her shoulder and squeezed gently. "About last night?"

"What about last night?"

It was as if she intentionally didn't want to remember. He persisted. "I had fun. Didn't you?"

"The food and ambience were great," Niki said, ever so softly. "I'd definitely try the restaurant again."

"I was talking about you and me. About the time we spent afterward. The meal paled in comparison to those kisses."

The blotches on Niki's throat were even more pronounced. Her face had turned fire engine red. "Why are you doing this? What's really your goal?"

"You don't know?"

"No, I don't know. You've spent a great deal of time and money searching for a mate. Why not put last night down to too much wine and leave it at that?"

Cary turned Niki toward him, crooked a finger, and tilted her chin. She was forced to look into his eyes. "Is that what you want?"

"You're my client. It's not important what I want."

"I'll show you what you want." Quick as could be, he dipped his head and gently brushed her lips, successfully silencing her. He kissed her again before she could utter another word.

When he released her, Niki's fingers outlined her lips as if in wonder.

"I've known what I've wanted all along," Cary said. "And so have you. But you're afraid to go after it. When you finally get the courage, call me. Till then, go ahead and set up my dates. Fix me up with every Deandra, Kendra, or Betty for that matter. It won't change a thing."

"You're . . ." Niki had finally recovered her voice.

"I'm interested in you," he said, silencing her with another kiss.

Turning, he left the room.

Chapter 8

Bill Morris perused the latest article, then snapped the newspaper shut. For the third day in a row, San Francisco General had made front-page news. Who ever would have imagined a little boy's death would garner such interest? The reporters, of course, all had different takes on the situation. Some thought Dr. Onika Hamilton walked on water, others thought she should be hanged and quartered. Bill had always thought she was a pain in the ass; that's why he felt not the slightest twinge of guilt. It was a dog-eat-dog world out there and only the fittest survived.

It was well over two weeks since the little Eldridge boy's death, and members of the press were still camped out on the hospital's grounds. They hounded anyone remotely looking like staff, vying to outscoop each other. As the days went by, the stories got wilder and wilder.

Bill had been surprised when so many advocacy groups had taken up Dr. Hamilton's cause. They'd picketed the hospital and gotten their share of media attention. It paid to volunteer in a poor part of town, he supposed. It definitely paid to have local backing.

Apparently Niki Hamilton had doctored a goodly share of San Francisco's poor and infirm. The liberals loved her. That meant three quarters of San Francisco was on her side. So were many of the politicians.

Bill heard the knock on his door as if from a distance. "Come in," he grunted, not bothering to look up.

Glenn Jacoby's rangy form took up almost every inch of Bill's office space. The hospital administrator waved a scrunched up paper at him. "Did you see this?"

Bill pointed to the newspaper he'd set aside. "Much ado about nothing, if you ask me. There's no way they can finger us."

"Even so, the hospital's being slaughtered. Phones are ringing off the hook. You would think we single-handedly murdered that kid. Now somebody's found out this is the third child under Dr. Hamilton's care to die in the past six months. That someone lodged a complaint with the state medical board. There's bound to be an investigation."

Bill scratched his earlobe with an uncapped Mont Blanc pen. "As long as the board's investigating her and not us. Hamilton's prescribed treatments are always highly unconventional, and she's prickly as hell."

"And so are three-quarters of the doctors on our staff. Dr. Hamilton is exceptionally bright. Her thinking's out of the box. She's saved twenty times more lives than have actually been lost, but no one sees fit to mention that."

"Actually, the advocacy groups have been quite vocal on that point." Bill capped the Mont Blanc and tucked it into his shirt pocket. Glenn, he suspected, had the hots for Niki Hamilton. Someone had once seen them out on a date. If Glenn was getting nookie from Niki, it stood to reason he would defend her.

"I don't like the idea of a full-fledged investigation," Glenn said.

"It could take years for the board to come to any conclusion. The rumor mill has it Niki Hamilton's in New Jersey visiting a friend. Supposedly she called the hospital looking for Phillip Jordan and left a 908 number."

"As a matter of fact she's on vacation. She's just put in for an extended leave."

"I hope you granted it."

"I did."

"Good. If she lies low, the reporters will eventually pack up and leave."

"We should be so lucky."

Bill shoved his chair back. "Enough talk about Hamilton. Time for lunch. My treat."

"You're on."

Under the guise of straightening up his desk, Bill planned his strategy. He needed to rid the hospital of Niki Hamilton. It would make life easier all around.

Niki examined the label of the huge manila envelope she'd gotten from the mailbox. When she'd asked the hospital to forward her mail, she'd never expected this much. She tore the flap open and withdrew a large stack of letters. Giving in to curiosity, she opened the first envelope she withdrew, removing a piece of yellow notepaper.

You shouldn't be practicing medicine. You've successfully managed to murder three children. You should be shot.

The message was unsigned. With a sinking sensation in

the pit of her stomach, she thrust the lot back into the envelope and concentrated on her breathing. No point in getting upset. Every time a hospital or doctor got negative publicity, hate mail usually followed. In this instance, the sheer volume was overwhelming.

Frustrated, Niki swiped a hand over her eyes. Surely there had to be some positive comments among them. She wasn't about to check, though. Not now. Not on the off chance that the next would be another ugly, derogatory missive. Not while the sky outside was the ideal shade of blue. Perfect beach weather.

An afternoon at the beach just might be the ticket. She let the thought roll around her head, liking it more and more. She'd been in a good mood, until now, and could be again. It was Saturday. Coffee Mates closed at noon. Kim's part-timers, having completed their calls to clients, were long gone. She'd already called Deandra Moore to set up Cary's date. She had nothing pressing.

Niki raced upstairs to change into a bathing suit and throw a few items, including her beeper, into a bag. Minutes later, when traffic slowed to a crawl on Ocean, she idled the rented Jeep past the huge mansions facing the beach. Maybe she should try Sandy Hook, as Kim had suggested during one of their phone calls. She liked the idea of a larger beach with a restaurant and nature preserve. Still, a smaller beach had a certain appeal. Fewer people, for one, and the nominal fee Monmouth Beach charged nonresidents was worth the more private experience.

Besides, she'd been enchanted by the tiny seaside community from the moment she'd laid eyes on it. She'd been especially taken by the picturesque homes. It was unusual to find fishermen's cottages next to modern homes with huge wraparound decks. Monmouth Beach was definitely a town worth exploring.

After circling several times and finding parking nonexistent, Niki found a spot on a side road. She followed two families armed with beach chairs and floats across the street and into the low, flat building housing the beach club. In the changing room, she stripped down to a red one-piece swimsuit. Though modest in cut, the suit left her feeling bare. Niki added a colorful cover-up, substituted prescription dark glasses for her horn-rimmed ones, and, with her towel draped over one arm, headed off to find a place on the small strip of beach.

She'd discarded her wrap and had just settled in with a best-selling novel when a child's voice floated her way.

"Hey, Dad, can I go play volleyball with the other guys?"

"I don't see why not, as long as you remain in clear view. Just don't get in the water without checking with me."

"OK. Hi, Miss Hamilton. Bye, Miss Hamilton."

Niki looked over in time to see the boy whizz by. "Hi, Brett," she called.

Seeing the child again had perked her up immensely. Such enthusiasm and unbridled energy reminded her of why she'd chosen pediatrics to begin with. As sad as her job sometimes was, she wouldn't trade it for the world. She'd always loved kids. Loved their honesty. But why, of all the beaches in central Jersey, had Cary Thomas and his son chosen this one?

Niki thought of how different her life could have been had she had a child of her own. Her ambition and commitment to her job had driven off more men than she could shake a stick at, including her ex-husband, who wanted her money but not necessarily her. At age forty-two, having a baby wasn't to be considered, especially with no man in the picture. Cary Thomas was playing with her, of that she was sure.

She must be losing her mind. Cary, even if he was executive material, was younger than she was. Her hectic lifestyle couldn't accommodate children. She sensed Cary's gaze on her and flushed. Sitting up quickly, she reached for her wrap.

"Fancy seeing you here," he greeted, leaning over and sucking up every last bit of fresh air. He handed her a bottle.

Niki couldn't pull her eyes away from his chest. It glistened with perspiration and suntan lotion. She moistened her lips and watched a single bead of sweat trickle between the bristly golden hairs, settling around his solar plexus. He smelled of sun. She forced herself to look away. Cary Thomas in a pair of cutoff denims was truly awesome.

"I could say the same of you," she said, trying her best to use the cover-up to hide her legs.

"You'll need this if you don't want to burn to a crisp," he insisted, his fingers curling around hers, placing the bottle in her palm.

"Thanks." Where their hands made contact tingled. She had no choice but to accept the sun block gratefully. She'd searched Kim's house, but hadn't been able to find anything remotely resembling lotion, much less block, and she hadn't thought to stop at a store.

"You're very welcome. It feels good to play, doesn't it?"

"Yes, it does."

He lowered himself down beside her and extended those long legs of his. The hairs on his legs were as golden as those on his chest. He was invading her space. She couldn't hear herself think. The heat coming off him enveloped her, befuddling her senses, weakening her resolve. She could smell sun, lotion, and man.

"I called Deandra Moore," Niki said, trying for conversation.

"Deandra who?"

From the expression on Cary's face, he didn't have a clue.

"One of the women you saw on the videotape. The stockbroker who wanted her man to take time out to smell the roses."

"Oh, her."

Cary reached across and uncapped the sun block she still held. He tilted the bottle and squeezed a goodly amount of liquid into his palm. His strong fingers kneaded her shoulders and arms. She was too taken aback to protest. His hands on her body felt good. Very good.

"Aren't you the least bit interested in Deandra?" Niki persisted.

Cary shrugged. "I'm certain she's a perfectly nice woman." He spread the liquid on her back and over almost every bare inch of her. "May I?" he said, indicating her legs.

"No, you may not. That I'll do myself." Niki reached over and grabbed the bottle of sun block from him. Forgetting modesty, she slathered on cream in haphazard motions. She knew her face and throat must be beet red. "Deandra's very interested in you," she persisted. "She seems to think you're quite the catch. She loved your video and thinks you are *the* one."

"I doubt that. I'll go on this date on one condition."

"What's that?" Niki asked.

"You come with me."

"I'm sorry?" She couldn't have heard him right.

"And why not? If we call it a double date it would take a lot of pressure off me. My buddy Aaron can be your date."

Niki scrunched up her nose. "Aaron of The Stone Pony? I hardly think I'm his type."

"You'd be surprised."

"Isn't it a bad idea to mix business and pleasure?" she asked, forgetting about her wrap and jumping up. It really was the most absurd proposition.

Cary was up beside her. His arm spanned her waist, bringing her close to him. "Hey, chill. Who's talking pleasure? You'll be coaching me along—supporting me, if you will. You'll be earning every dime of the money I paid Coffee Mates, and then some."

"Mr. Thomas, Mr. Thomas," shrill boyish voices called. Cary's head swivelled in the direction of the high-pitched tones. He relinquished his hold on Niki and followed the progress of the agitated boys heading their way. The little band kicked sand in every direction. Angry sun worshipers shouted at them.

"Watch where you're going."

"Whose kids are you, anyway?"

A sturdy lad, a good two inches taller than Brett, came to a skidding halt in front of them. "Mr. Thomas, Mr. Thomas, Brett hurt himself."

Cary's face paled under his summer tan. He barely got the words out. "Where is he?"

The boy and his little group pointed in the direction from which they'd come.

Niki immediately went into doctor mode. "Let's go." She fell in step with Cary as they raced off.

The thing he'd dreaded most had happened. What if Brett was seriously hurt? How would he cope? The child meant everything to him. Brett was his life, practically his reason for living. He'd tried his best not to cosset him, to remember that boys needed to be boys.

Elsa, the boy's mother, no longer played a major role in her son's life. Brett saw her maybe two times a year. Cary saw her even less, if he was lucky. Still, if Brett had been badly hurt, she would have to be told.

Elsa, a web site designer, had been contracted by several of the resorts in Grand Cayman. She was living the high life and loving every moment of it, from what he could glean.

"Mr. Thomas?" The same, sturdy boy who'd broken the news tugged on his shorts. "Brett's over there."

Cary saw several boys huddled over a body on the side of a makeshift volleyball court. Niki had already raced ahead and was shouting instructions to the children to move away and give the boy air. By the time he made his way over, she'd squatted down and was examining Brett's ankle like a pro.

"Get ice," she directed.

"I'm on my way," one of the boys who'd come to fetch them shouted back.

"Are you all right?" Cary asked. His son's too-bright eyes sparkled with unshed tears.

"My ankle hurts, Dad."

"He's twisted it," Niki confirmed. "I'm fairly certain it's not fractured."

"How would you know?"

"I'm—" Niki touched the swollen spot surrounding the ankle gently. "I have a medical background."

"You're a trained nurse?"

"Something like that."

"I think we should take him to the emergency room," Cary persisted.

"If you'd like. But I'm sure it's not necessary. Get him

home to bed, give him a couple of children's Tylenol, and apply an ice pack. If he stays off his ankle, he'll recover in a day or so."

She certainly seemed to know what she was talking about. He'd learned something new about Niki. She'd gone to nursing school, but had obviously not completed her training. That would explain her unemployed status. He could call Brett's pediatrician and see if he was available, but it was Saturday, and most doctors' offices weren't open past noon. The thought of spending hours in an emergency room didn't hold much appeal.

"What do you think, squirt?" Cary directed the question to Brett. "Shall we try reaching Dr. Zeig or should we listen to Niki?"

"No, Dad. I just want to go home."

"Home it is, then. Help me get him up," Niki directed, taking over. "Brett, don't put that foot down. Your father will carry you, if necessary. It was smart of you to come get us," she said to the boys standing off to the side. "Definitely the right thing to do."

Cary felt he should have insisted they see a doctor, but he was torn. Clearly his son was petrified and making him see Dr. Zeig would only add to his angst. Besides, Niki sounded like she knew what she was talking about. Some of that nurse's training must have paid off. He scooped Brett into his arms. The boy laid his head against his shoulder and closed his eyes. "Please take me home, Daddy."

Brett hardly ever called him Daddy, not unless he was scared to death.

"It hurts badly, doesn't it, son?" Cary said, softly, so as not to embarrass his child.

"I'm in agony."

"The hurt will go away soon," Niki promised, kissing the child's cheek. Cary wished she was kissing him. He wished she looked at *him* like that. Imagine being jealous of his own son.

"I'm going to go back and get our stuff," Niki called over her shoulder. "Meet you at the entrance of the beach club in a few minutes."

"You're coming back with us?"

"You bet. Don't even try stopping me."

He didn't want to analyze what that meant. Having Niki with him would be comfort enough. He was beginning to realize that parts of her story didn't add up. He remembered the beeper she wore constantly, the long phone call, and now this new information about her medical background. Even so, he enjoyed her company, and Brett liked her, too—not, of course, as much as Cary liked her. Deandra Moore didn't stand a chance.

Chapter 9

"Are you feeling better?" Niki asked Brett, placing a hand on his still warm forehead.

"A little." Although the child's eyelids drooped, he smiled at her.

Bending over, Niki kissed his cheek. He was running a fever, and Cary had gone off to get him more water.

Niki had insisted Brett be put to bed the moment they'd gotten home. Cary had started second-guessing himself, muttering that he should have taken the boy to the emergency room. He'd wanted to call his son's doctor, but she'd convinced him not to. The child had a sprained ankle, but nothing was broken. In a day or so he would be up and about, acting as if this little mishap had never happened.

Cary was back. He bore a pitcher filled with ice cubes and water. He set the container down, and in his hurry, sloshed water all over. He poured liquid into a glass and handed it to Brett. The boy gulped greedily. In a few minutes he would be fast asleep. The mild pain killer in the Tylenol would slowly begin to take effect.

"Sit," Niki ordered, pointing to the wing chair next to Brett's bed.

"I'm OK."

"No, you're not." She could tell his son's accident had taken an emotional toll. She'd never seen him this tired.

"Brett looks like he's about to fall out," Cary said. "Let's leave him to get some rest."

In silent agreement, they headed for the living room. Cary took a seat on the sofa and after a while began worrying his lip. It was apparent he was concerned about his son. Overly so.

"Brett will be fine," Niki reassured him, taking his hand. When his fingers curled around hers, she didn't feel the need to pull away. Who was she to begrudge him a little comfort?

Cary held on to her hand as if it were a lifeline. "That boy's all I have. I don't know what I would do if anything happened to him."

"You won't have to worry about that. Brett's fine. His ankle will throb for a day or two, but that's about as bad as it will get."

"You sound so sure."

"I'm used to being around kids. I told you I had a medical background."

She was prepared for a slew of probing questions. He surprised her by letting it go. She used this agreeable mood to ask the question foremost on her mind. "Does Brett have a mother?"

At first she thought he wasn't going to answer. Finally

he said, "She's in Cayman. Elsa and I never married. We had a relationship of sorts, but were never in love."

"As in Grand Cayman?"

"You're on the money."

Niki squinted her eyes at him. "Is she a native?"

Cary chuckled. "She's as American as they come. She found herself a very nice job designing web sites for upscale resorts."

"Leaving you to raise your boy on your own."

"That was my choice. I love every moment of it."

Cary Thomas had risen immensely in her estimation. He'd just admitted he'd taken on the role of single parent willingly—and was doing a bang-up job of it, from what she could tell. Most men she knew didn't want to support a child, much less raise one. Most didn't want the responsibility. That Cary'd willingly assumed this role said something about him. Had things been different, they might have had a future together.

Who was she kidding? A doctor and a landscaper had little in common. *Gardener,* an inner voice said. Albeit an articulate, sensitive one, with a lot to recommend him. Her ex-husband had been a house painter. She'd hired him to spruce up her townhouse. He'd ended up sprucing up more than that. He was one smooth talker. Two weeks later he'd moved in with her. Two months after that they were married, and three months later divorced.

Cary continued. It seemed he'd forgotten she was there. "Elsa showed up on my doorstep four years ago carrying Brett. He was four years old then. When she told me he was mine, I wanted not to believe her. That was before I took one look at him and fell in love. He was such a sad child. In fact, he barely spoke. I sensed he'd had a hard life. Later, I learned he'd been abused by a number of baby-sitters. And even though paternity hadn't been established, when I found out what he'd been through, I was determined to fight Elsa tooth and nail for custody. I didn't love her, but I did love that boy."

"You're remarkable," Niki said, squeezing his hand.

"Am I?"

"I think so."

His smile warmed her. Her opinion apparently carried weight.

She hadn't realized how much depth Cary Thomas had to him until now. Her pompous cohorts usually talked about nothing except investments and material things. But this man, who earned far less than any of them, had so much more to offer. He had substance.

Oh, God. She couldn't afford another emotional entanglement. Not now, when it made no sense. At most, she could stretch her leave another couple of weeks. So what would be the point of encouraging him?

Cary stood and held out his hand. Niki fitted her hand in his and followed him through the kitchen.

"It's too beautiful a day to sit inside," he said. " Let's go out to the back deck."

As if it was the most natural thing in the world, they took a seat on a raised deck holding two teakwood chairs, a table, and a Jacuzzi.

"I'm starving," Cary admitted, lowering himself into one of the chairs. "How about you?"

"I could munch on something."

"It's close to dinnertime. What if we ordered pizza?"

"Pizza sounds great. Brett would probably enjoy a couple of slices when he wakes up."

"Then pizza it is."

Cary left to call in the order and returned a few moments later. "The pie will be here in about twenty minutes. How about we enjoy the Jacuzzi until then?"

Jacuzzi? She couldn't have heard him right. She wasn't ready for this. "My suit's still wet," she said, referring to the bathing suit she'd slipped out of and hastily stuffed into her bag.

"Who needs suits?"

The blatant come-on hung between them. How had they gotten here?

"You're not implying we get naked?"

"We're adults. I won't tell if you don't."

Despite its being totally uncharacteristic, Niki was tempted to discard all her clothing and join him in whatever act he saw fit. Who would ever know the normally uptight Dr. Hamilton had willingly ditched her clothes and hopped into a hot tub with a gardener? She was hundreds of miles from San Francisco with an attractive man who turned her on. She might never have such an opportunity again.

"Someone needs to stay dressed to get the pizza," Niki said, chickening out.

"The delivery person will ring the bell. We'll have plenty of time to get it together." With that he stood and began yanking the shirt over his head. "Don't be a party pooper. Join me."

Oh, God. What had she gotten herself into? Mesmerized, Niki stared at his bare chest. At his washboard belly. At the crisp hairs curling around his pectorals and dipping below the waistband of his shorts. It would be so easy, so very easy to fall in with his plans, to strip down to nothing and jump into that Jacuzzi with him.

In one swift motion Cary kicked off his shorts. Niki averted her eyes as he swung his long muscular legs over the edge of the Jacuzzi. She did manage to get a quick peek at his butt—and what a butt it was. Taut, white, and tempting like the devil. She could almost forget that Cary, despite his light skin, had two African-American parents. Why should the shade of his skin matter to her? He was secure in himself and knew who he was.

"Coming in?" Cary inquired from the depths of the Jacuzzi.

She didn't respond quickly enough.

"I'll close my eyes and be a gentleman."

She grunted something. At the beach club, Niki had changed into capri pants and an oversized T-shirt. She examined her options. Jumping nude into a Jacuzzi with a man she barely knew was asking for trouble.

"All right," she called, "I'm coming in. Keep your eyes closed."

She stepped out of her capris and her panties and unsnapped her bra. She slid the straps down her arms. No point in getting her undergarments wet. Tugging the T-shirt down way past her knees, she placed one leg over the edge of the hot tub and tested the warmth of the water with her big toe. It was tepid to the touch. With temperatures soaring into the eighties, having hotter water made no sense.

Cary's eyes were shut when she plunged in next to him. The T-shirt billowed around her. Niki yanked at it and perched gingerly on the edge of the ledge, letting the cascading jets ease the tension in her lower back. She wouldn't think about the hateful mail she'd left behind. Time enough to deal with that later.

"You can open your eyes now," she said to Cary.

"At last." Quickly realizing he'd been duped, his expression changed from anticipation to incredulity. Recovering, he joked, "To think I was conjuring up these fantasies of a naked Niki, her long legs brushing mine, her head tilted back, enjoying the late evening sun. Instead I get a clothed woman acting as if I'd bite."

"Sorry to disappoint you."

"Ah, but I'll only have more to look forward to the next time around."

"There won't be a next time."

Cary threw back his head and roared. "How can you be so sure?" The water around him rippled.

"What a beautiful day this is," Niki said, changing the subject.

"Things are bad when we're reduced to talking about the weather." Cary flicked water at her, splashing her in the face. "Come closer so we can talk."

"I'm perfectly capable of hearing you from here."

He crooked a finger at her. "Stop being a pain in the butt. Just come."

She slid closer to him, albeit reluctantly.

Why did she get the feeling he was up to something? She was practically sitting on top of him, uncomfortably aware that, under the bubbling surface, he wore nothing. Cary's elbow brushed hers. The rough hairs of his legs rubbed against hers. Placing an arm around her shoulders, he whispered in her ear, "When was the last time you were with a man?"

"You are impertinent." She slid away from him, sputtering.

"Am I?" He arched an eyebrow.

She wasn't sure whether to be insulted or angry. Was he implying she was inexperienced—or worse, needy?

The doorbell rang, a jarring sound, one that brought her back to earth. She should have known better. Cary Thomas had no real interest in her beyond the obvious. He simply wanted to get laid.

"Saved by the bell," Cary joked. He stood and reached over the side for the towel that had fallen.

Niki's eyes swept his golden chest, focusing on the damp

hairs that had flattened into a velvet mat and trailed downward. She couldn't believe his gumption. She kept her
gaze on his torso, not daring to look lower. He wrapped
the towel around his waist and headed off to answer. When
he was safely out of sight, she stepped from the tub.

At the door, Cary accepted the pie and paid the delivery
man. He set the box on the kitchen counter and went
to check on Brett. The child was still sleeping. Quickly
changing into jeans and a polo shirt, he retraced his steps.
Niki was nowhere to be seen.

"Niki," Cary called. "Niki, where are you?"

Puzzled by her sudden disappearance and lack of
response, he went back inside. A quick look around confirmed she was nowhere to be seen. Would she have left
without saying good-bye? There was only one place left to
check. He started up the hall toward the bathroom.

The door was closed. Cary thought about knocking. No,
that would definitely be crossing the line. He decided to
go back to the kitchen and find some plates to accommodate the slices of pie. He'd just set out portions of pepperoni and white pizza and poured Cokes when he heard
footsteps behind him.

"Uuuumm. Smells wonderful," Niki said. "I didn't realize how hungry I was."

"Want to eat here or outside?" Cary asked without looking up.

"Outside. It's a glorious day, and I love your backyard."

He handed her the Cokes, balanced both plates in one
hand, and didn't even try to hide his smile. "You're wearing
my shirt." He'd left it hanging on a peg in the bathroom.
He eyed the two top buttons that remained open. "You
must be warm."

Niki blushed the same becoming pink he was quickly getting used to. "I know I should have asked, but you'd gone off to answer the door and I—well—I needed to get dressed. I didn't think you would mind."

"I don't. That shirt fits you better than it does me. Keep it." He eyed the two open top buttons again.

Niki quickly buttoned them up and followed him outdoors. "I'll launder it and get it back to you."

They sat under a billowing umbrella on two teakwood chairs. Niki looked around Cary's spacious backyard in quiet assessment. "Beautiful."

"I bought this house primarily because I loved the yard. I wanted privacy and a yard filled with flowers and trees," Cary said, in answer to her comment.

"You chose well. Those morning glories are divine. Just look at the way they cover that fence. You must have done the landscaping yourself."

"I had quite a bit of help, actually." That had been the case. He'd designed the yard, but his men had done most of the hard work. "What's your place like in San Francisco?" He envisioned utilitarian furniture and everything in its place. People's homes were so often an extension of themselves.

Niki smiled. She was on to him. "Austere. Sterile. Nothing like this. I'm seldom there and have no time to decorate."

"Most people make time for what they want to do."

She sighed. "I'm afraid I'm much too busy."

What could an unemployed woman be doing to keep that occupied? Sounded like an excuse to him. "Busy doing what?" he probed.

"Stuff. My life in San Francisco is quite full."

He wondered if this busyness had something to do with

the beeper she never left home without. Should he continue to press her?

"Dad?" Brett called from inside.

"Yes, son." Cary was already on his feet, heading into the house. "Pizza's here. You have a choice. White or pepperoni."

"Pepperoni and a large bottle of Coke."

"Coming up."

"Is Niki still with you?" the little boy asked.

"I'm still here," Niki shouted back.

"Good. Bring her in with you, Dad. I like her about as much as I like pizza."

Cary stuck his head in the refrigerator, searching for the bottle of soda. He wondered what it would take to convince Niki Hamilton he liked her even more.

Chapter 10

The phone on Glenn Jacoby's desk rang for what seemed like the hundredth time. He'd gotten so used to its incessant jingling that for the most part he'd relegated all calls to voice mail. Today was different, though. He was expecting a call from Niki Hamilton. She would let him know when she was coming back.

"Hey," Glenn said, deepening his voice in the fashion someone once told him was sexy.

"Uh, I'm calling for your hospital administrator, Glenn Jacoby."

Glenn quickly became all business. "This is he."

"My name is Sharon Lewis, with the California Board of Medicine. What can you tell us about Dr. Onika Hamilton?"

Glenn went instantly on the alert, not that it was unusual

to hear from someone at the state board. Patients or relatives too often contacted them to lodge complaints about their doctors.

"May I inquire as to why you're asking?" he said, playing the game.

"We've been asked to review several cases involving Dr. Hamilton. This is a courtesy call to let you know we're about to launch a formal investigation."

Glenn scratched behind one ear. Any investigation could take years. The process would require a peer group to review Niki's cases and pass judgment. Meanwhile, she would be free to practice medicine. What concerned him more was the press getting hold of this information and using it to discredit the hospital and its hard-working staff. Damnit! Things were beginning to heat up. He needed to talk to Bill.

"I appreciate the call," Glenn said, preparing to disconnect. "Please keep me posted."

"I'll do that."

After he'd hung up, he sat for a long time, fingers drumming on the desk. Niki had lost three patients in a relatively short period of time. Even so, she was a conscientious and ethical doctor who'd been in the running for Chief of Staff Pediatrics until this. His job was to preserve the hospital's good name, and at the same time make sure his butt was covered.

The blinking red light on the answering machine got Niki's attention. Even though Kim had said it was perfectly acceptable to check for messages once a day, old habits died hard, and her Hippocratic oath inevitably kicked in. It could be a matter of life and death.

Cary and Brett still very much on her mind, Niki

depressed the rewind button, listening to the tape whirr. Despite Brett's mishap and the time spent caring for him, she'd enjoyed being with father and son. They'd devoured pizza, watched a video, and eaten more of Cary's delicious ice cream than she cared to think of. Then they'd played Monopoly and conspired to let Brett win.

When Niki realized she was getting much too comfortable, she'd decided it was prudent to go home. Despite Cary's efforts to convince her otherwise, she'd said her farewells and left.

Even now, images of Brett's and Cary's disappointed faces surfaced. The more she got to know the man, the more she liked him. His easy manner made her comfortable. His sense of humor kept her in stitches. He was warm, personable, and caring. What was the problem, then? She'd never considered herself a snob, but could a doctor and a landscaper really make it? A doctor and a house painter hadn't. Cary was looking for a mother for his son. She, with her busy lifestyle, would be a horrible fit.

The tape had fully rewound itself. Kim's voice came through loud and clear.

"Hey, girl, figured I'd check in with you." Kim sounded a lot more upbeat than she had in a long time. "Ma's doing real well. The doctor says if she continues with therapy she should be fully recovered. I'm considering hiring a nurse, and my sister-in-law's offered to stop by every day. If things go smoothly, I'll be back in a couple of weeks. Can you hang in until—" There was a loud beep as the machine cut her off.

Niki knew she should be delighted Kim was thinking about returning to take over the business, yet sadness engulfed her. Kim's return would be a reminder that she needed to think about her own departure for San Francisco. She couldn't hide in New Jersey forever. She had her career to think about—what was left of it. The hospital had granted her a leave, but not indefinitely. Besides, it was time to start thinking about facing the real world again. She missed her patients. Missed volunteering at the clinic.

God, she'd vowed not to let work intrude, but she couldn't help wondering how Robyn, the baby diagnosed with HIV, was doing. Phillip, while a dedicated and caring doctor, didn't have the same bond with her patients. He tended them diligently but felt that the solution to most of their ailments lay in the prescriptions he wrote. She, on the other hand, thought of her patients as friends. She listened carefully, realizing that much of their hurt was more mental than physical. She was always careful to limit the pills.

Ignoring the manila envelope with its stacks of mail, Niki listened to other business-related messages. She jotted down names and numbers, making notes to return calls, set up video viewing times, and check on those clients who'd been out on dates. This dating service business was certainly busy, but a far cry from what she'd been trained to do.

The next message got her attention. "Kim, it's Lisa. Call me back."

Lisa Williams, her artsy college suitemate who now ran a successful jewelry business out of Seattle. Lisa, with her wispy voice and off-the-wall ideas. Lisa, who clearly thought out of the box. Niki decided to return the call and surprise the heck out of her friend. That would take her mind off Cary and the unopened mail still waiting to be sorted through.

It was six o'clock in the Pacific Northwest, dinnertime. If she tried now, she just might catch Lisa. The phone rang for what seemed an interminable number of moments.

"Hello."

Her friend sounded out of breath and harried. Niki pictured her in one of her billowing thrift-shop purchases, wild hair framing her face. The divorcee had never remarried and swore she never would.

"Thought I'd surprise you," Niki said.

"You did, Ms. Thang. You did. To what do I owe this pleasure?"

"I'm filling in for Kim. Her mother's sick. I got your message and thought I'd return the call. Is there something you needed?"

"A good dose of Kim's humor. I'm starting to feel stressed. Making jewelry's supposed to be fun, but lately all I want to do is go sit on a beach and veg. Is Kim's mom all right?"

"The recovery process has been slow." Niki went on to explain that she was running the place in Kim's absence.

Lisa's loud laughter filled the receiver. "Level-headed Dr. Onika Hamilton, running a dating service? This I must see."

"Then come visit. Believe it or not, I'm enjoying it immensely. You should see the characters I meet."

"Any good men?" Lisa asked coyly.

"That depends on how you define good."

"Now there you go again, being the rational doctor. Just answer the question, hon. Are there any Mr. Finer Than Fines with halfway decent jobs?"

"Like I said, come see for yourself. It's the Fourth of July in two weeks. You've got that extra day. Kim might be back, and we'd love the company."

Lisa paused, apparently considering the invitation. "I suppose I could do that. Flying's hardly costly these days. I just got a huge advance from a commission. I'll check my calendar and get back to you."

"Do that. It's been a long time," Niki said. "Too long." She ended the call.

Taking the manila envelope with her, she headed upstairs, making a mental note to call the hospital and have Phillip or the cleaning lady check on her apartment. Thankfully, she kept a spare key at the hospital.

It was still fairly early, and Niki began straightening up the bedroom, another task that would delay her sorting through that mail. She sat cross-legged on the bed watching the evening news. Eventually she took a deep breath and tackled the stacks. Anything business-related went in one pile. She could not take this personally. She'd done everything in her power to prevent that boy from dying. Her conscience was clear.

The first letter made her feel a whole lot better. It was from an ex-patient offering his support. The second was from someone venting about the disservices of HMOs. So far no threatening, hateful mail, as she had anticipated. Feeling somewhat relieved, Niki slowly worked her way through the piles. There were angry people who felt she should have taken more of a stand, but a large number were from advocacy groups, people she'd heard of, or people she knew. People who supported her.

She exhaled a pent-up breath and allowed herself to relax. She could handle this. Everyone was entitled to his own opinion. Toward the bottom of the stack, she found a poorly typed envelope with her name misspelled. She'd received correspondence like this before, filled with hateful, venomous words. Was there no end to it? She'd concluded the sender was barely literate, perhaps someone she'd inadvertently upset. Niki inserted a thumb under the flap and removed a torn page.

Murdirer! I'm goin' make sure you don't hurt no other childrin.

The spot where there should have been a signature held a splotch of red that looked suspiciously like blood.

Niki set the letter aside. Her temples throbbed and little pinpoints of light flickered before her eyes. She'd been deluding herself, expecting the hate mail to abate. The phone calls were bound to come next.

Squeezing her eyes shut, she tried to think rationally. The mail had been forwarded from San Francisco. No one knew she was in New Jersey except for Glenn, Phillip and her friends. Her head pounded. No prescribed drug would soothe that ache. From a distance, she heard the ringing phone. It only added to her discomfort. She was tempted to roll over, place the pillow over her head, and let the machine pick up. What if it were Phillip? He'd call rather than beep if one of her patients' lives was in jeopardy.

Niki groaned and reached for the receiver. "Hello."

"You sound awful, hon. Everything all right?"

Hon? The pounding in her head didn't even begin to match the thumping of her heart. What was Cary doing calling her when they'd only been apart a few hours?

"I'm OK. Just fighting a headache."

"I'll be glad to come over and take care of you. You must have some Tylenol in the house." He sounded concerned, as if her hurt was his hurt.

"Thank you, but I'll feel a whole lot better once I get some sleep." His offer was lovely, but she couldn't accept. She did not need Cary Thomas visiting at this hour. Much too tempting.

"OK, if you're sure. Did you by chance leave something at my house?"

Niki's fingers circled her forehead. What could she have forgotten at Cary's? She made a mental inventory. They'd thrown her wet shirt into the dryer, and she'd folded it and brought it with her. She had her purse. She'd used the keys to get into the house. What was he talking about?

"You left your beeper behind," Cary informed her.

"Did I?" Niki's hand instinctively reached for her waistband and the pager she never left home without. It wasn't there. How had she become so forgetful? Wearing that beeper was like wearing underwear. She never left home without either.

"I'll bring it by tomorrow," Cary said, "unless you'd prefer it tonight. We need to talk about our double date, anyway. I've already convinced Aaron to come along. He owns the largest pharmacy in town."

She wanted that beeper. Badly. But she couldn't risk having him drag Brett out. The child was still running a low-grade fever. Phillip knew where to find her if it was critical.

She came to a decision. "Thanks, but tomorrow's good enough. I'm going to try getting some sleep. Do me a favor. If my pager goes off, call me immediately."

"See you tomorrow, then. Sleep tight. Don't let the bedbugs bite."

Niki chuckled. She hadn't heard anyone say that in years.

Cary Thomas had thrown her normally orderly life off kilter. He was responsible for her forgetfulness. His presence, even the sound of his voice, affected her rationality and made her breathing escalate. Maybe it was time to think about getting back to San Francisco.

Cary dressed carefully. It was important to him to make the right impression. Gray slacks, collarless shirt, navy blazer. Casual chic or the country gentleman look, which was it to be? Would Niki even care?

A glance in the mirror confirmed he was presentable.

Aaron had been instructed to choose the place for their date. Man around town, he knew every upscale establishment there was and then some. The supper club he'd eventually selected in nearby Seabright was intimate but not stuffy.

A touch of cologne to the jaw and Cary was ready. He hadn't felt this unsure of himself since—since he'd taken his first crush to the movies. His edginess had nothing to do with Deandra Moore. He could care less about her. Aaron could be counted on to make her feel special.

Definitely no pickup truck tonight, Cary thought, searching for and locating the keys to his BMW. The vehicle spent more time in his garage than on the road. If he planned on impressing Niki Hamilton and getting her to change her mind about him, he would pick up Deandra Moore in style.

Meanwhile, Aaron had been dispatched to get Niki. It had been five whole days since Cary had seen her—an eternity, it seemed. Even when he'd dropped off her beeper, their conversation had been limited. He'd been rushing off to smooth out a misunderstanding with one of his clients and she'd been on the phone. She'd paused to open the door and thank him, and then returned to her conversation.

Twenty minutes and a few wrong turns later, Cary pulled up in front of an elegant home in Atlantic Highlands. From the vantage point on top of the bluff, the lights of New York City twinkled. Deandra was doing well for herself, obviously.

He followed a stone-strewn path to the front door and rang the bell. Seconds later, a woman's silhouette could be seen through the frosted glass pane. The door was thrown open. It took Cary a while to adjust to the blinding light spilling from the house. Deandra Moore slowly came into focus. She stared at him, a welcoming smile on her face.

In person she was even more gorgeous than in her video. Her curve-hugging red dress with its plunging neckline stopped midthigh. Shimmering hose covered ample but shapely legs, the envy of even Tina Turner. He had the feeling Aaron was in for a treat.

"Hi," Deandra said, eyeing him up and down. "When I saw your video I thought you were a white boy. You look even more so in person."

"Is there a problem with that?" he asked, managing to keep his smile fixed. He was sick to death of hearing people say that.

"No problem. So long as you know who you are."

"I've never forgotten," Cary said smoothly. He extended his hand. "Cary Thomas."

"Deandra Moore. Come in. I'll be ready shortly."

Cary followed her across marble floors and into a sitting room that looked like it was from *House Beautiful*. His expert eye told him a professional had been called in to do the decorating. Deandra had disposable income, obviously. Why was she having a hard time finding a man?

"I chose to go the route of using a dating service," Deandra said, as if reading his mind, " because I am an extremely busy woman. Commuting back and forth to New York leaves me little time for meeting people. How about you? Why did you use a service?"

He couldn't tell her the real reason. It wouldn't go over well to say, *Because I wanted to get to know the person running Coffee Mates*. Instead he said, "Like you, I'm extremely busy."

"Have a seat. Help yourself to a drink." Deandra gestured to an elegant white couch that looked as though no one had ever sat on it. Before departing, she pointed to a lacquered entertainment center that held a bar.

Cary sat. The evening would not be boring. Of that he was certain.

Chapter 11

"How long have you known Kim?" Aaron Smith asked, clearly making conversation. All the while, his eyes darted to the entrance of the upscale little supper club he'd brought Niki to.

"We went to school together," Niki responded, doing her best to keep her focus on Aaron. "How long have you and Cary been friends?"

Niki tugged on the hem of the black silk dress she'd borrowed from Kim's closet. It was the most demure outfit Kim had. Even so, it ended a good four inches above the knee, leaving her feeling exposed. She tucked an escaping tendril of the hair she'd blown dry behind one ear. Why had she chosen not to wear her glasses tonight?

Aaron stirred his vodka and tonic with a finger. "Cary and I have known each other since nursery school."

"That long?" Talking about Cary had piqued her interest.

"Yup. Since we were four. That's thirty-four years, if you can believe it. We were joined at the hip until Cary went off to college." Clearly bored, his gaze wandered again.

"Cary's a college graduate?" Niki knew her tone said it all. "What's he doing landscaping?"

"Landscaping?" Aaron seemed to find that amusing, "Cary's a—there they are." He leaped up, waving at the two people who'd just walked in. "Over here," he shouted, his tone escalating a couple of decibels. He ogled the woman accompanying Cary.

Niki's stomach clenched. Deandra Moore was beautiful, her carriage regal. How could she hope to compete? What on earth was she thinking of? She'd agreed to this double date only because she didn't want to lose the business for Kim. Kim's contract had a satisfaction guaranteed clause. She didn't want to have to refund Cary's money because he was displeased with the service.

Niki's eyes were riveted on Cary as he headed their way. In his navy jacket and crisp white shirt, he looked like any successful Fairhaven banker. Better. She willed her breathing to settle. This was Deandra and Cary's date, not hers.

Cary held the stockbroker by the elbow and guided her their way. As they advanced, heads turned. Niki admitted they were a striking couple, but was that the only reason why they'd gotten the patrons' attention? She'd grown up the child of mixed parentage. She was used to the curious looks thrown her parents' way. In this case, they were mistaken.

"You made it," Cary said, coming to a full stop in front of their table. Introductions completed, he held out a chair for Deandra.

"Thanks." The stockbroker slipped into the seat and tilted her head back, flashing him a smile.

Niki wanted to throttle her. She squelched the ugly feelings that were beginning to surface. She didn't have any claim on Cary and had no reason to react this way. She smiled brightly at Aaron. The pharmacist ignored her. His tongue hung to the floor as he gaped at Deandra, who looked like no stockbroker Niki had ever met before. Although she was dressed in Kim's sexy black number, Niki felt mousy and unattractive beside this woman. Time to remember her role was solely to play chaperon.

"That outfit is extremely becoming," Cary said, leaning across the table and beaming at her.

Deandra's eyebrows rose. She shifted in her seat as if to say, *Remember me? I'm your date.*

Aaron came to the rescue. "We're a lucky pair, escorting the two best looking women in the house."

"That we are," Cary said, apparently finding his manners.

"Drinks?" A waiter's arrival put an end to further conversation. He took their order, then disappeared.

During the course of dinner, Niki learned Deandra was an overachiever. Not only did she have a successful career, she skied, played tennis, and was the president of the local branch of African-American Women in Business. Accomplished, but a tad overbearing, Niki thought.

They made it through the meal with Deandra monopolizing the conversation. Cary now seemed to hang on her every word, as did Aaron. Even though Niki silently congratulated herself for making a successful match, she found herself getting depressed.

With coffee and dessert out of the way, Aaron suggested they head for the dance floor. Niki squelched a brief moment of dread. Here were two men clearly interested in the same woman, leaving her the outsider, the unwanted fifth wheel.

Her toe tapping, she hovered on the periphery of the crowded dance floor, listening to a loud 'N Sync tune. Cary had managed to maneuver a spot beside her.

"Let's dance." It was more an invitation than a question.

Why wasn't he asking his date to dance? Remembering her role as chaperon of this fiasco, she prompted him, "Shouldn't you be asking Deandra?"

"Deandra who? Oh, that Deandra. Aaron's got that covered."

Niki couldn't help but smile when his fingers circled her arm, and he propelled her out to the floor and found them a spot. She had never been big on free form, didn't have the time to keep up with current moves. She did her best to ape Cary, but when his steps became too intricate, she pulled back. Watching Cary dance told her a lot. There was no doubt in her mind he was black.

She glanced over to see Deandra and Aaron one-upping each other. With loud whoops and a series of hollers, they bumped shoulders, hips, and butts. The two were well suited for each other in every way. A stockbroker certainly had more in common with a pharmacist than a landscaper, even if Cary was an educated one.

Niki had been shocked to hear about Cary's degree. On perusing his application, she'd noted he was looking for an educated woman, but that's all it'd said. She'd assumed he was hanging his hat high, aspiring to find a woman with the credentials he lacked.

Deandra shimmied in front of them. The straps of the red dress hung to midarm, her generous assets pouring over the neckline. Everything jiggled. Niki decided a discreet disappearance was in order. She turned to go, but Aaron enveloped her in his arms. The music slowed.

Niki was pressed up against Aaron's chest, encased in his sinewy arms, overcome by the cloying smell of a powerful cologne that made her slightly nauseous. Aaron's hands dipped lower, coming dangerously close to cupping her buttocks. Niki remembered counting the four, maybe five, vodkas he'd downed during dinner. This sudden interest in her was fueled by alcohol, designed to get Deandra's attention. How to delicately retreat without causing a scene?

Aaron halted when Cary tapped him on the shoulder. "I'm cutting in, buddy. Help me out with Deandra."

This time she was thrust into the arms she wanted to be in, her head resting against a broad chest. She inhaled the clean smell of a freshly laundered shirt and let his strong arms circle her waist. Cary's curly head dipped. Niki thought he was going to kiss her out here for all the world to see. She remembered the fleeting touch of his lips, the intensity of the passionate second kiss they'd shared. She couldn't let it happen. He was on a date with another woman.

Inches from her mouth, Cary stopped. "You looked like you needed saving." His breath smelled ever so slightly of citrus, like the screwdriver he'd been nursing all night long.

"Was it that obvious?"

"Obvious to me."

They continued to dance. Her heart pounding, all her senses in overdrive, Niki followed his expert lead. She closed her eyes and saw Cary clear as day, his dark curls shining, his skin the color of fresh cream. She heard the sharp intake of his breath as their bodies melded, smelled his expensive cologne, and tasted the salt on his skin. The coarse hairs on his arms rubbed against her flesh. God, she was bowled over by the man. It didn't make sense.

The song ended and reality slowly returned. Aaron and Deandra waited off to the side.

"Uh-oh. Looks like trouble in paradise," Niki said, when she was able to talk.

"We'll soon find out."

Still holding her hand, but looking increasingly grim, Cary sidestepped the still exuberant dancers and made his way toward the couple.

Deandra's smile was a tad strained when they approached. She crooked a finger at Niki. "I need to use the ladies' room. Will you join me?"

Inside the powder-blue lounge, Deandra confronted Niki. "What exactly are you up to?"

"I beg your pardon?"

"Don't play little Miss Innocent. This is supposed to be my date, yet the sparks coming off both you and Cary can ignite a fire."

Niki'd been denying it all along, yet here was a third party confirming what she already knew. She and Cary Thomas had a strong physical attraction to each other. Where that would lead, who knew?

"You're mistaken," Niki said. "Mr. Thomas asked me to accompany him on this date only because he felt double dating would take the pressure off you."

"BS. He asked you to accompany him because he wanted to spend time with you. Look, I'm not mad. Aaron and I are probably better suited to each other anyway. But for gawd's sake, be adult enough to acknowledge the attraction." Deandra kissed her on the cheek. "Go after it, girl, if that's what you want."

Suddenly Niki realized it *was* what she wanted. Despite their differences, she wanted Cary Thomas. Wanted him with every fiber in her body. Needed him like the air that she breathed. He made her feel alive.

* * *

Niki returned from the ladies' room in a strange mood. Cary couldn't help wondering what had gone on between the women. Whatever, the results were clearly in his favor. Deandra had promptly latched on to Aaron, and Niki seemed more amenable to being with him. They'd danced a few more sets, exchanged partners occasionally, and finally decided to call it a night. Aaron had asked to take Deandra home, leaving him free to drive Niki.

Now Niki sat in the passenger seat of the BMW, no sign of a beeper visible. He wondered if it had been relegated to the small purse she carried. The evening she'd left her pager at his place he'd been consumed by curiosity and guiltily punched the memory button, noting the same number coming up repeatedly. He'd dialed and gotten a Dr. Phillip Jordan's office.

Naturally he'd hung up. It had made him wonder if Niki was ill. That would certainly explain why she didn't have a job and why her stay on the shore had been extended indefinitely.

"Nice car," Niki said, touching the wood trim on the dashboard. "Is it a rental?"

"No. It's mine."

From her sharp intake of breath, she seemed surprised that he might own such an expensive vehicle. "What did you think of Deandra?" she asked, changing the subject.

"She's a good looking woman. Certainly upbeat and personable. . ."

". . . but not for you?"

"Definitely not for me. She's better suited to Aaron."

"Maybe the next one will work out better," Niki said.

"There will be no next one."

What kind of game was she playing? Was she deliberately

ignoring his interest in her? His eyes strayed to the legs she'd crossed one over the other. Beautiful legs. He liked the sexy black dress that was so becoming, but would hazard a guess it wasn't hers. Onika Hamilton didn't normally wear that kind of outfit.

He pulled up in front of Kim's Victorian and put the car in park. When Niki reached for the handle on the passenger door, he leaned across, stopping her. "I had fun tonight. Did you?"

"Yes."

That one word spoke volumes. He dared to hope. "What are we going to do about us?"

"There is no us."

She was sending mixed messages again. Inside the club, they'd danced as one. She'd melted into his arms. Frustrated, Cary exploded. "What's the problem? I'm not good enough? Or are you just determined to ignore the chemistry between us? Not many people communicate without saying a word."

"So what if we do connect?"

What did it take to get through to her? He tried again. "Is it every day you find someone who turns you on physically and mentally? Is it that easy to find a compatible mate? Someone who likes your son and he likes her back?"

Niki shifted uneasily and reached for the door handle again.

Cary was quicker. He had no right to pursue this. No hold on her. Maybe if he told her what he did for a living, that would make the difference.

She turned back to him, her voice low. "What would be the point in our embarking on a relationship? I live in San Francisco, and I have to start thinking about getting back."

"Sounds like a good excuse. Make geography an issue.

People have long-distance relationships all the time. They manage. Is it that you're scared of becoming too attached? Emotionally dependent on me?"

"Maybe."

"You're afraid of getting hurt?"

Niki shifted uneasily. Cary reached across and folded her into his arms. Her entire body quivered. "Don't be scared," he said. "Get rid of the stone wall around your heart and give me passage."

Before she could utter another word, he kissed her.

It was a mistake. From the time his mouth made contact with hers, he forgot where they were, forgot he had a business to run, forgot he had a son—well, almost. He slid his tongue into her mouth, circled, and urged her to join him. Tentatively at first, her tongue met his. Advance. Retreat. A sophisticated tango. A murmur of longing came from her throat. His pants felt as if they were sizes too tight. Under that hard exterior was a vulnerable woman.

Niki Hamilton wasn't as tough as she would have him believe. Even if there was something about her that didn't add up, he wanted to get to know her better. San Francisco wasn't that far away.

Chapter 12

From the moment their mouths made contact, Niki chastised herself for allowing it to happen. How did a practical woman turn to mush in this man's arms? Why had she allowed him to kiss her? She couldn't breathe, much less think. One of Cary's hands was now on her thigh, manipulating her flesh, driving her wild. What had happened to her resolve?

"We should go into the house," he whispered. "Get more comfortable." Even as he spoke, his fingers drew question marks against her inner thigh, then slowly crept upward.

Unable to answer right away, she moaned. What little there was left of her brain cautioned her not to invite him in. But they couldn't just sit out here in the driveway, making out like teenagers. What if Kim's neighbors saw them?

"OK, just for a second. I have an early day tomorrow," she said.

He slid out of the driver's seat and came around to her side. But even in that brief moment of separation she felt abandoned. Missed his touch.

Inside, they faced each other awkwardly. Niki stared at Cary's tousled head of hair, the way his clothes were mussed, and wondered if she also had the look that said, *We just shared some pretty good loving.*

It was Cary who first broke the charged silence. He held his arms wide. "Shall we pick up where we left off?"

Like a puppet on a string, she was pulled toward him, drawn by some invisible force. He met her halfway, folded her into his arms, and kissed the tip of her ear. For what seemed hours, they remained that way, holding each other. Listening to each other's breathing.

"I think we should sit," Cary said after a while. "I'm beginning to cramp."

Not a good idea, her head said, though her heart thought otherwise. If she made Cary too comfortable, it would make it increasingly harder for her to ask him to leave.

Against her better judgment, she said, "Let's go into the den."

In there, Cary sank onto an oversized camel-back couch loaded with pillows.

"Come sit," he invited, patting the space next to him.

"Let me fix you a drink," Niki offered, turning on the lamps and bathing the room in a soft pink hue. Delaying would buy her time and allow her hormones to settle.

"I've had my fill. Quit stalling and get over here."

"What?" She'd never been spoken to like that. She blinked at him, wishing she had her glasses to hide behind. For years they had provided her security.

"Do I sound Neanderthal?" Cary's whiskey-colored eyes

twinkled. "I want you next to me. I want to smell that sexy fragrance that's been driving me crazy from the moment I met you."

She'd never met a man quite like him. There'd always been a certain reverence when men addressed Dr. Onika Hamilton. But Cary didn't know she was a doctor. What's more, she had the feeling he wouldn't care.

Niki sat carefully. Immediately Cary nuzzled her shoulder. His lips brushed her neck and his hands began a slow exploration, trailing up and down her arms, roaming her back. His hands caressed her legs, manipulating the soft flesh. Driving her wild. The little black dress hiked thigh high.

She'd never felt like this before. None of the three men she'd allowed into her life had made her feel this way— certainly not her ex-husband. Niki's breathing came in little spurts. Her entire body felt flushed. Her center throbbed, a pulsating ache that wouldn't go away, preventing logical thought. Nothing and no one had ever felt this good.

Cary moaned, a deep rumbling sound. Niki decided to throw caution to the wind. So what if a relationship with him seemed impossible? For the second time around, why not follow her heart?

As if from a distance, Niki heard the creak of the zipper on the little black dress. Cary's kisses on her neck were moist and passionate. He slid the straps of the dress down and ran a hand across her skimpy lace bra. Bending over, he laved her nipples through the lace. Niki groaned when his palms cupped her breasts, stroking, manipulating, caressing.

They moved into a prone position with her on top of him. The dress was bunched around her waist. Cary's palms kneaded her buttocks, pressing her into him. She could feel his erection. Pulsating, huge, hot. Oh, God. She should make him stop.

"If you don't want this to go any further, you'd better say so now," he said.

But she wanted it to go further, needed him to keep touching her. He'd made her realize she was capable of feeling again.

"Niki?"

Cary's hands wrapped around her waist, lifting her slightly. He looked into her eyes.

"Do you have protection?" she asked.

A wide smile broke across his face. "I think so. Old, but still serviceable. I'll need to get up for a moment."

She got up and watched him undress. He took his wallet from the pocket of his trousers, removed a foil package, and set it on a nearby table. "Couch or bed?" he asked.

"Couch," she automatically responded, knowing if they changed locations she might chicken out.

"Come," Cary said. "I need to hold you."

He'd stripped down to his briefs, and a swirl of hair matted his golden chest. Only the barrier of their underwear separated them. Niki stroked his muscular back, her fingers outlining each muscle. Cary kissed the sides of her neck before putting her away from him briefly. His tongue found her cleavage. She felt a sudden rush of air as he unsnapped her bra and his mouth fastened around one nipple.

"I want you so badly, it's a physical ache, honey," Cary said. "I've wanted you from the moment I laid eyes on you and heard that intriguing accent."

"Is that a fact?" Her voice sounded husky. Sexy.

"That's a fact."

Cary's fingers played with the waistband of the matching panties she'd so carefully selected. She slid her hand under the elastic of his briefs, the final barrier separating them. She could no longer deny it. She wanted his skin against hers. Needed to feel his hands on her. Needed him.

They collapsed on the couch and began loving each other. Nothing else registered except them. When Cary entered her, Niki felt a moment of trepidation. She'd taken the final leap and there was no pulling back. She was loving every moment of it. Loving just being with him.

In less than forty minutes, her entire world had changed. It would never be the same again.

Cary had just shrugged on his shirt and was thinking of going home when a series of sharp beeps got his attention. Niki, who had changed into a robe, sprinted toward the purse she'd tossed on a nearby table. She dug through the interior, removed a compact and tissues, and found her pager. After depressing the button and peering intently at the number that had come up, she turned back to him.

"Something wrong, hon?" Cary asked. He came up behind her and kissed the back of her neck.

"I'm not sure." She walked away from him.

Niki had a look on her face he'd never seen before. It was as if there were two Niki Hamiltons—the warm, loving woman he'd just made love to, and the detached, business-like version.

"Excuse me. I need to return this call," she said, heading off.

He knew it was privacy she sought. But did she have to be that abrupt? If it was bad news, he would be there for her. Cary tugged on his socks, stepped into his loafers, and went off to find her.

She was seated at the kitchen counter on an antique wrought iron chair, the receiver pressed to her ear. Cary paused at the entrance, observing, trying his best not to listen to the one-way conversation. Given his location, it was virtually impossible.

"Who are you?" Niki asked in a tight little voice.

The mystery caller must have said something unpleasant, because Niki's tone escalated. "Where did you get my beeper number? Why are you doing this to me?"

She grew increasingly more agitated. The person on the other end was no friend. Niki's body language indicated that.

"Damn it," she screamed, now dangerously close to tears. "Damn it! Why can't you leave me alone?"

Cary didn't wait to hear anything else. He raced across the floor and yanked the receiver from her hand. The man on the other end snarled, "Uppity bitch. You need to pay . . ."

"Who is this?" Cary snapped.

There was a resounding click as the call disconnected.

Before replacing the phone in its cradle, Cary hit the redial button. After a half dozen or so rings, someone finally picked up.

"You bastard," he shouted, "where do you get off calling someone and threatening them?"

"Whoa, hold it a minute, bro. This is a pay phone. I just happened to be walking by."

Cary slammed the phone down and turned back to Niki. She stood, arms folded, looking completely stricken. "Is bozo an old boyfriend? How long has he been at it?" He enfolded her in his arms. "Start from the beginning. Tell me everything."

She sighed, and her whole body relaxed into his. "He's not an old boyfriend, just some guy who gets his jollies harassing me."

"Then you need to call the police and report him."

Niki ran a trembling hand across her face. She'd aged ten years before his eyes. "He's never called my beeper before. I don't even know how he'd get the number. Only a few people have it."

"You'll need to get a new pager," Cary said quietly. "The other alternative is to get rid of it."

"I can't do that."

"Why not?"

"I need my beeper," she insisted.

No explanation. She simply shut down on him. There was nothing to be gained by pursuing this line of conversation.

"As you wish," he said, giving up and kissing the top of her head. "I'm going to have to leave. I promised Brett's baby-sitter I wouldn't make a night of it. Will you be OK?"

"Of course."

"Tonight meant a lot to me," he said, on his way out. "It was made even more special by the present we shared."

"I enjoyed it, too."

He held on to her for another precious moment. "If you ever need a shoulder, I'm here."

"I'll remember that," she said, offering him a watery smile. "I'll remember that."

"Rough night?" Lourdes Gonzales asked the moment he walked through the door.

Cary acknowledged her comment with a smile. Not all of it had been bad. In fact, most of the evening had been wonderful, up until that weird, threatening phone call.

"How was Brett?" he asked, counting out bills, then handing her a couple.

"Kinda quiet. He's still running a fever off and on."

"Hmmmn. It's been going on much too long. I'll have to take him to the doctor."

Lourdes nodded. "You might want to do that." She gathered her purse and the stack of magazines she traveled with.

Cary yawned loudly. "Tomorrow I'll make the appointment."

"Good night." On her way out, Lourdes added over her shoulder, "You got a coupla messages on the machine."

"Anything important?"

"Play them back and judge for yourself." She suddenly seemed in a hurry to leave.

After checking on Brett and making sure he was sleeping soundly, Cary played back his messages. Elsa's voice came across loud and clear. Why did he sense his life was about to change, and not necessarily for the better?

"I'm coming into town on the Fourth of July weekend," she said. "I want to see my son. You've got my number. Call me."

The tape whirred again. Elsa's voice, this time more strident. "Damn it, Cary, where are you? I want to see my son. Call me back."

The third time she was definitely angry. "It's near midnight and you're still not there. Where are you, anyway? What will I need, a court order to see my child?"

Cary was furious. The nerve of Elsa. Since when did she decide to play the role of concerned mother? Four years ago she'd been happy to dump Brett off on him. She'd barely looked back, except for popping into his life a couple times a year and sending the obligatory holiday and birthday gift. Yes, she phoned occasionally. So what?

Elsa's almost total disappearance from Brett's life had suited Cary perfectly. He'd worked diligently to make the boy feel secure. With the aid of a therapist, he'd helped the child erase the memories of abuse suffered at the hands of pedophiles calling themselves baby-sitters.

He would never refuse Elsa the opportunity to see her child. As minuscule a role as she played in his life, what could it hurt? Brett needed reassurance his mother existed. Elsa, on the other hand, finally wanted to acknowledge she had a son. It was too late to call her now. Better wait until tomorrow.

Chapter 13

"I can't wait to see you," Lisa Williams gushed into the receiver. "I got myself one of those e-tickets and I'm counting the days to Fourth of July weekend. Any chance you could pick me up?"

"Absolutely," Niki said. "Oh, Lise, it'll be just like old times."

"Well, not quite. Unless, of course, we can convince Charlie and Kim to join us."

Niki thought for a moment. Could they swing it? Kim had said she might be back, and Charlie could easily be persuaded.

"It would be an expensive weekend," Lisa said, breaking into her thoughts.

"Charlie has tons of frequent flyer miles. I'll ask. She can only say no."

"It would be such fun to have all four of us together again," Lisa said before hanging up.

A mini reunion, that's what it would be. That hadn't happened since the class of '80's cruise aboard the M.S. *Machination*. They would lie in the sun, drink, gossip, and relax. It would help take her mind off the weird calls and threatening letters. She would be too distracted to think about returning to San Francisco.

Niki made a mental note to call Charlie tonight. She'd try to convince her to cash in her frequent flyer miles and join them. Now it was time to get back to work. She had people to interview and calls to return. *Keep busy, Niki. Don't think about Cary.*

Yet how could she not? He'd contracted with Coffee Mates. She still owed him several dates. What to do? Go ahead and set them up, or refund the man's money?

After what they'd shared the other night, the thought of seeing Cary with another woman was simply unbearable. Niki found his work number and dialed. A sense of trepidation engulfed her as the phone continued to ring. It would be the first time they'd spoken since that night. He'd called, but, needing time to think, she simply had not returned his calls.

"Carett Designs," a strange female voice answered eventually.

"I'm trying to get in touch with Cary Thomas," Niki said, omitting any mention of her association with Coffee Mates. Most people weren't big on advertising the fact they'd hired a company to find them dates.

"Cary's not in," the woman said. "He took his son to the doctor. May I help you?"

Niki's heart did triple loops. "What's wrong with Brett?"

"I don't know. Cary just said he was running a temperature. May I have your name? May I give him a message?"

Niki left her name and number, then hung up. She hoped Brett was OK and wished she could help in some way. What had happened between her and Cary had shaken her to the core. Dr. Onika Hamilton didn't have casual sex. Though, truth be told, there'd been nothing casual about the sex they'd had. It had been deep, intense, powerful, and moving. No one before had made her feel this way.

She was scared of the new feelings Cary had unleashed in her. Scared that despite her efforts to guard her heart, she'd permitted him entrance. How could she have allowed this to happen? How had she allowed herself to fall in love with another blue collar worker? Why couldn't she find someone with a better position? Clout?

Love? Had she really fallen in love, or was it deep like? Was she confusing good sex with deeper emotions? Whatever, she needed to get over it, and fast. Soon she would have to start thinking about getting back to San Francisco. Her leave couldn't go on forever. Phillip, good friend that he was, wasn't superman. He could cover for her only so long before getting burned out.

Determined to blank her mind, Niki methodically punched data into the computer. Work would keep her occupied. She paused briefly to pet Scarlet, who was making catlike noises at her feet. In the back of her mind, she acknowledged her beeper number still needed to be changed. Was it worth the trouble? Would the man dare call again?

The phone rang, startling her. Niki squelched her jittery feelings and picked up. Kim had a business to run. She couldn't let it suffer on account of one idiot.

"Coffee Mates," she said, forcing her voice to sound upbeat.

"Yo, girlfriend."

At hearing Kim's voice on the other end, Niki's entire

body relaxed. Her friend sounded like her old self. It must be good news.

"I'm coming home, girl, I'm coming home," Kim sang. "I'll be there to bring in the Fourth of July with you."

"That's great," Niki said. "Lisa's planning a visit and I'm trying to convince Charlie to come. I figured you wouldn't mind."

"Cool. It'll be like old times. All the homegirls together."

Until then, Niki hadn't realized how stressed she was or how much the threatening phone calls and running Coffee Mates had taken their toll. She hadn't minded helping Kim. She'd been grateful to keep occupied, though admittedly it was a far cry from what she was trained for. Still, she'd learned a valuable lesson from all this. She hadn't realized what business acumen it took to manage a dating service. Professional matchmaking meant you had personal responsibility and accountability for other people's lives.

"I'll see you in a week, then," Kim said.

"Can't wait," Niki responded. "Can't wait, girl. I've missed you." She hung up.

"Where were you?" Elsa griped. "I left several messages. You could have at least returned one call."

"I did," Cary answered, his attention still focused on the design he'd been working on. "Brett wasn't well and I needed to get him to a doctor. When I got around to calling you back, no one answered."

As Elsa continued to berate him, Cary's mind wandered. He'd finally joined the twenty-first century, abandoning his drafting table for the newly purchased Landcadd program. The software had made his life so much easier. It created estimates, provided an inventory of plants, and even produced site plans. The serenity garden he was working on was looking better and better.

"Cary, I'm the one doing all the talking," Elsa railed.

"That's because I can't get a word in edgewise."

"You said Brett was sick. What's wrong with him?"

Cary explained the child had been running a low-grade fever.

"Is he better now? I'll be in town the Fourth of July weekend. Any possibility of seeing both of you?"

"His doctor prescribed antibiotics," Cary answered carefully, still processing the news of Elsa's imminent arrival. "He should be fine by the time you get here. It's been a while since he's seen you."

"What about you? Will you make time to see me?"

Cary had always made a point of not being around when Elsa came to the house. Lourdes Gonzales had grown quite adept at handling her.

"What would we have to discuss that can't be said over the phone?" Cary said evenly.

"Quite a bit. For one, I'm thinking of moving back to Long Branch. My boy's getting older, and I plan on playing a more prominent role in his life."

Cary felt as if someone had driven a nail through his head. Elsa's announcement had served to fan his already rising temperature. Where did she get off wanting to reenter Brett's life at this late stage? Her return would only disrupt the orderly life he'd created for himself and his child. He was processing new feelings for Niki Hamilton, trying to determine when exactly he'd fallen in love with her. Now, without warning, his ex was coming back to town.

"Why are you coming back to Long Branch?" he asked.

"My son's there. So is the man I love."

The pounding in his head escalated. There was a time when he'd wanted her badly, when he'd thought they stood a chance, and that maybe, just maybe, they could create a life around Brett. But he'd quickly been stripped of his illusions. Elsa was a user, a supreme manipulator of people. He doubted she'd changed with age.

"So when can we get together to talk?" Elsa asked.

The pounding had turned into a persistent drumming. "I don't know, Elsa. I mean, what would that really accomplish? I've got custody of Brett. I've allowed you to see him any time you've asked."

"That's not good enough. I want to be a part of his life. I want him to know his mommy is there when he needs her."

"You forfeited that right the day you walked out on him," Cary couldn't stop himself from saying.

"It wasn't like that. I needed to make a living."

He closed his ears to her pleas. "And you did. You've made a good living for several years now. That's why I don't understand the sudden interest. I have to go now."

He hung up before she could say another word.

"This is quite an impressive proposal," Bill Morris said to the man seated across from him as the *che-ching* of a cash register went off in his head. Glenn was going to be pleased. "Give me some time to review it and I'll get back to you." He stood, holding out his hand, signaling the meeting was over.

The man winked. "Of course there'll be the usual finder's fee, if you decide in our favor."

"Of course."

They shook hands and Bill escorted him to the escalator.

Returning to his office, proposal still in hand, Bill sat for a moment contemplating. If he could push this contract through, he stood to make a bundle.

The phone rang. He was tempted not to pick up. It was way past his lunch time, and he wasn't in the mood to deal with persistent vendors.

But, conditioned to answering, he reached for the phone. "Bill Morris."

"Glad I caught you," Glenn Jacoby said. "Do you have time for lunch?"

"Are you buying?"

"I could be persuaded to."

God moved in mysterious ways. Glenn, as always, would be a useful tool in getting the hospital to make this purchase. "Meet you in the cafeteria in ten," he said.

When the two men had gotten their food and sat facing each other, Bill commented, "Glenn, you seem awfully distracted. Is anything wrong?"

The administrator ran a pale hand across his neatly styled hair. "Todd Eldridge's parents have filed suit. The hospital and HMO are under the gun. They're citing corporate negligence. I've been talking to our lawyers all morning."

Though this hardly came as a surprise, Bill frowned. "I would have thought they would have gone after Hamilton, since she was the attending physician."

"Indirectly they *are* going after her. They're taking the tack that an HMO has a duty to exercise reasonable care in ensuring the competency of any physician working in a hospital."

"I thought the Eldridges liked Dr. Hamilton."

"Liking her has nothing to do with it. Their son's dead. Now they're bitter and angry. They've figured they'll probably get a bigger settlement if they sue the hospital. They've also filed complaints with the Department of Corporations and Public Relations."

"I always knew the Eldridges were bloodthirsty," Bill

said, biting into his meat loaf. "They demanded a review the moment HMO denied their boy treatment."

What he didn't say was that someone had sent the Eldridges an anonymous letter urging them to do so. That someone was him.

"And they were denied," Glenn said dryly.

"True, but not a day goes by that the parents' faces aren't plastered over the front page of some paper. It's bad for business. When's Niki Hamilton returning, anyway?"

Glenn shrugged. "I granted her a leave of absence indefinitely. Most likely she'll be back in a couple of weeks. Phil Jordan's overdue for vacation and the poor guy's beginning to burn out."

"Cute that she can conveniently disappear, leaving San Francisco General to face the heat." Bill continued to shovel food into his face.

"I don't think you're being fair." Glenn picked up his bottled water and chugged it. "Niki's had an extremely difficult three months. Until now, she had a good shot at Chief of Staff."

"I'm not being fair, or you aren't being objective? It's common knowledge you're hot for her."

He took one look at Glenn's face and knew he'd crossed the line.

The administrator gulped the remaining water and abruptly stood. "Gotta run, Bill. I'm late for my meeting."

"Give me Niki's number and I'll call and see how she's doing?"

"Why?"

"Because it's the right thing to do."

"You've never had a conscience before."

"Who said I have a conscience now?"

"That figures," Glenn commented, not bothering to look right or left, and left the room.

Chapter 14

"So, girlfriend, do I have lots of new clients?

Kim had arrived only moments ago, and the office practically sizzled with her presence.

"I don't recall being in charge of marketing," Niki joked.

"What if I were to rephrase the question?" Kim dug through the huge piles of mail that had accumulated in her absence. "Did you make lots of good matches? Are my clients happy? Am I happy where it counts?" She patted the oversize purse she'd flung onto a nearby chair.

"Maybe we should do a survey," Niki said, tongue in cheek. "I'm game if you are."

"Wise ass. My sources say you did a bang-up job without me." Kim picked up Scarlet, who'd been rubbing against her ankles, and nuzzled the cat. "By any chance did you meet Mr. Fine while screening my clients? Did he make your socks go up and down?"

"Don't be ridiculous." She knew Kim was fishing. Even so, the telltale heat in her cheeks told her she was beet red and her neck was mottled. "How's your mother?"

"Mom's doing much better." Kim went on to give the details of her mother's progress. "She's got almost complete mobility in one arm and her diction's fairly clear."

"I'm so glad. Sounds like she'll make a full recovery."

"You're avoiding answering my question," Kim persisted. "Did you or did you not meet a potential Mr. Right?"

Niki chuckled. "I thought I was supposed to be running Coffee Mates, not looking for a match as well."

Kim cut her eyes at her, then set Scarlet down. "Let's not forget, I know most everyone there is to know in Long Branch, honey. One day when I couldn't get you, I called Aaron Smith's pharmacy to find out about some medicine Mom was prescribed. He filled me in about you and Cary. Who would have imagined you'd have hooked up with my landscape. . ."

The shrill ringing of the phone cut the conversation short. Niki reached for the receiver, but Kim was quicker. "Hello, Coffee Mates."

Niki could tell from the look on Kim's face that the person on the other end was unpleasant.

"Call again, hotshot, and your butt will be turned over to the police so fast you won't know what hit you," she threatened, slamming down the phone and turning back to Niki. "How long has this idiot been calling?"

Niki's stomach churned. She felt the nausea building. The thing she'd dreaded most had happened. The crank caller had tracked her down. How he'd found her number in New Jersey was anyone's guess.

* * *

Making a point of getting to Monmouth Beach early had paid off. Cary plopped down the two folding chairs and took the cooler from Brett. They'd found a prime spot a little way from the beach club. In less than an hour, the place would be packed. Fourth of July weekend always brought noisy crowds.

As he unfolded the chairs, he watched his son race toward the ocean. The boy's ankle had healed nicely and medication had controlled the lingering fever. Not a word from Elsa. So much for her concern.

"Easy, son," Cary called as Brett kicked sand at another boy who had joined him. It was a picture-perfect day—not too hot to make sitting out uncomfortable, not too cool to avoid venturing into the water. He was looking forward to relaxing.

He'd all but given up on Niki. How many times could a man call and not have his calls returned? Eventually he got the message. Niki hadn't struck him as being fickle, but neither had Elsa. Cary fished a pair of sunglasses out of his knapsack, plopped them on, and prepared to lather on lotion. Brett was still standing at the edge of the surf in animated conversation with his friend.

"I knew eventually you'd show up," a female voice behind Cary said.

So much for peace and quiet.

"Elsa. What do you want?" he said, somewhat rudely.

"What a way to greet a friend."

She was dressed in a teensy little bikini. Knowing she looked good, she strutted her stuff.

Her preening was wasted on him.

"Where's Brett?" Elsa asked, as she lowered herself onto the empty chair next to him.

Cary pointed in the direction of the ocean. "Over there."

With a well-tended hand, Elsa shaded her eyes and looked. "Is that really him? He's gotten so big."

"That's right. You haven't seen him in what, several months?"

"Eight months," Elsa said curtly. "Hardly an eternity. I've been busy earning a living. What's in the cooler?"

"Drinks," Cary said rather abruptly, watching her settle in. He fumbled in his knapsack and found the novel he'd packed.

Elsa reached over and snapped the book shut. She'd always been pushy.

"What the hell?" Cary yelled.

"It's rude reading when you have company. Brett! Brett!" She stood waving at her child.

Her loud shouts got Brett's attention. All smiles, the boy came scurrying across the sand. At that age children were so forgiving.

Elsa met her son halfway. She embraced him, holding him as if he was the most precious thing in the world. Cary swore he saw tears—crocodile ones. To someone who didn't know different, it was the most touching thing in the world. To Cary it was just another staged demonstration, designed to make him think she cared. She was desperate to worm her way back into his life. Something must be going on with that job of hers.

"Dad, Dad!" Brett said, practically hopping from one foot to another. "You knew Mom would be here. Why didn't you tell me?"

Cary couldn't exactly say, *If I'd known your mother was going to be here, we wouldn't be.* He managed a smile somehow. "It's a nice surprise, isn't it?"

"The best." Brett now had a tight hold on his mother's

hand. He tugged her along. "Come on, Mom. Let me introduce you to Jason. He doesn't believe I have a mother."

The child's pride was obvious. Cary guessed he'd been taunted mercilessly by his classmates. Kids could be cruel. After shifting the fashionable sunglasses perched on top of her head to a more secure position, Elsa headed off with Brett.

Cary exhaled a breath and reclined back in his chair, then reached over into the cooler and extracted a beer. It wasn't quite noon, but he sensed it would be a long day. Under normal circumstances, he needed libation to deal with Elsa. These weren't normal circumstances.

"I may very well consider moving to the central Jersey shore," Lisa Williams said when she got her first glance of the beach. "This is too cool." Dressed in a filmy caftan and huge straw hat, Lisa surveyed the pristine white sand and blue-green water. "I say we take up residence right over there." She pointed to a spot under a huge pink and white umbrella.

"Sounds good to me. I'm glad you guys convinced me to come. My talk show's in good hands. A colleague's filling in." Charlie Canfield-Spencer trailed the group while Kim led the way.

After settling onto beach chairs, drinks in hand, Kim said, "What's with you, Nik? You're awfully quiet."

"Am I?" In retrospect, maybe she was. She had a lot to think about, like getting home and resuming her job. Cary Thomas didn't fit into her life. Not that he seemed to want to fit. He hadn't even made the time to call her back. Tit for tat, she supposed. He was probably ignoring her since she'd taken this long to return his calls.

"You've been pensive since I got here," Lisa added. "Sure there's nothing you want to talk about?"

"Leave my girl alone," Kim said, coming to her rescue. "Women tend to get moody when they've fallen in love."

"Kim, stop it," Niki warned.

"Hush your mouth, girl."

"Oh, come on, spill it," Charlie demanded. "I've finagled three glorious days to be with you people. Least you can do is catch me up. I'm meeting Devin in Frisco after this. Niki, any chance of using your place?"

"By all means. I'll give you the key."

"Niki in love?" Lisa Williams chanted, simultaneously raising both eyebrows and making her hat jump up and down. "This I have to hear."

"Kim," Niki warned again, louder, "stop it!" The girls would tease her mercilessly until she gave them details.

"It's like this," Kim said conspiratorially. "Niki met this awesome guy who does work for me. He's a . . ."

"Who's the fine thing heading our way?" Lisa interrupted.

Niki peered through her glasses in the direction Lisa stared. She saw all two-hundred-plus pounds of Aaron Smith bearing down on them.

Lisa whistled softly. "Whoo-whee. Ain't he something?"

"Down, girl. That's Aaron Smith, ex pro football player," Kim supplied. "And don't think of going there, or I'll put a serious hurting on you. He owns the largest pharmacy in town, as well as several pieces of prime real estate."

"Just my luck. You always seem to snap up the good ones," Lisa grumbled.

Aaron came to a quick stop in front of them. "Hey, sweet thing," he said to Kim. "Cary never once mentioned you were back."

Niki wondered what had happened to Deandra. Things

obviously hadn't worked out, or Aaron wouldn't be acting as if the sun rose and set on Kim.

"Who's Cary?" Lisa asked. "By the way, I'm Lisa Williams."

"Aaron Smith. Niki hasn't told you about my buddy Cary? The two of them are tight." He winked at Niki and, despite wanting to strangle him, she smiled back. Aaron Smith was a character, but truly delightful. "What are you lovely women doing on the beach alone?" he asked.

"Probably the same thing you're doing," Kim said, eyeing him up and down and practically licking her lips. "Scoping out the possibilities."

Aaron squatted down, his tight thigh muscles bulging. "I haven't had the pleasure." He held out his hand to Charlie.

"Charlotte Canfield-Spencer," Charlie said, emphasizing the Spencer, telling him she was a married woman and clearly off limits.

Niki hid a smile. Aaron's arrival had taken the heat off her, at least temporarily.

"What are you ladies drinking?" Aaron asked.

Kim patted the still full cooler beside them. "Margaritas, piñas, you name it. Can we offer you a drink?"

"How about a beer?"

"You got it." Kim reached over and dug out a Michelob. "Will this do?"

"That'll do nicely," Aaron said, in a voice deeper than Old Man River's and equally as smooth. He turned back to Niki. "When was the last time you saw Cary?"

"Cary who?" Charlie and Lisa said simultaneously.

Aaron and Niki ignored them. Niki shrugged. "It's been a while."

"You do know Brett's been ill?"

"Who's Brett?" Lisa lowered her harlequin sunglasses, hanging on every word.

"Cary's son," Aaron offered. "The prescription the doctor called in to my pharmacy seems to have worked. He's here today."

Did that mean Cary was at the beach as well? Niki's heart pounded and her limbs felt leaden. "What prescription was that?" she asked, unable to stop herself.

"Ampicillin."

"I would have thought amoxicillin in liquid form would have been a better choice."

Aaron seemed surprised she was so knowledgeable, but didn't pursue it. He pointed to a spot up the beach. "You should go over and say hello to both of them."

"*We'll* go over and say hello," Kim said, bounding up and linking an arm through Aaron's. "Come on, girls."

"I'm there," Charlie said, leaping up to join her. "Any guy who's caught the eye of the elusive Onika Hamilton is definitely worth viewing."

There was no stopping Kim when she put her mind to it. Niki wanted to dig herself a hole in the sand, crawl into it, and hide.

"Coming, Niki?" Charlie stood before her, a twinkle in her eye. "Don't let her get to you," she whispered. "You and I will walk by, nod, and keep going."

Resigned to the fact there was no way out of this one, Niki reluctantly followed Aaron and the women.

Elsa had made herself very comfortable in the chaise longue next to him and showed no signs of moving. Dressed in her itsy-bitsy bikini, she was very distracting. Cary continued to leaf through the lackluster thriller while keeping his eye on the ocean. Brett splashed noisily with a group of kids who had joined him.

This was no accidental meeting. She'd somehow found out he and Brett were coming here and had obviously followed them. He couldn't shake her unless he was rude.

Cary had contemplated packing it in, but Brett was having too good a time. Was it really fair to deprive his son of his mother's attention? His child so rarely saw her. Brett had been so proud to introduce her to his friends. He'd proven to the other children he was normal, that he did have two parents.

Out of his peripheral vision, Cary spotted a small group heading their way. The man's long strides reminded him of Aaron's. That quarterback's body was hard to miss. Cary sat up and shaded his eyes. Elsa, sensing his interest, did likewise. He could almost feel her bristling.

Aaron's loud voice boomed at him. "Cary, my man, look who I found."

He'd garnered the attention of others. Heads turned their way.

Elsa scooted her lounge chair closer and said, "My, Aaron Smith hasn't changed a bit. He always was a hustler. Who are the hootchie mamas with him?"

Cary found himself getting angrier by the moment. Elsa's razor-sharp tongue was at it again, slicing down anyone who made her feel insecure. Cary bolted upright when he recognized two of the women. Kim Morgan and Niki. An unexpected bonus.

Kim skipped the preliminaries. She waved at him. "My yard looks good, but when will it be done?"

"As soon as you pick out more plants. I wasn't about to choose without your input." He slid off his lounge chair and came toward them. Niki and Kim were accompanied by two women he'd never seen before.

"Is that white guy yours?" he overheard one of the strange women whisper. "God, he's fine."

"Shush." This came from Niki.

"Cary Thomas," Cary said, sticking out his hand.

A cinnamon-skinned beauty with a shiny cap of curls shook it. "I'm Charlie and this is Lisa." She pushed forward a woman dressed in a wild print bathing suit that looked like it came from another era.

"I'm Elsa Viera," Elsa said, joining them.

Niki's face paled and she blinked behind her glasses. Cary wanted to strangle Elsa. "Elsa's a friend," he offered by way of explanation.

"A very good friend," his ex interjected.

"Mommy, Mommy," Brett yelled, racing across the sand toward them. "Did you meet Niki? She's real cool. Even Daddy says so. She plays the most awesome Internet games."

Stony-faced, Elsa assessed Niki. Neither woman looked happy. Time to take charge before things got further out of hand. He had to redeem himself in Niki's eyes. "Elsa, this is my friend, Niki. These are her friends." Cary allowed each woman to introduce herself. "Elsa and I sort of ran into each other."

Aaron, trusty friend that he was, stepped in to save the day. "You're looking well," he said to Elsa, eyeing her shapely body. "Good enough to eat."

She thanked him and flounced off. "Come with me, Brett. I'll get you a hot dog."

Reluctantly, the child followed. "Will you come by later?" he said, turning back to Niki. "I miss you."

When both mother and child were out of earshot, Cary said to Niki, "So how come you haven't returned my calls?"

"This is where we exit, girls. Coming, Aaron?" Kim said.

"Wherever you're going, I'll follow."

Amongst a flurry of "Nice meeting yous," the group made a U-turn and headed off.

Niki still hadn't answered. "Well?" Cary prompted.

"Well, what? I called. Clearly you were not interested in returning my call."

She sounded more British than ever, a sure sign she was ticked.

"You left a message?" Cary came closer, his hands encircling her shoulders. Niki stiffened. He had the feeling he would have to do a lot of talking to soften her up. "I didn't get any message," he said. "You know I'd never ignore you. I called you several times. You could have done the same."

He could tell she seesawed back and forth. Against her better judgment, she wanted to believe him. How must it look? He and Elsa, the mother of his child, at the beach together, lounging in adjacent chairs.

"Elsa and I barely speak to each other," he said.

"Didn't appear that way to me."

"Trust me, it's not how it looks."

"Trust is something I've learned not to associate with men. I trusted my ex-husband and what did that get me? I came home to find the skunk in bed with the neighbor's maid."

"I'm not your ex-husband."

He wanted to shake some sense into that pretty head of hers, kiss the dusting of freckles made even more pronounced by the sun, and convince her that he was sincere. Fidelity meant a lot to him. He ran the back of his thumb across her lower lip. "We need to talk, but not here, and not now. How about dinner?"

"It will have to wait until my friends leave."

"When will that be?

"Tomorrow night."

"Plan on Wednesday, then."

"I'll check my schedule. Kim may still need help."

Cary's body sagged with relief. At least she hadn't turned him down flat.

Chapter 15

"How are my patients doing?" Niki asked Phillip. She'd initiated this call and held her breath waiting for his answer.

"Overall, pretty good. Robyn Saunders, your HIV baby, has had her ups and downs, but seems to be holding her own."

"Poor little one. You sound beat."

"I am," Phillip said. "I'm envisioning a long cruise in the very near future."

"And you'll have it. Soon as I get back."

Phillip sighed. "I'm not putting pressure on you, Nik. You've scratched my back enough times for me to scratch yours."

"You're the best. But I can't keep expecting you to do my job plus yours. Have you had time to stop by my apartment?"

Phillip groaned. She could tell the answer was negative.

"Don't worry. You're off the hook. Friends of mine are flying in for a couple of days. If there's a problem, they'll call."

Phillip caught her up on news at the hospital; then the conversation centered on their patients again. When Niki ended the call, the phone rang almost immediately. Lisa and Charlie had left for their respective homes the evening before. Kim was at a massage and pedicure appointment: afterward she was meeting Aaron for a drink. Niki tamped down on her trepidation and reached for the receiver.

"I wasn't sure you'd be in," Cary greeted.

"Why ever not?"

"I thought you might be avoiding me. Look, I'm calling about our dinner plans. I've gone ahead and made reservations at The Channel Club. The seafood is outrageous and the view's even better."

"Sounds lovely."

"Then it's set. I'll pick you up at seven. Does that give you enough time to get dressed?"

"Plenty of time."

Glancing at her watch, she realized she had exactly two hours to get ready. Did that give her enough time to do a total makeover? *Stop fussing, Nik.* But she couldn't stop worrying. Cary liked his women sleek and elegant. One only had to look at the woman at the beach to figure that out.

Even now she could see Elsa strutting her stuff in that minuscule bikini. The mother of his child had looked like a model, with her slanted eyes and equally slanting cheekbones. Not one hair on her well coiffured head had been out of place. She had skin the color of warm cinnamon buns and light eyes edged in kohl. She was stylish and beautiful.

What could she wear that would catch Cary's attention? Nothing she'd packed was suitable. None of her serviceable clothing made her feel desirable or even faintly sexy. Niki went to Kim's closet. Kim wouldn't care if she borrowed a dress. She shifted through rows and rows of shimmering evening clothes, needing something that would make Cary sit up and notice her. Kim had plenty of eye-catching outfits, but given her rather generous bustline, most wouldn't fit Niki.

Niki went through the closet a second time before finding a sleeveless linen number. The hemline skimmed mid-thigh, and the back was barely there. If she wore bone pumps and borrowed a purse from Kim, it just might be the ticket. That decided, she stepped into the shower and turned it on full force, allowing the warm water to beat down on her. After a moment or two, she loofahed her body and shampooed her hair, deciding to let it dry naturally.

Niki had never been big on makeup, but this was a special occasion. She dusted her face with a shimmering powder Kim had given her because it was the wrong shade, outlined her eyes with the slightest hint of sienna, and used the same color on her cheeks. By then her hair had dried into an unruly mass of curls which she fingered into an even more tousled state. She slipped on her pantyhose, lowered the turquoise dress over her head, and stepped into pumps. Dare she look in the mirror?

A quick peek revealed someone she did not know—a virtual stranger. A tantalizing vamp. Outside, a car door slammed. No time to change. Her two hours had been eaten up. She found her beeper and threw it into Kim's bag. A gold foil package winked at her from the interior. Trust Kim to always be prepared. Niki decided not to remove the condom. She headed for the door.

"My God, you're beautiful," Cary greeted, helping her into the passenger seat of the BMW. His sharp intake of breath said even more than words.

Niki managed a breathy, "Thank you."

They were off, making the short drive to the restaurant in record time.

At the entrance, a hostess greeted them, then escorted them to a table overlooking the Navesink River. Luxury boats were moored at the dock, and tiny white lights twinkled from expensive homes on the shore. The whole scene was breathtaking. Awesome. Romantic.

Niki focused on the flickering lanterns. She inhaled the salty air, fingered the single rose in the bud vase, and drank in its heady perfume.

"What would you like to drink?" Cary asked, snapping her back to the present.

He'd tanned nicely and wore a black collarless shirt and matching cuffed pants. His cream linen jacket had been flung carelessly over the back of the chair.

"Wine would be nice."

"Champagne's even better. Perrier Jouet OK with you?"

Niki raised an eyebrow. "That's a bit rich."

"Nothing's too rich for my lady." Smiling at her, he summoned their waiter.

"*Your lady*?" Niki said, when she could find the words. "Aren't you taking a lot for granted?"

"Am I?"

His eyes roamed her face. The patrons around them ceased to exist. She barely registered the waiter's return with the champagne and glasses.

"What kind of game are you playing?" she asked, softly.

"I never play games. I know what I want, and I go after it."

"Only a few days ago you were with another woman. Do you want her, too?"

"Elsa?" Cary said, chuckling. "Elsa and I were over with a long time ago."

Niki gulped her champagne and set the glass down. "Didn't look that way to me."

Cary broke off a bit of bread stick and crumbled it between his fingers. He brought the pieces to his lips, and chewed slowly. That mouth. Those lips. God, could they work magic.

"Elsa bails out at the first sign of trouble," Cary said. "She always has and always will. She went chasing after some guy the moment she found out she was pregnant. She'd hoped to get him to marry her. That failing, she departed for parts unknown. She was quick to drop Brett off when he became a problem and she could no longer control him. She's probably back in town because her personal life's in turmoil."

"Interesting. But what do you really know about me?"

"Enough. I know you're warm, kind, and relate well to children. I know you're beautiful but prefer to hide it under disfiguring glasses." He leaned in closer, his champagne-scented breath fanning her face. "I know you have a secret you're reluctant to share. And I know under that frigid-looking exterior is a passion on slow burn."

Niki's breath caught in her throat. Either he was a smooth operator or extremely sincere. She'd never met a man quite like him.

"Tell me, Niki Hamilton," Cary continued, "what's the problem? You're intrigued by me, maybe care for me more than a little. Isn't that something worth exploring?"

"I'm not looking for a quick hop in the sack," Niki said, surprising even herself.

The expression on Cary's face was priceless. Their waiter's return prevented him from saying another word.

"Ready to order?"

Neither had glanced at the menu.

"Give us another minute," Cary finally said.

They perused their respective menus and made their selections—calamari for the appetizer, salmon for Niki, prawns for him.

Cary waited until the waiter was out of earshot. "Making love with you meant a lot to me," he said. "It told me something . . ."

"What?"

A loud voice bellowed, "Cary Thomas, fancy running into you here."

Cary turned to acknowledge the large man in a hideous plaid jacket who waddled their way. The man eyed Niki curiously. "Don't mean to interrupt, but I figured you must have heard about the Little Silver deal. I'm about to break ground any day." Obviously pleased with himself, he patted his ample stomach. "Got these fancy-pantsy condos planned. I need you to do a site inventory and design me something wonderful. Look, I'm disturbing your dinner with this beautiful young lady." His hungry gaze roamed over Niki, leaving her feeling naked.

"Vinnie, this is Onika Hamilton," Cary said, rising.

Vinnie's huge mitt enveloped Niki's hand in a bone-crushing squeeze. "Nice to meet you, lovely lady. Your man's a keeper. Landscape designers with Cary's talent are hard to find. I'll count on you to convince him he'd be better off with me than running his own business." Vinnie guffawed.

Niki simply nodded. She felt as if someone had compressed her lungs, rendering her speechless. Cary was a landscape designer, not a landscaper? She felt like a prize fool. She'd seen him getting dirty and, snob that she was, had concluded he worked with his hands, so consequently was beneath her, and that he was a gold digger. Appalling. Unforgivable.

Niki thudded her palm against her forehead. Carett Designs. Cary. Brett. Carett. How dense could she be? The pieces all fitted together—his simple but beautiful home, the tasteful furnishings, the expensive car. She'd screwed up big time.

Their waiter returned with the appetizer.

"Enjoy your dinner," Vinnie said, leaving them.

Niki's appetite was gone, but Cary ate with relish. There was a twinkle in his eyes when he looked at her. "Have I risen remarkably in your estimation?"

Could the man read her mind?

"I owe you an apology," she said, feeling like a complete idiot.

"For?"

"My incredible stupidity. For being a total ass."

"Apology accepted," he said, clinking his glass against hers. "Now can we talk about us?"

Now was the perfect time to tell him that she had misled him, too. But something stopped her. Maybe it was the beautiful night filled with infinite possibilities. Maybe it was the way he looked at her. Whatever the reason, she decided to leave things as they were. She was enjoying his company, loving every minute of the attention he paid her. She wanted to see just how far things could go.

Her vibrating purse signaled her pager had gone off. Niki sighed. So much for an enjoyable evening. She removed the beeper and quickly scanned the digital message.

Call me when you get a chance. The message came from Phillip.

It didn't sound urgent. Later, even tomorrow, would be good enough. Niki turned her attention back to Cary.

"Problem?" he asked.

"Nothing that can't wait."

"I thought we might go for a stroll on the boardwalk," Cary said when they had finished their meal.

"I'm game. Sounds like fun. Tell me about the boardwalk."

"It's like something out of the past. It has the usual arcade games, fortune-tellers, fun stuff. I'll buy you a cotton candy if you're good," he said, leering at her.

"I'll hold you to it." She leered back.

After Cary settled the bill, they drove off in his BMW.

Finding a parking spot wasn't easy. They circled for several minutes, eventually parking on a side road. Cary eyed her high-heeled pumps. "Those can't be easy to walk in."

"I'll manage."

"I can carry you."

"I don't think so." Walking with purpose, she kept a respectable distance from him. Ahead was a brightly lit Ferris wheel, and Niki heard barkers working the crowd.

"Come try your hand at horseshoes!"

"Win a stuffed toy for your love!"

"Cotton candy!"

As they came closer, Niki smelled buttery popcorn and the tempting aroma of caramel apples.

Cary took her hand. "Reminds me of my childhood," he said. "My parents used to bring me here a lot."

"Where are your parents?"

"Dead."

"I'm sorry. How's Brett?" she said, changing the topic quickly.

"Doing better."

"His fever's all gone?"

"Yes. The antibiotics seem to have worked."

"Is he home with his mother?" Niki asked.

Cary shot her a strange look. "No. He's home with Lourdes Gonzales."

When they reached the boardwalk, their pace slowed. A half moon bathed the ocean in silver, and Cary's arm tightened around her shoulders.

"When are you going back to San Francisco?" he asked.

"Probably in another few weeks."

Leaving wasn't something she wanted to think about. Going home meant returning to a life of fielding threatening phone calls and battling HMOs. Going home meant being apart from Cary.

"I wish you wouldn't go," he said.

Was he asking her to stay? She was tempted, but what did she really know about him? Cary came with his own share of baggage: a child who desperately needed a mother, and an ex who didn't want to be an ex.

Cary's thumb traced a path across her bottom lip. She shivered.

"Cold?" he asked.

"Not at all." Her treacherous body pulsated in places she hadn't even known existed.

"Shall we go back and buy you your cotton candy?" he asked.

She shook her head. "No. It's beautiful here."

"Take off those shoes and ditch your hose," Cary ordered, rolling up his pants legs and taking off his own shoes and socks. He pointed to the dark entrance of a vacant building. "Change over there. We'll walk on the beach."

Niki scooted into the shadowy entrance way. She made short work of her shoes and hose and then took the hand

Cary offered, following him down a steep flight of stairs to the beach.

The salty night air titillated her senses. The pounding surf made it almost impossible hear. Only the two of them existed. Cary's steps slowed as they made their way under the boardwalk.

"I've been dying to do this," he said, taking her shoes, purse, and hose from her and setting them down next to his things. He leaned in for a kiss.

Niki closed her eyes and savored the feeling of his tongue circling hers, the heady taste of him. She wanted to lose herself in that kiss—lose herself in him. They continued to explore, taste, and savor. Cary's hands flitted across her breasts. Niki moaned. His knee parted her thighs and her dress hiked up. Her back was pressed up against a column, and Cary's hot kisses roamed her face. When his hands cupped her buttocks, she moaned again. The erection pulsating against her belly was a huge one. A serious one.

Niki struggled to regain her composure. Why was she feeling so much better about him? Did this new knowledge about his occupation make that much difference? Here she was again, thinking of him, throwing caution to the wind, and just going with it.

"Niki?"

"Yes, Cary?" Her breath came in little spurts.

"I want to be inside you. Right here. Right now."

"Not a good . . ."

"Shush." He pressed her against the column and kissed the sides of her neck. "No one can see us. No one knows we're here."

Kim's dress was bunched up around her neck, probably ruined. But Niki didn't care. Cary bent to kiss her exposed belly. He ran a hand across her mound before slipping that same hand beneath the elastic of her panties. She moaned loudly.

"This is crazy," she managed.

"Nothing crazy about this." Cary cupped her buttocks and lifted her slightly, pressing her up against the full, long length of him. She smelled the musk coming off his skin when he nibbled her shoulder.

"Ouch," Niki said. "Wait!"

He stopped immediately, turning serious. "Did I hurt you?"

"No. I need my purse."

Realization slowly dawned on him. "Sorry, I didn't plan this well." He handed her purse to her.

Niki retrieved the foil package and handed it over. "I have it covered."

He would probably think she had an active sex life, carrying a condom with her. Little did he know.

Cary's zipper screeched and in seconds he'd protected himself. He pushed her underwear aside. His sheathed, throbbing flesh probed hers, his need very palpable.

"Oh, God," Niki said, opening up, and giving him access. "Oh, God," she said, when he plunged inside. He took a nipple into his mouth and bit down gently.

Niki squirmed under him. Each entrance and exit brought ecstasy. The dress was ruined. She'd have to explain it to Kim. Cary nipped the sides of her neck and found her mouth again. Niki molded her body against his. Contract. Release. Contract. He trembled.

The ocean roared in her ears, the smell of brine reminding her of where they were. Somehow Cary Thomas had gained access to her heart, making her feel things she didn't want to feel, leaving her a quivering mass of desire.

"Oh, God," Niki repeated, "oh, God."

"We're close, honey. Almost there."

Together they exploded.

When they came back to earth, he kissed her. It was the type of kiss she'd always dreamed of, tender and reverent. Cary smoothed her clothing and tidied himself.

"Ready?" he asked, taking her hand.

"Ready."

But she hadn't been ready for Cary Thomas. Not by a long shot.

Chapter 16

"Nik, is that you?" Kim called out the moment she walked into the house.

"Yes, ma'am."

Niki looked up to see all the lights ablaze and Kim at the top of the stairs in a sexy red nightgown. Remnants of facial cream still clung to her skin. Niki smothered a grin. Kim in the role of anxious parent was a ridiculous sight. It wasn't that late, either, just a little past one.

"Niki," Kim said, taking the stairs two at a time, "Charlie's called several times. There's been bad news. You better sit down."

Niki's heart stopped. "My parents?" Her fingers plucked at the hem of the ruined dress.

"Your parents are fine," Kim hastily assured her. "Let's go in to the kitchen, have a drink, and talk."

Niki followed Kim into the kitchen and took one of the glasses of Coke Kim poured.

"Sit," Kim ordered.

Niki sat across from her.

"Your apartment's been broken into and vandalized," Kim said without preamble.

"How could that be?" Niki felt the blood drain from her face, and the room began to fade in and out.

"Breathe, girl. Breathe. Charlie and Devin called the police immediately. They walked into a mess. Your doctor friend also phoned. He left you a message on the machine. Claims he beeped you. Charlie called him after she realized the place had been broken into. You'd given her his number."

Niki remembered Phillip's page and the message he'd left. Even though it hadn't sounded urgent, why hadn't she called?

Kim embraced her. "Look, girl, whoever did it is bound to get caught. They left the place in shambles and left some sort of note. Devin and Charlie are now booked into the Fairmont. Here's the number if you want to call them."

Niki accepted the paper the message was written on. She tried to steady herself by taking a deep breath.

"I'm here, girl. I'm here," Kim said, handing her the cordless phone. "You'll get through this."

Niki dialed, waited for the hotel operator to come on, and asked to be put through to the Spencers.

"I hope I'm not calling too late," she said the moment she heard Devin's soothing voice.

"Not at all, Doc. Don't forget the time difference. It's a little past ten here. How are you holding up?"

Charlie's voice came from the extension. "Not to worry, hon. Everything's under control. The police came as soon as we called. They're still questioning people and scouring your place for clues."

"Do they have any idea as to who might have done it?"

A pause on the other end. "Based on the note, they've concluded it's a disgruntled patient," Devin said.

Niki pinched the spot between her eyes and the bridge of her nose. When would it end? She'd thought with time the threatening phone calls would stop, but they'd started up again. She'd come across the country to decompress and had managed somewhat successfully until tonight, when reality had reared its head in an ugly way. Why couldn't she get away from the hatred? Even worse, she didn't have a clue as to what she'd done to bring it on, except try to save lives.

"I'm coming home," Niki said. "Tomorrow first thing I'll be on a plane."

"Your town house isn't in the best of condition," Devin warned.

"It's a mess," Charlie confirmed. "Hon, you'll need to find yourself a hotel or better yet, stay with a friend."

Niki thought about the austere apartment she'd grown accustomed to—the pristine walls, the white on white furniture. She had a few nice antique pieces left after the divorce. They were probably in shambles. She didn't want to think about it.

"We'll be here when you get in, and we'll stay as long as you need us," Devin offered.

"I'd appreciate that."

She disconnected the phone, laid her head on the table, and closed her eyes.

"Should I call Cary?" Kim asked, her hands kneading the back of Niki's neck.

"No, he doesn't need to be involved."

They'd made no commitment to each other, hadn't

talked about a long-term relationship. Her problems weren't his problems.

Kim picked up the phone again. "I'll book you a flight."

"OK," Niki said wearily. "I'm going upstairs to pack."

Cary let the phone ring. On a weekday morning, someone should be answering at Coffee Mates. After what must be the fifteenth ring—he'd actually counted—Kim picked up.

"Coffee Mates."

Cary identified himself. But instead of Kim's normally enthusiastic greeting, he received a careful, "You must be looking for Niki."

"Yes, I am."

"She's not here." Kim's voice sounded guarded.

"When do you expect her back?"

"Uh. . . well. . ."

Kim at a loss for words? Must be something going on.

"All right, spit it out," Cary demanded.

"Niki's on her way to San Francisco," Kim said, exhaling audibly.

Cary couldn't stop the crude expletive that slipped out. "Tell me it was an emergency. I saw her last night. She never said a thing."

"It was rather sudden."

"Then you can give me the details in person. I'm on my way over." Cary slammed down the phone.

Not bothering to change out of the T-shirt that still held remnants of gooey sap from when he'd tagged specimen trees, he found his keys and jumped into his truck. Who cared if he looked a mess? Driving the short distance in record time, he ran every amber light he encountered.

Kim waited for him in the foyer of Coffee Mates.

"Boyfriend, you sure got here quickly," she said. "You want a beer or something?"

Ignoring her offer, Cary demanded, "Why did Niki leave?"

Kim motioned with her head that her part-timers were probably listening. "Let's go into my office. We can talk there," she said.

Kim's office was as flamboyant as she was. Chinese red walls held an assortment of fans, plus happy photos of the couples she'd matched. There wasn't an empty surface on her desk. Stacks and stacks of pictures and applications had literally taken over.

Kim cleared a path and set her elbows down. Her manicured hands cupped her chin. She leaned in, peering at him. Cary flopped onto the couch, eyeing her warily.

"Niki's apartment was broken in to, boyfriend," Kim said when she was sure she had his full attention.

"No! That explains why she left in a hurry. Was anything stolen? Damaged?"

Kim nodded. Her braids swung back and forth. "It's a mess, from what I can gather. Poor kid, the last few months have been rough. Lesser mortals would have broken under the stress."

Kim obviously thought he knew something. Best to play along. She would feel comfortable speaking freely and he might learn something more.

"I know she's had a difficult time," Cary said carefully.

Kim's long red nails tapped the desk before her. "Difficult is putting it mildly. How would you would feel if you lost three children in three months? This last child's death was especially difficult. Niki told me she did everything to keep that boy alive."

"Niki has children?" He couldn't keep his eyebrows from rising.

Kim squinted her eyes. "I thought you knew what she did. Niki's a pediatrician, boyfriend. She was only helping me out."

"Niki's a what?" Cary knew his mouth must be hanging open and his eyes practically bulging out of his head.

"A doctor. As in someone whose medical specialty is children."

Cary punched the arm of the sofa. A string of curse words followed.

Kim let him vent, silently waiting for his tirade to end.

How could Niki have misled him into believing she was unemployed? He remembered the beeper she never left home without, remembered the way she'd tended to Brett, remembered her saying she had medical training. It all added up, but did nothing to alleviate his feelings of anger and betrayal. His hurt. Why hadn't Niki told him? Why had she chosen to string him along? *Why didn't you tell her you were a landscape designer?* a little voice said.

"Cary." Kim's voice made him focus. "I don't think Niki intentionally meant to mislead you. She came to the shore looking for a little R and R, wanting to forget about all the bad stuff going down in San Francisco. For the short time she was here, she was able to relax. In all the years I've known her, I've never seen her this loose. You played a large part in that."

Kim filled him in on the situation in San Francisco and told him about the threatening phone call Niki had had.

"It's not the first. I can't believe she didn't trust me enough to tell me what was going on," Cary said, shaking his head sadly. "Where do we go from here?"

Kim spread her hands wide. "I don't know about you, boyfriend, but I sure as hell know what I'd do."

"What's that?" Cary stood facing her.

"I'd go after her. Offer my support. If I want something

badly enough I go for it. How do you think I got five husbands?"

Even though Cary was still upset with Niki, he couldn't help laughing.

"See, I always knew you were da bomb," Kim said, scribbling furiously. She rose from behind her desk and slapped a piece of paper into his hand. "That's Niki's address. Now get your butt on a plane to San Francisco. Call me when you get there."

Cary sat staring idly at his monitor. The note Kim had given him lay on the desk in front of him. He was still undecided what to do. Would Niki welcome his presence, or would she think he'd overstepped his boundaries? He'd tried burying himself in work, hoping that would keep him busy, but he couldn't focus. He simply stared vaguely at the before and after digital photos of the serenity garden he'd been working on.

Could he put all his projects on hold and just take off for San Francisco? Could he get someone to cover for him at the shelter while he was gone? His adults had gotten used to him being there. He didn't want their reading to fall behind.

For so many years, in addition to running the business, he had been the sole landscape designer. But these last two summers, a student from Monmouth College had apprenticed with him. Mason had shown interest in a job after graduation. Surely he could hold down the fort for a week or two. The supervisors were experienced and could handle the landscaping crews, and Cary could twist Aaron's arm. Have him go to the shelter in his place. Work with his adults teaching them to read.

Behind him a door slammed. Another walk-in customer,

perhaps. His secretary would handle that. He heard the low drone of conversation but couldn't quite make out the words. The pitch of his secretary's voice escalated, and he heard her shout, "You can't do that."

"Watch me." There was a flurry of movement before the door swung open behind him.

"What now?" Cary turned in time to see Elsa, all five-foot-six of her, striding toward him, fire flashing from her eyes.

She slammed her purse down in front of him and placed a hand on one hip. "I went to your house to pick up my son. He wasn't there."

"I don't remember your calling to arrange this," Cary said calmly.

"Then it's obvious you don't check your machine. I left you a rather lengthy message explaining I would be stopping by. I'd hoped to take Brett to the city with me."

"On a day when he has baseball practice?"

Cary clicked the save button, closing the program. Elsa was right, he hadn't checked his answering machine at home in ages. Ever since hearing Niki had taken off, he'd been preoccupied and determined to bury himself in work. Niki could easily have called when he was out.

"Yes, on a day when he has practice," Elsa said. "That child needs to get out and about."

"Elsa, Brett's been into Manhattan on several occasions. He doesn't care for it."

"He's never been there with me."

The intercom buzzed. "Onika Hamilton's on the line for you," his secretary announced.

Cary's mood lightened immediately. Hallelujah, Niki had called. "OK, put her through," he said. "Will you excuse me?"

Elsa ignored him. "Who's that, the woman on the beach? One of the floozies?"

"You're way out of line," Cary said, covering the phone's mouthpiece. "Our business is just about completed. You should be on your way. Brett's going to baseball practice, so that ends any plans for an excursion."

"I'm not going to let you do this to me," Elsa huffed.

"Do what?"

"Keep me away from my son." She jabbed a finger at him before storming out.

Cary's fingers kneaded his aching forehead. Blast the woman and the broom she flew in on. In a New York second, she had taken him from elation to irritation. Elsa could do that to a man.

"Hello, hon," he said into the phone. "How are you holding up?" He was still angry with Niki, but his anger was colored more by hurt. She hadn't seen fit to tell him her true profession. She didn't trust him. They would talk about this sometime in person.

"Hi." Niki's voice sounded strained, as if she hadn't had much sleep. He'd never heard her so shaken.

He took control of the conversation. "Kim told me what happened. She told me you're staying at a hotel."

"Yes, my place was defaced pretty badly. I notified my insurance company. My housekeeper isn't able to handle the task on her own, so I called in a cleaning service. The walls will need to be painted and most of the furniture replaced."

"Do the police have leads?"

"Not that I know of." She sounded truly exhausted, like she needed someone to lean on. That someone should be him. He'd been sitting on the fence for far too long. Time to get off it.

"Hang with me, babe," he said, clicking on to the

Internet. "I'm booking plane reservations as we speak. I'm coming to San Francisco."

"Oh, Cary, you can't."

"Try stopping me," he said, quickly disconnecting the phone.

Chapter 17

"So I heard Niki Hamilton returns to work Monday," Bill Morris said, clearly displeased.

Bill had run into Glenn in the hallway. Glenn nodded his head.

"It's about time," Bill continued. "Let her handle her own questions. You must be sick to death of consumer service analysts quizzing you about her quality of care."

"It's been a busy time," Glenn admitted, attempting to slide by. "You know my first loyalty is always to the hospital."

Bill faced him. "Between the California Medical Board, the board's investigative offices, and the zillion and one requests from PR asking for Hamilton's files, you must be swamped. Good thing the press has died down a little."

Glenn ran a hand over his carefully styled hair. Bill

Morris's constant digs at Niki were beginning to get to him. "How's that deal you discussed coming?" he said smoothly.

Bill's face lit up. He rubbed his cocoa-colored hands together. "It's coming. It should be signed, sealed, and delivered shortly. Then we're in the money."

"Morning, gentlemen. Did you say money?" His white coat flapping behind him, Phillip Gordon attempted to hurry by.

"Just a moment, Dr. Gordon," Glenn called, using Phillip as the perfect excuse to get away from Bill.

"Yes?" Dr. Gordon perused him through tinted eyeglasses. "You have an update?"

Glenn cleared his throat and ignored him. "You've been covering for Dr. Hamilton at the hospital, plus filling in for her at that clinic."

"Yes, I have." Phillip waited expectantly.

"Then you've heard from her since she's back in town."

"Yes. Her home was broken into and she's been staying at a hotel."

Bill Morris whistled. "I thought her fancy neighborhood was safe. Was anything taken or vandalized?"

Phillip seemed to regard him with a keener eye. "I really don't know. What I do know is her place was almost completely destroyed. She's due back at the hospital soon. You may want to try being compassionate and offer your support. She's had a rough time lately."

"Onika Hamilton is as tough as nails," Bill Morris interjected. "She's got the survival instincts of an alley cat."

Phillip tilted his head to the side and looked at him, but remained silent.

"Give Niki our regards," Glen said, slapping the doctor's arm. "Tell her we missed her and are looking forward to having her back on staff."

"That I will do," Phillip said hurrying off.

When he was out of earshot, Bill whispered, "There goes our next chief of staff."

Niki stood on the balcony of the rented hotel room, looking out onto the surrounding hills of a city she'd come to love. Temperatures held firm in the low seventies and a cool breeze skimmed the trees.

For the first time since moving here, she felt isolated and just a tiny bit lonely. She'd welcomed Devin and Charlie's presence and support, but after a few days, she'd sent them home. Both had business to take care of.

Now she waited for the phone to ring. Two undercover detectives had been assigned to her case. They'd scoured her town house for clues, but other than a stray button and the note, they'd come up dry. From what Niki could gather, this latest missive had read:

Take heed bitch next time I goin' make sure your inside.

A blood red thumbprint had been left in lieu of a signature.

Niki shivered. How could she ever feel comfortable in her place again? The thought of someone sifting through her stuff, touching her valuables, fingering her clothing, was downright repulsive. The thought someone hated her enough to do something like this was even more upsetting. For a fleeting moment she considered it might be her ex-husband's doing. What would he hope to gain?

The door bell jingled. Niki jumped. Could the police have come to deliver more bad news in person?

She squinted into the peephole. A bellman waited outside.

"May I help you?" she called.

"I have a delivery for Dr. Hamilton."

It took a while to process the information. She hadn't ordered a thing, not even room service. Somehow she'd lost her appetite.

"ID please," Niki demanded.

The bellman pressed his photo up against the peephole.

Niki fumbled with the latches and slid the chain aside. Nodding his greeting, the bellman wheeled in a trolley piled with flowers. She must have been his first delivery. Who would be sending flowers to her? The only people who knew where she was staying were Kim and Phillip.

The bellman began to unload his cart. The entire room was perfumed by what seemed millions of fragrances. Roses competed with lilies and lilacs. Rare orchids were grouped with birds-of-paradise and sunflowers. Such a colorful profusion she'd never seen before—baskets upon baskets everywhere.

Why was the bellman taking so long to find hers? He'd unloaded every single arrangement from his cart and now stood waiting his hands behind his back.

Niki dug through her purse and found a couple of bills. "Shouldn't you be loading those flowers back on your cart?" she asked, while tipping the employee.

His caramel-colored face broke into a huge grin. "They're all for you."

"That's impossible."

He reached across to pluck a card from an oversized arrangement with trailing vines. "Says here Dr. Niki Hamilton. Aren't you Dr. Hamilton?"

"Yes, I am."

"Looks like somebody's in love," he said, pocketing his tip and inching his way toward the door.

Niki stood with her back toward the door after the bellman had left. Every possible surface now had a basket or flowering pot on it. The mini suite she'd booked into had turned into an indoor garden in less than ten minutes, and she had a sneaking suspicion she knew who was responsible. She would kill him.

Even so, she reached with some trepidation for the card placed in another arrangement and slowly withdrew it from its envelope.

Thinking of you.

Love,
Cary

Love? Did he really mean it? The thought of Cary's being in love with her made a tingle ricochet up and down her spine. She knew now with certainty she was in love with him. It had come to her during the flight home, when she'd had nothing to do but think, when her efforts to read a magazine had been futile. The print blurred, and Cary's face had come clearly into focus, his whiskey-colored eyes twinkling. During that time she'd acknowledged none of the men she knew had made her feel this way. None of them had made her want to have his baby.

A silly thought. At age forty-two, she was far too old to think about bringing a child into the world, much less raising it. *It's done all the time,* the imp inside her argued. *Older women are having children.* She thought of several movie stars and colleagues, who, having married late in life, started a family immediately.

You're not cut out to be a single parent, the imp lectured, vacillating back and forth.

But what if you were married to the man of your dreams?

Damn it, she had to stop. Her imagination was whirling

way out of control. She'd slept with Cary twice, and already she was leading him down the aisle.

The tip of Niki's nose itched and her nostrils tickled. She felt the sneeze come on, but was powerless to stop it. The flowers, lovely as they were, were too much at once. Some would have to go.

Niki threw the French doors wide and trudged back and forth, placing huge arrangements on shaded areas of the balcony. She carted armfuls into the bathroom and arranged them around the tub. When she'd almost cleared the bed-sitting area, she decided it was time to call Cary.

A woman answered after a considerable number of rings. Niki's first thought was of Elsa. Nonsense. Must be the same secretary she'd spoken to previously.

"Thank you for calling Carett Designs," the voice said. "May I help you?"

"Cary Thomas, please."

"Who may I say is calling?"

Niki gave her name. There was a slight pause on the other end.

"Is he there?" Niki insisted, wondering what that was all about.

"No. Mr. Thomas has been called out of town unexpectedly."

Disappointed, she disconnected. She'd so looked forward to hearing Cary's voice and speaking with him. Niki picked up the receiver and dialed again. This time Kim's joyful greeting filled her ear.

"Coffee Mates. Where you find your mate, soul or otherwise."

Niki couldn't help smiling. Kim had the gift of spreading sunshine over the gloomiest of days.

"I'm glad I got you," she said by way of greeting.

"How's it going, girlfriend? Wish I could leave the business and be there for you."

Kim probably felt guilty. Niki had helped Kim out in her time of need; now Kim couldn't reciprocate. Niki quickly reassured her she was doing fine. Having Charlie and Devin here initially had made the difference.

"I'm trying to get in touch with Cary," Niki said, "but I've been told he's out of town."

"He was by here yesterday, making sure his guys were finishing up. We had coffee together. Listen, I've got clients waiting. Glad to hear you're doing OK. I'll call you later." Kim hung up the phone before Niki could get in another word.

Why did she have the uncomfortable feeling Kim had rushed her off the phone? It wasn't like her to be so dismissive.

The doorbell rang. There was no end to the disturbances this morning. Niki straightened her sweater and padded in sock-clad feet to the door.

"Who is it?"

"Bellman."

Not again. No more flowers, she hoped. While they were a thoughtful gesture and she was flattered, enough was enough. A quick peek through the keyhole revealed dark clothing but no face. She didn't bother asking for ID this time. Niki unlatched the door prepared to face the bellhop.

"I didn't order ... oh, my God, Cary! You're here. I didn't believe you would come."

Her mouth hanging open, she backed into the room.

Cary followed. He pulled her against him, then picked her up and swung her around. "I came to find you," he said kissing her soundly. "Kim gave me your address. I missed you, honey."

Tears caught in her throat. She was unable to speak. Winding her arms around his neck, she let go. All those days of holding her emotions in, of carefully answering the policemen's questions, were beginning to take their toll. Her tears flowed freely.

"Hush, baby, hush," Cary said, setting her on her feet. He punctuated his words with kisses. "Have you eaten?

Niki shook her head. Words still wouldn't come.

"Good. Put on your shoes. We're going to Fisherman's Wharf. Yes, I know it's filled with tourists. Today *we're* tourists."

Three hours of roaming the wharf left them worn but sated. The first thing they'd done was stop at a little seafood place for a glass of wine and a long leisurely lunch. After that, they'd held hands and walked the waterfront. When Niki spotted some trendy new boutique she'd never been into, she'd dragged Cary in and poked around. In one store, he'd surprised her and bought her a pair of candlesticks she'd admired. The hours had flown by easily, effortlessly. By the time they got back into Cary's rental car, they were exhausted.

"Where are you staying?" Niki asked as Cary navigated one of San Francisco's famous hills. Cary's garment bag had been tossed onto the backseat.

"With you. Is that a problem?"

Niki's heart did a triple jump. She'd gotten the answer she wanted. Cary had left his business and come all this way to find her. She had to let him stay.

"Not unless you make it a problem," she teased.

He wiggled both eyebrows. "Does that mean I should behave myself?"

"Did I say that?"

They parked in an underground garage and, still holding hands, made their way through the lobby. Cary slung his garment bag over one shoulder. As they passed the front desk, one of the clerks called, "Dr. Hamilton, I have messages for you." She waved a fistful of white.

Niki walked over to retrieve them, briefly glancing at the scribbled lines. One was from Phillip, the others from the officers assigned to her case.

"Everything OK?" Cary asked, spotting her frown.

They were at the door of her suite before she answered. "The police want me to contact them."

"Good. Maybe they've uncovered something new."

"Could be."

Even so, when would it all end? When could she return home without worrying? In a couple of days she'd be back at work, faced with a huge headache. The medical board had requested all records pertaining to her deceased patients. She'd have to provide written summaries of their care.

"Stop worrying, hon," Cary said, kissing the nape of her neck, then drawing her down onto the couch to sit next to him. "I hear you're a pediatrician," he said softly. "Why didn't you tell me?"

He must have found that out from Kim. Funny thing was, he didn't sound mad. He'd taken the news in stride.

"My credentials intimidate a lot of people," Niki said.

"They don't intimidate me. I used to think I wanted a stay-at-home lover, a woman I could adore and protect. I've changed my mind. I've decided an independent woman is far more intriguing, just so long as she remembers to pay attention to me. I need lots of loving." He undid the top buttons of her sweater and nuzzled the hollow of her throat. "Initially I was really angry with you, but not for the reasons you think. I thought you didn't trust me, and I couldn't figure out why you'd initially set out to deceive me."

"I wanted to be accepted for myself. I was married to a man who loved the idea of my being a doctor but didn't love me. God, I was so sick and tired of being Dr. Onika Hamilton. I came to the shore looking for anonymity. Peace. Fun."

"And you thought my knowing what you did would make a difference?" He released another button. His warm hands cupped her breasts, his fingers teasing the nipples.

"It could have."

"Then you really don't know me. Aren't you the person who thought I was a landscaper?"

"Touché."

"Clearly out of your league."

"I never said that."

"But that's what you thought," he whispered, settling on top of her, the bulge of his erection pressing into her, demanding its own response.

"I'd say the more I've gotten to know you, the more convinced I am you're very much in my league."

"It took you forever to realize that," Cary said, kissing her soundly while reaching into his back pocket for one of the condoms he remembered to bring along.

Chapter 18

A day later, Niki sat in the living room of her hotel suite holding Cary's hand.

Michael Edwards, one of the officers assigned to her case, was perched on the couch facing her. He tapped a pen against his notebook, knitted his brows, and asked, "What about your ex-husband, the men you've dated over the last couple of months? Any rejected lovers? Unhappy patients?"

Cary's entire body went rigid. The question had gotten his attention. Still holding her hand, he leaned in, waiting for her response.

"I haven't dated that many men," Niki said carefully. "Since my divorce I've had little or no time for a personal life. As for patients, there are always a disgruntled few."

Edwards eyed her skeptically. "Come on, Doc, an attractive woman like you must have had a dinner or drinks with someone."

Niki replayed the last several months. There really hadn't been anyone serious. Fred Willis, the classmate she'd become reacquainted with on the reunion cruise, had called a couple of times. But eventually, her less than enthusiastic responses and geography had taken care of his interest.

"Let's see. I had a short-lived relationship of sorts with Oliver Stanton, an old classmate," Niki admitted. "Then there's Glenn Jacoby, our hospital administrator. He's asked me out several times, but it's never gone further than one dinner. When Dr. Phillip Gordon first joined the staff we tried dating, but we decided we made better friends. Even the Spencers tried fixing me up with a colleague, but nothing ever came of it."

Michael Edwards had uncapped his pen and was busy taking notes. "Did any of these men become unpleasant when you decided they weren't for you?"

Cary's grip on her hand tightened.

"I can't really say that. Glenn was disappointed when I kept turning him down, but I think he's gotten over it. He's not a bad chap."

"Mmm-hmmm," Edwards said, busily scribbling. "What about Jordan? You two are still close." He peered up as if expecting her to refute it.

"Phillip and I are friends. He covered for me during my absence. He would have no reason to want to hurt me. He feels the same way I do about health maintenance organizations. He would do almost anything to ensure a patient receives appropriate care, regardless of the cost factor. If the medication he prescribes happens to be expensive, so be it."

Though his hold on her hand tightened even more, Cary sat quietly listening.

"What about patients at the hospital or clinic?" Edwards asked. "Anyone disgruntled or making threats?"

"Unpleasantness often comes with the territory. People are hurting, especially when they're diagnosed with a serious illness." Niki provided him with the names of several of her more challenging patients.

"What about the Eldridges? They've become pretty bitter people."

Niki countered, "Wouldn't you be? Your child's been ill for most of his young life. Experimental or not, you're given an opportunity to reverse his death sentence, and your HMO turns you down flat."

"But why would their anger be directed at you? You were their advocate. You were the one pushing for gene therapy. Why would they turn around and sue you?"

"Those people are suing you?" Cary interjected, sounding outraged. "What an ungrateful bunch."

"They're not exactly suing me. Glenn Jacoby tells me they've filed suit against the hospital, citing corporate negligence. Yes, I'm mentioned, and, yes, my competence is being questioned. But it's interesting they haven't sued me personally. They're doing what they think they have to do, and a pretty savvy attorney is guiding them."

"That might well be." Edwards slapped his notebook shut. "I'll be speaking to the Eldridges anyway. Anything else?"

Cary spoke for the first time. "What about the blood print on that note? Niki's told me this isn't the first time she's received a message with blood on it."

"It was paint. The perpetrator was trying to scare her," Edwards said matter-of-factly, rising and brushing imaginary lint from his pants legs. "By the way, there was no visible sign of forced entry. I'll be in touch."

After the officer had departed, Niki and Cary stood on the balcony looking down on the city. "Do you get the feeling this is someone you know?" Cary asked.

"None of my friends would be that vicious." She changed the topic. "You never did tell me how long you planned on staying."

"I wish it could be forever. Realistically, probably two weeks. Then I have to get back to my business."

"I can't thank you enough for being here," she said, winding an arm around Cary's waist. "I don't know what I would have done without you."

He gave her a sad smile. "Wouldn't it be nice to have this animal apprehended? You could move back into your place and start feeling safe again."

"I'd like nothing better. The painting's already been completed, Phillip oversaw that. Both the cleaning service and my lady took care of what they could. I need to get over there and figure out what's salvageable and what's not. Maybe we could stop by and check it out later."

"Good. I'll get to see how you live." Cary kissed her cheek. "Can't wait to see Niki Hamilton's taste."

"You'll be disappointed," Niki warned. "I haven't had much time for decoration. My furnishings are based on practicality more than aesthetics."

"I'll be the judge of that."

Inside the phone jingled.

"Want me to get that?" Cary asked.

Niki nodded. A ringing phone still produced a certain amount of tension. Would she ever get over that? Probably not until the person threatening her was caught.

"Sure."

She remained on the balcony, letting the cool morning

breeze blow across her face. After a while, when Cary didn't return or call for her, she went in search of him. He was still speaking to whomever it was. By the grim expression on his face, and his tight grip on the receiver, she could tell this was no friend. Niki's gut clenched.

"Who . . ."

He placed a finger to his lips, cutting her off.

"Repeat that, you bastard," she heard him say. He was red in the face, almost sputtering.

A string of colorful epithets followed before he ended the call.

"What was that all about?" Niki ventured, though in her gut she knew.

"I'm calling the cops," Cary said, punching in numbers. "This has got to end."

Edwards wasn't back and his partner was on a day off. Another officer suggested having the operator screen all calls. Niki didn't plan on staying around long enough for that to happen. She was too sick to her stomach to do that.

"We need to take charge," Cary insisted, hugging her quivering body against his.

"What did you have in mind?"

"Let's assess what your place looks like. If it's in reasonable condition and we can move back in, we'll have the locks and phone numbers changed. I'll stay with you as long as I can. If need be, I'll buy you a dog."

"That wouldn't be necessary. I'll ask Phillip to stay, if it comes down to it. He's a good friend."

"This Phillip guy is starting to make me jealous." Cary smiled, but she sensed genuine concern underlying his smile.

"You have nothing to worry about," Niki said, standing on tiptoe and reaching up to circle his neck with her arms.

He tried grabbing her and pulling her closer, but she scooted away.

There was no point in staying in the hotel room. Anxious to get going, Niki began haphazardly tossing items into a suitcase.

"I take it we're leaving?" Cary asked.

"Yes. It's time I went home."

He gathered his own stuff and shoved it into a garment bag. "I'll call a bellman," he offered when they were done. Picking up both sets of car keys, he handed her one. "I'll follow you."

"How did I manage before I met you?" Niki said, meaning it.

"You managed. You just didn't live."

Keeping a respectable distance behind her, Cary tailed Niki's Range Rover through her elegant Nob Hill neighborhood. *Snob Hill,* he thought, while admiring the well-tended gardens and attractive landscaping.

He probably wasn't being fair. He was relying on the memories of his student days at Stanford. The guys would all pile into one car and head for *Snob Hill,* the neighborhood they'd all aspired to move into.

As Niki steered her vehicle up a treacherous-looking incline, Cary concentrated on following. The rented Taurus let out a few groans. Then, resigned to the fact there would be no turning back, it continued uphill with only a halfhearted protest or two. Niki parked and hopped out. Cary followed with the suitcase and garment bag.

He trotted behind her up a cobblestone walkway made beautiful by roses just beginning to bloom. When they got to the entrance of an attractive Spanish-style town house, Niki stopped and fumbled in her purse for her key.

"Your home's got style," Cary said, eyeing the intricate architecture.

"I wonder what you'll think of the inside."

They entered a room with an open floor plan and an overhanging loft. Fans whirred from cathedral ceilings, and the overall impression was of the outdoors being brought in. Niki's cleaning service and housekeeper had done a good job, but piles of stuff they weren't sure what to do with had been stowed in every corner. Even so, the home was very livable.

"So what do you think?" Niki asked, throwing her hands wide.

"I like it." Cary looked around and, with his artist's eye, saw the potential the place had. The copper funnel fireplace alone was to die for. If he were to decorate, he'd angle a wraparound couch against that wall and fill every inch of living space with trailing plants and vines. He'd do it Southwestern.

"Let's see what condition the bedrooms are in," Niki said, leading the way.

They entered into a room that by virtue of its size must have been the master bedroom. It was sparsely furnished and held a bed minus a headboard, a chest of drawers, and a rocker with no cushion.

"I guess the headboard wasn't salvageable, and the cushion bit the dust," Niki said, looking like she wanted to cry. "That headboard was one of my favorite pieces. I bought it at a little antique store on Market Street."

"I'll buy you another," Carey offered. "Honey, by now you have to know I'd buy you the world."

"You're sweet."

He meant every word. He'd never felt this way about a woman. If anyone needed him, Niki obviously did. Behind that independent exterior was a woman who needed pampering.

They entered the second bedroom. The bed frame was intact, but the mattress was missing. The walls had been treated to a fresh coat of white paint and the fumes still lingered. The carpeting looked new.

"I see they destroyed the mattress," Niki said sadly.

"You'll buy another. First things first. Let's see if we can get a locksmith out here right away. Then we'll tackle the business of the phone."

It took the remainder of the day to have the locks changed. There was some difficulty finding someone to do the job immediately. Companies that were willing wanted to charge an exorbitant fee. Finally they settled on a company whose charges weren't too outrageous.

Changing the phone number was relatively easy in comparison, and they were able to obtain a new unlisted number which Niki immediately shared with the hospital. Later that week, Cary had said, they would go shopping for a replacement answering machine. Hers had been destroyed by the intruder.

"We've done as much as we can do, hon," Cary said as Niki sorted through the last pile of stuff in the living room. She tossed anything she didn't want into a large plastic bag. "Let's go to dinner."

Neither had eaten since breakfast, Cary recalled, and a nice leisurely dinner followed by a long hot bath might be the ticket.

"Sounds wonderful, as long as it's not anywhere fancy," Niki said, slipping into a pair of black slacks and tugging on a sweater. "I'm working tomorrow. I've got an early day."

"How about Chinatown?"

"Perfect." She tossed him a quizzical glance. "I can't believe how familiar you are with the city."

"I'll tell you about it over dinner." Cary located her car keys. No point in taking the rented Taurus. The Range Rover was much better at negotiating San Francisco's steep hills.

Dinner was at one of the smaller restaurants in the congested section of the city where Chinatown was located. Niki seemed fine with having him order, giving the nod to tasty dim sum, succulent Peking duck, and melt-in-your-mouth lo mein noodles. After the meal, they both grabbed their fortune cookie served on top of a scoop of vanilla ice cream, breaking it open eagerly to retrieve the message inside.

"What does yours say?" Niki asked.

Cary read his aloud. "Confucius say a smart man will go after the woman he wants."

"It doesn't say that." She smiled at him, eyes twinkling. "Want to hear mine?"

"Sure."

"Happy days are just around the corner," Niki read. "You were going to tell me how you know San Francisco like the back of your hand." She sipped on the soothing green tea.

"I used to live here. In fact, I got my master's here." He could tell from her expression she was surprised, maybe even shocked.

"When was this?" Niki said carefully.

"At least twelve years ago. Remember, I'm thirty-eight."

"What did you major in?"

Cary chuckled. "International relations. Back then I planned on saving the world."

"And now?"

"I'm concentrating my efforts on raising my son and

helping adults to read at the shelter. You'd be surprised at the number of people who aren't able to, even at the most elementary level."

"Nothing surprises me," Niki said, her hands covering his. "It's a worthy thing you do, Cary Thomas. Many of the adult patients at my clinic can barely read, much less write. It's difficult for them to decipher a prescription."

"It's hard for most literate adults to read most doctors' writing," Cary joked.

"You're right."

The conversation changed to other topics before Cary carefully brought up the issue of the break-in.

"I can't help but think it's all related," he said. "The threatening phone calls, the notes. I'd hazard a guess it's someone you know. Didn't the police say there weren't signs of forcible entry? Is there anyone who might have your key?"

Niki thought for a moment. "I keep a spare set at the hospital, and my housekeeper has a set. Charlie and Devin now have keys. That's how they got into the place to begin with."

"How long have you had your housekeeper?"

"Ages. Anna Jenkins and I go back a long way. She's always been trustworthy and loyal."

"Yet you didn't depend solely on Anna to clean up. You hired a service. How did they get in?"

"I knew it would be too much for her. The woman's in her sixties. Phillip came by to let in the service."

"He seems to make himself very available."

Niki laughed. "That's Phillip. There's no reason he would want to hurt me. Besides, I'm pretty sure whoever's doing this is uneducated. You've seen some of the notes."

He had. Niki had shown them to him. But had they

been intentionally written that way, designed to throw her off track?

"Time to get you home," Cary said, signaling for the check. "Tomorrow's a big day. You'll need your sleep."

Niki yawned. "Yes, it's going to be pretty hectic, but then I get to come home to you. I will, won't I?"

"You will," he said, quickly assuring her. "If it were up to me, you'd come home to me every night."

She sighed. It just wasn't possible.

Chapter 19

"Good to have you back." Glenn Jacoby flashed Niki a welcoming smile. "You brought your medical records with you, I hope?"

Niki slapped down the thick folder on his desk and peered at him from behind her horn-rimmed glasses. "What was so urgent it couldn't wait until later?"

Glenn didn't answer; he simply gestured for her to take a seat. When she remained standing and looked him square in the face, he blushed and ran appraising eyes over her.

"You look nice and relaxed," he said at last. "Looks to me like you've lost weight, too."

"Is that a good thing?" Niki waited for him to get on with the reason he'd summoned her.

"Sit." Glenn pointed to the chair across from him.

To ignore him completely would be rude. He opened the folder and began flipping through papers. Niki took the vacant seat he gestured to.

"What's going on?" she asked when his brows knitted together. "I haven't had time for a turnover, and I get this message from you."

"I didn't mean to alarm you." Glenn's worshipful smile told her more than she wanted to know. She'd tried so hard not to mislead him. "I missed you," Glenn said, his gaze raking her face. "I've done my best to protect you from scandal. The service analysts from the medical board are extremely persistent. They keep calling, requesting information about the care and treatment you provide. I'm guessing this was brought on by the publicity generated from the Eldridge boy's case. I've pushed them off so far. I can't push them off forever."

Glenn paused, appearing to do a visible double take at one of the records before him.

"Something wrong?" Niki asked.

He held the page out to her. "I've never known you to use Wite-Out."

"It's very unlikely I would."

"Look here." Glenn tapped at a spot with his index finger.

Niki zeroed in on the section where she would have written the diagnosis. She glanced at the patient's name. Zachary Adams had needed a liver transplant, but had died before a suitable donor was found. She didn't recall him having juvenile diabetes, and she certainly didn't remember writing it down. She also didn't recall recommending aspirin. She wouldn't have. It was probably one of the worst things you could give to a patient with liver problems. They could end up bleeding to death. Whoever had done this knew her well. They'd copied her handwriting exactly.

"Mmmmm," Niki mumbled, "I'll have to check the records in my computer. Normally I record each diagnosis there, then list the recommended treatment."

"You've always been very thorough," Glenn said, rising and squeezing her shoulders. "You're a wonderful doctor and an all-around terrific person."

Thankfully, the phone on his desk rang. Niki exhaled a sigh of relief. Her life was complicated enough. She didn't need it further complicated by Glenn's unwanted attention.

"Jacoby," he said, picking it up and appearing to listen intently. "No. Not again. I thought they'd gone away." He covered the mouthpiece and turned back to her. "It's Public Relations on the other end. They want to talk to you."

"What about?"

"Reporters are camped out on the front lawn again. They're demanding a statement. Someone must have leaked the information you're back."

Niki took the receiver from Glenn with some reluctance.

"Dr. Hamilton?" The hospital PR director's resonant voice boomed through the earpiece. "Leland King here."

"What can I do for you, Leland?"

Niki remembered King as a tall, extremely good-looking man who wore double-breasted suits and wild ties. He was known to sashay flamboyantly down the hall, chasing one doctor or another.

"The break-in at your place has made the news, and the reporters see it as a good opportunity to revive an old story. I'll handle statements on your behalf, so don't hesitate to send the paparazzi my way."

"I appreciate that. What do I do if I'm confronted by one of these pests?"

"Avoid them at all costs. Use the back entrance when you leave. If reporters stop you, tell them to contact me, and give them my number. Under no circumstances say, 'No comment.' It makes it sound like you have something to hide."

Niki thanked him and hung up. The enormity of the situation finally hit her. Would she be dodging reporters for the rest of her life? Now foremost in her mind was getting out of Glenn's office and avoiding his fawning gaze. Bile began to build in the back of her throat, and there was a tightness in her chest that hadn't been there earlier. Excusing herself, she raced out. She needed support. Just hearing Cary's voice might help.

In the relative calm of her own office, she cradled the receiver between her ear and shoulder and dialed her home number. The phone rang for an eternity. They hadn't yet gotten around to getting that answering machine. Where was he? Only a log could sleep through that ringing. Disappointed, Niki gave up. Time to be professional and go back to work.

Niki booted up her computer and typed in her password. After several unsuccessful attempts, she concluded she'd been locked out. How could that happen? The hospital couldn't have kicked her out of their system. It wasn't as if she'd quit the job. She'd been on leave. When she got a moment, she would contact the info systems team and see what was wrong.

A knock on her door got her attention. Phillip hovered.

"Come in," Niki politely invited.

"You're pale as a ghost. Are you ill?" Phillip crossed his arms and rested his butt against the arm of her chair.

"I've had a couple of unsettling things happen."

"Like?" His brows knitted together.

Niki told him about Zachary Adams's medical records, about not recalling him having diabetes or being prescribed aspirin.

"Am I going crazy?" she asked. "To top that off, I can't even access my computer to check my records and verify my sanity. Looks like I've been locked out."

Phillip crossed over to the computer. "Let me take a look. What's your access code?" He asked.

Niki blinked at him. Her password was something she didn't give out, not even to her family.

"You can always change it afterward."

Niki gave it to him. After several tries, Phillip gave up.

"Yep, looks like you might be right. Someone must have tried accessing your computer while you were out. They probably needed some information. Rather than disturb you, they opted to try getting in themselves."

It sounded like BS to her. "Patient information is confidential," Niki said, "Any doctor entrusted to care for my patients could simply have called me or at the very least gotten in touch with Glenn."

Phillip sighed. "You're right, I suppose. Maybe they just wanted to use the computer."

"I'm not buying it. If that were the case, why not use their own password?"

"Dr. Jordan. Dr. Jordan," a deep male voice boomed over the intercom. "You're needed in emergency."

His white coat flapping behind him, Phillip raced off, looking glad to be gone.

The phone rang, pulling Cary from a deep sleep. After fumbling for the receiver, he placed it carefully to his ear.

"Hello," he croaked.

"Oh, Cary, Cary, I don't know where to begin." Cary's numb brain registered Lourdes Gonzales's hysterical screams on the other end. He was instantly awake.

"What's wrong with Brett?"

"She *took* him. She *took* him."

"Who's *she*? And where did *she* take Brett?"

"All I know is that he's gone. She up and left with him. No one knows where they went."

"Lourdes, you're not making sense."

"Oh, Lord, Cary you left him in my care, and now he's up and disappeared."

Cary closed his eyes, hoping that when he opened them again, the room would come back into focus. Pinpoints of light flickered behind his closed lids and the beginnings of what would be a doozy of a headache started somewhere at the base of his skull.

He clenched and unclenched his fists. *She* probably meant Elsa. Damn the woman! Why had she chosen now to pull this nonsense?

"I'm on the next plane," he informed Lourdes before hanging up.

Next Cary dialed the number Niki had left for the hospital. It rang and rang. He hadn't thought to get her beeper number. He raced around, throwing the few items of clothing he'd brought into his garment bag. He would head for the airport and buy his ticket from there. He looked for a piece of paper, anything, to leave Niki a message on, and found a brown paper bag in the kitchen. Quickly scribbling a note, he set the bag down on what he believed to be a prominent place on the counter. It would suffice until he got home to New Jersey, when he'd try calling again.

For an exorbitant sum, he managed to pick up a ticket in business class. Not his choice, really, but the plane was almost completely sold out. For another five agonizing hours, he endured what seemed to be the longest flight in history, one filled with air pockets. He had no idea where Elsa could have taken Brett. Back to Grand Cayman was always a possibility. Finding his child might require police intervention, but if it came down to that, he'd simply do what he had to do.

The ride home from the Newark airport took less than the normal fifty minutes, largely because he pushed the speedometer to eighty. By the time he walked into the house, Lourdes looked like she'd been crying for days. Cary tossed his garment bag on the floor and opened his arms to her.

"Hush. It'll be all right. We'll find Brett," he said, sounding more confident than he felt.

Lourdes, glad to unload, told him all about waiting for Brett to get off the camp bus and finally giving up, about calling the camp herself, only to be told that Mrs. Thomas, bearing a note of authorization, had already picked Brett up.

Cary grew increasingly angry. How dare Elsa pose as his wife, forge her own note, and go to his son's camp? No point in getting crazy now. What was done was done. His primary goal was to find Brett. Hopefully Elsa had not taken him out of the country.

Forcing himself to concentrate, Cary pinched the skin between his nose and eyes. It was a safe bet that Brett was no longer in Long Branch. Even so, it was a place to begin. Elsa had mentioned taking a room at the Hilton on Ocean. Cary quickly dialed the operator to get the number.

"Elsa Viera's room," he demanded once the hotel operator picked up.

Keys tapped as the employee attempted to locate the name on her computer.

"I'm afraid there's no one here by that name," she said finally.

"V-i-e-r-a," Cary said, spelling it out. "Check again."

More tapping on the keyboard as she continued her search.

"Ah, Elsa. She's no longer here, sir. She checked out."

"Damn it." Cary slammed down the phone and turned away. He paced the room, planning his next move.

Lourdes stood, arms crossed, staring at him. Sobs ripped from her throat. She sounded like an animal awaiting slaughter.

"It's not your fault," he said, touching her arm. "Elsa was determined to take Brett. Trust me, we'll find him."

Cary drummed his fingers on the nearby coffee table. His second call was to Aaron, whom he tracked down at the pharmacy, and who came to the phone after considerable paging.

"What's up?" his friend asked.

Cary told him. "Any ideas where I might track Elsa down?"

"She may have just moved hotels," Aaron suggested. "I'd call around locally. Then I'd try the City."

That floored him. Searching for Elsa in Manhattan would be a formidable task. There were hundreds of hotels, and it would be virtually impossible to find one adult and a little boy there.

He thanked Aaron and hung up. Clearly he was left with no other option. He'd wait a full twenty-four hours. Then he'd call the police.

"Cary," Niki called softly. When there was no answer, she repeated his name, this time louder. "Cary?"

The town house had been blanketed in darkness when

she pulled into the driveway. The rented Taurus was nowhere in sight. Niki initially thought Cary might have moved it into the garage. Still, that didn't explain the dark house or the silence. Methodically, she checked every room. Soon it became apparent he wasn't there. She'd given him keys. Could he be out getting dinner?

Niki returned to the bedroom, removed her shoes, and slowly climbed out of her clothing. What a brutal day it had been. She'd been away just long enough to forget the long hours, constant understaffing, and high patient load. She'd been forced to dodge aggressive reporters camped out on the front lawn and flooding the hospital with calls. Thanks to the intervention of two security guards, she'd made it home. Even now she wasn't entirely convinced she hadn't been followed. Where was Cary when she needed him most?

Another hour went by without hearing from him. She grew worried. It was pitch-black outside. She had new locks and a new unlisted number. That should provide some modicum of security. Too bad they'd never gotten around to buying that answering machine.

Niki heard every outdoor noise clearly: the whistle of the wind through the huge oak tree on her scrap of a lawn, the crack of twigs, the sound of muted conversation as neighbors hailed each other while walking their dogs. Even the chirping crickets sounded ominous in the night. She was suddenly starving and wished Cary would return so they could eat.

When eleven o'clock rolled around with no sign of him, she wandered into the kitchen, took two slices of bread from the refrigerator, and set them down on a brown paper bag on the counter. She spread on a liberal amount of mustard, slapped in a couple of slices of bologna, a piece of cheese, and a generous slice of tomato, and transferred her sandwich onto a plate. She balled up the greasy paper bag and threw it into the garbage, wolfed down the sandwich, and chased it with generous swigs of juice.

There was no one she could think of to call, no one who would know of Cary's whereabouts. She returned to her bedroom and turned on the TV. The silence was oppressive inside. Maybe noise from the TV would help.

Was that sound a car? A quick peek through the window revealed flickering taillights disappearing into the neighbor's driveway.

Looking around at the bedroom, Niki realized something was different. It seemed neater than she had left it. Realization struck with such finality she almost stumbled from the blow. Cary's clothing was missing. His striped polo shirt was no longer thrown casually over the rocker, nor were his jeans draped over the chest of drawers. His shoes weren't parked next to hers on the floor.

Niki flung open the closet doors. Just as she'd thought. The few clothes he'd hung up were gone. She felt betrayed. Used. Abandoned. He'd left with no note, not even a phone call, saying where or why he was gone. She deserved better.

What might have brought this on? He'd been her rock. In the short space of time they'd gotten together, she'd learned to lean on him. She was surprised he'd taken the coward's way out, sneaking out on her when she'd gone to work. She needed to talk to someone, to be reassured that she wasn't crazy or easily taken in. She would call Kim.

The phone rang and rang until Kim's answering machine picked up. Niki opted not to leave a message. It was close to midnight by then, but tired as she was, she was still too wound up to sleep. Tomorrow would be time enough to deal with all this. Tomorrow, she might try locating Cary in New Jersey. Then she would give him a piece of her mind.

Leaving the lights on, Niki stripped off her clothes and got under the covers. Mentally and physically, she felt beaten up. It had been one long, aggravating day. She pulled the bedclothes up to her chin, closed her eyes, and drifted.

"Mirdirer! You killed my child." The image came closer. An elongated finger jabbed the air, pointing at her.

Niki focused on the face. The features weren't clear.

"I goin' git you. We all goin' git you," the apparition chanted.

Accusatory fingers pointed at her, stabbing the air, jabbing at her. Mouths opened into an obscene O, the M word rolling off each tongue. "Mirdirer."

She searched the crowd for a friendly face, an advocate, someone to support her. But all she saw were the same distorted features, yelling at her, calling her names.

"Mirdirir. You call yourself a doctor."

In the background, a shrill ringing penetrated. She bolted upright and brought trembling hands to her chest. She tugged at the covers, brought them up to her chin, and waited for her breathing to regulate. What was that thumping she heard? A loose shutter? Her heart? Footsteps? Niki gulped air.

The ringing sound ceased. She needed a glass of water.

Halfway off the bed, the creak of a floorboard stopped her. The seriousness of the situation hit her. She was alone in a house that had already been broken into, no one to come to her rescue except for neighbors who were probably dead asleep by now. Even Cary hadn't remembered his promise. Where was the dog he'd said he would buy her?

A light flickered across her windowpane and spanned the room. Someone was outside her home. Could another person possibly be inside? Niki licked dry lips and concentrated. The town house was old. That might very well explain the creaking boards, but the light playing across her bedroom window was another matter. She looked around for something to protect herself with, and remembered the golf clubs at the back of the closet, the ones she never used.

Trying to keep as quiet as possible, Niki crept from her bed. She opened the closet and searched around. Eventually her hands wrapped around cold steel. The breath she didn't know she was holding escaped.

Taking a club with her, she padded over to the chest of drawers, managed to find the phone, and dialed nine-one-one. When the operator came on, she whispered her address and hung up. No way was she going to remain stationary while someone ransacked her house again or tried to kill her. Let it not be said Niki Hamilton was a pushover.

That decided, golf club in hand, she crept down the hall. The police would show up soon, hopefully before she was murdered.

Chapter 20

Toting the golf club with her, Niki crept through the house. Initially she had some difficulty adjusting to the darkness, so she edged around objects, doing her best not to bump into things. In the living room, she stood stock-still trying to listen, trying not to breathe. A floorboard creaked again. She sucked in a breath, waiting—for what, she wasn't sure. After a while, when no monster loomed out of the darkness, she positioned herself next to the window and pressed her nose against the pane.

Lights swept across her tiny front lawn, the type of beams flashlights might put out. Someone was definitely out there. Carefully, Niki made her way back to the kitchen. She pressed herself against the wall and peered out the back window. Footsteps crunched across the yard, and a deep voice swore. Whoever it was had stumbled over something. The police had better get here soon.

Niki wiped her sweaty palms on the nightshirt she'd worn to bed. Her underarms had gone damp. Much as she tried to regulate her breathing, her breath still came in quick, erratic bursts. There was nothing she could do to stop that. The kitchen swam before her eyes. She was dangerously close to hyperventilating.

She heard the footsteps. Louder. Closer. There was no place to hide.

Her brain shut down, and she simply couldn't think. She found herself backing out of the kitchen and heading toward the front door. Would a burglar have the gumption to let himself in through the front? Stranger things had happened.

She was halfway to the door when heavy footsteps crunched their way up the walkway. Arcs of light swept the living room and played across her face, then moved on. She froze. Niki opened her mouth to scream, but nothing came out. She was fairly certain more than one person was out there. She was outnumbered.

The footsteps were closer now, and eerie lights revolved in circular motions. She ventured toward the window again and pressed her nose against the pane, squinting into the darkness. There was a car out front. Her burglars were bold.

A loud bang on the front door caused Niki's heart to almost leap from her chest. Reaching out a trembling hand, she tried steadying herself. There was nothing to hold on to. The golf club went flying as her knees buckled. The floor rose to meet her. She pitched forward. There was no one to call out to.

Cary let the phone ring eight, maybe nine, times, before hanging up. Unless there'd been an emergency at the hospital, Niki should be home by now. Maybe she was dead to the world and couldn't hear the phone.

A quick glance at his watch revealed it to be four o'clock his time, one o'clock hers. A little late to call, but he'd felt he needed to. He'd scribbled that quick note and raced off without telling her where he was going, comforted only by the fact that new locks had been installed and her phone number changed. Even so, Niki must be furious with him. He'd left her alone, even though he'd promised not to.

Cary knew there would be no sleep for him until he found Elsa and Brett. He couldn't think about Niki now—wouldn't, despite the fact that her being alone in the town house bothered him. He wandered into the room he'd converted into an office, sat down at the drafting table, and began designing the way he'd first learned, with pencil and paper. The old-fashioned way. Afterward, using a large gridded piece of paper, he completed the same sketch to scale.

By the time he was done, his eyes burned, and his head felt as if it were sizes too large. Cary laid his head down on the table and closed his eyes. Niki's face filled his vision. The scent of her subtle perfume tickled his nostrils. It was the last thing he remembered before falling asleep.

Hours later, a ringing in his ears woke him. Cary reached out a hand and felt for the phone, slowly bringing the receiver to his ear. "Hello," he croaked.

"Dad?"

He was instantly awake. "Brett? where are you?"

"Some place in the city. Mom and I rode the train. Then we took a taxi. We got in late at night."

He wanted to strangle Elsa. "Where's your mother?" he said, instead.

"Asleep in the bedroom. I slept on a pullout couch in another room."

Cary tried focusing on his watch. What time was it? He finally made out the numbers. Somewhere around seven o'clock. Early. Elsa had always been a late riser.

He spoke quickly. "Son, are you at a friend's house or at a hotel?"

"We're at a hotel, Dad. We checked in at a big desk. Mom gave the man her credit card."

"I take it your mother doesn't have a clue you're calling me?" Cary asked.

"No, she said this trip was a surprise and it should be our little secret. But I couldn't sleep, and I miss you."

"I miss you, too," Cary said, realizing Elsa could wake up any moment and he still wouldn't know where his son was. "In fact, I miss you so much, I'm coming to visit. It will be our surprise. Our little secret. What do you say?"

"I say I love it."

"OK. Now this is what I need you to do. Look on the coffee table or desk, whichever there is. Get a notepad and read me off the address at the top or bottom. When you're done, give me the extension listed on your phone."

Cary hung on while Brett went off to do his bidding. In seconds he returned.

"I have it, Dad. The room number's 640."

"And the address?"

Brett read off the midtown address while Cary scribbled.

In a few hours, Elsa Viera was about to receive a very rude surprise, one he planned to deliver in person.

"Police. Open up!"

Niki heard the words from a distance, but her limbs just plain refused to cooperate. A ringing sound came from some place in her subconscious. Focusing in, she realized it was the phone.

"Ms. Hamilton, Ms. Hamilton, are you all right?" Voices from outside penetrated the door.

Niki's throat tightened up on her. She couldn't get the words out to even acknowledge she heard them. The ringing stopped.

The thumping on her front door increased. "Ms. Hamilton, please respond. Let us know if you need assistance." A barked set of orders. "We're giving you thirty seconds. Then we're coming in."

"I ... I'm ... OK." Had the police even heard her? Her next words came across a little stronger. "Give me a minute."

"Are you hurt?"

"No." She'd managed to get the one word out loud and clear.

Crawling on all fours, she made it to the door, found the knob, and propelled herself slowly upward. Her legs felt like jelly as she fumbled with the latches and security chain. She found the energy to tug the door open and sagged against the frame. She squinted into the blackness, gulping the cool night air.

"Ms. Hamilton, do you need a doctor?" A burly policeman reached out with large paws, steadying her.

"I *am* a doctor. I'll be OK. I blacked out for a short while. Probably too much stress. All the tension."

"Let's get you sitting. Get you a glass of water," the policeman bringing up the rear offered.

When she was seated on the sofa in her living room, sipping on water one of the officers had brought her, she began to put things into perspective. She'd awakened to noise and lights in her front yard. She'd panicked and called the police.

"How did you get here so soon?" Niki managed.

"We didn't. Ever since the break-in, we've been

instructed to increase patrol of your neighborhood. My partner and I''—he gestured to the other officer—''were taking a look around the property when we heard our dispatcher on the radio saying you'd just placed a call to nine-one-one.''

Niki shook her head in disbelief. ''It was *you* out there all this time? *You* were the ones roaming around my property?''

''We've made a point of doing that every night. Vandals, thieves, whatever you want to call them, often return to the same house.''

Niki replayed the early morning events. She'd been pulled from a deep sleep, rescued from an awful nightmare by a shrill ringing. Immediately, her imagination had gone wild, and every sound in the house had become amplified. She'd peered outside and saw the lights, heard the footsteps, and reacted. Obviously the stress of the long day had taken its toll. She'd overreacted. Time to buy a dog, as Cary had suggested.

Just the thought of him made her angry again. He'd let her down, taken off and disappeared without leaving word. But that didn't mean she couldn't buy her own dog. She was an independent woman with money of her own. She didn't need a man to do that for her.

''Try to get some sleep,'' the burlier of the two policemen said, standing. ''We'll be patrolling your area for the rest of the morning. You won't be needing that.'' He pointed to the golf club she'd dropped.

Niki smiled wanly. ''You're right. Now if you gentlemen will excuse me, I'm going to try to get some much needed shut-eye.''

* * *

Cary walked into the lobby of the Sheraton with a folded copy of the *New York Times* under his arm. Before arriving, he'd called the hotel on a cell phone and asked the operator to put him through to Elsa's room. The moment she'd answered, he'd hung up.

Glad to find her still there, he'd raced from the parking garage. Lucky for him Brett had provided the room number. Now all he had to do was to figure out how to approach her without having her bolt.

Cary took a seat in the lobby and buried his head behind the paper. Whatever plan he came up with needed to have the element of surprise on his side. He flipped through the pages of the newspaper, not even seeing the print. Perhaps he could pretend to be room service. That might get Elsa to open the door. The more he mulled around that idea, the more he liked it.

After a while, he rose, folded the paper, and headed for the elevator. He needed to pull this off without having Elsa make the type of scene she was notorious for. What could be going on in her mind? She'd never wanted the responsibility of a son. For years she'd never even wanted a son, period. Why the sudden change of heart?

Cary exited on the sixth floor and looked to see where the rooms with even numbers were located. Sidestepping maids with carts filled with cleaning supplies and amenities, he eventually found room 640. He paused before the door, debating whether to announce himself as room service. But what if Elsa or Brett recognized his voice? He made a U-turn as a better plan began formulating, and proceeded back up the hallway.

"I need a favor," he said to a Latino-looking maid with dangling earrings and an elaborately made-up face. "I'll make it worth your while."

"Sí. Pero me no hablo ingles, señor." She pointed to another maid. *"Teresa she habla ingles."*

He needed someone who spoke English well, not Spanglish.

Cary approached the maid the girl had referred to as Teresa. She smiled brightly at him. "What can I do for you, sir?"

This one was more on the ball. Cary peeled several bills from his wallet and placed them on top of her overflowing cart. "Look, I need you to knock on 640. If a woman answers, identify yourself as the cleaning service and tell her you need to get in. When she opens the door, I'll take over."

"That's it?"

"That's it," Cary confirmed, as Teresa cheerfully counted the money he'd dropped on top of her cart. She clicked her tongue. "This could get me in trouble. I could lose my job."

"If it comes down to it, you could always say I pushed past you and forced my way in. Would this make it easier?" Cary peeled another set of bills from his wallet and set them on the cart in front of her.

"It might. OK, *chico*, now we go. Just pray I don't get into trouble and lose my job."

Teresa tucked the money he gave her into her ample cleavage and led the way down the hall. Her friend, the maid he'd first spoken to, shook her head and wagged a finger at Teresa. The maid parked her cart in front of room 640. He pressed himself against the wall and held his breath as Teresa's staccato raps shook the door. A rustling came from inside, followed by footsteps.

"Yes?" Elsa called. "Who is it?"

"The maid."

Cary held his breath. Hopefully, Brett had kept his

mouth shut and had not mentioned their earlier conversation to his mother.

"I'm not checking out today. Can't you come back?" Elsa sounded peevish.

Cary hadn't anticipated that. How would Teresa handle this new twist? The maid pursed her lips and shot him a speculative look. He motioned to her to try again.

"Yes, madam. But don't you want fresh towels, shampoo, soap? I'll give them to you now. That way you won't have to wait."

Elsa's sigh was audible. "OK. Yeah, that makes sense."

Cary heard her fiddling with the locks. Teresa hunched over the cart, taking the time to select towels and pick out shampoos, conditioners, and soap. The door was thrown open. Elsa, still wearing her bathrobe, faced Teresa.

"One moment, ma'am, I'm getting it for you." Teresa bent over to gather yet another bar of soap.

That was his cue. Cary lunged forward and slapped both palms against the door frame, trapping Elsa. "I want my son," he shouted.

"You . . . you can't have him." She tried to push the door closed, but Cary's body was in the way. She opened her mouth as if to scream. Cary quickly placed a hand over her mouth and forcibly maneuvered her back into the room. Using the sole of his shoe, he pushed the door shut.

"Dad, Dad. You came like you promised," Brett cried, scampering into the suite's living room. "I'm so happy. Will you take us to breakfast?"

"You knew about this?" Elsa sounded indignant.

Cary released his hold on Elsa. He did not want it to appear as if he were manhandling the boy's mother. It was a poor example to set, and one that could leave an indelible imprint on the child. For a second or so, he felt ashamed it had come down to this. He'd been taught to respect women, not push them around. Why had he allowed Elsa to put him in the position of aggressor?

But what choice had he really had—either come alone, talk some sense into her, and try to reclaim his son, or get a court order and get the police involved. That would only create hostility. Brett would be deprived of a mother he obviously loved.

"I can't believe you knew your father was coming," Elsa repeated, sounding horrified. She glared at her son.

"Brett called me," Cary confirmed. "And a lucky thing he did."

"I thought we were having fun," Elsa reasoned. "You said you enjoyed the train ride. Today we were planning on roller blading in Central Park."

"Can't we still do that?" Brett pleaded. "Now that Dad's here, it will be even more fun. Wouldn't it, Dad? We can rent one of those rowboats, just like last year. We'll go out on the lake."

"What do you say?" Cary quickly interjected, trying to be amenable. Much as he wanted to strangle Elsa for what she'd just put them through, she was still the child's biological mother. He'd save the angry words for later when they were alone. Once he'd straightened her out, he would send Brett to his own sister, then hop on a plane for San Francisco to be with Niki. He missed her.

This brief time apart had convinced him of one thing. He needed her in his life—not just for the short term. Forever.

Chapter 21

"Doc. Niki, Doc. Niki. Where you been, sister?" A tall, skinny young man with braids pointing north, south, east, and west waylaid Niki the minute she stepped out of the Range Rover. He gave her an ear-to-ear grin and high-fived her. "Want me to watch your vehicle?"

"I'd love it if you would, Akbar." She squeezed his shoulder. "Good to see you again."

"You know I'll always watch your back. Matter of fact, I got something to tell you."

"Can it hold? I'm terribly late. I should have been at the clinic half an hour ago."

"It'll hold, but it's important. I'll be right here when you're done."

She was already several minutes late for her two-hour stint at the clinic. Niki sprinted the last few feet uphill. It couldn't be helped. She'd had an emergency at the hospital and couldn't leave until relief arrived. Although she was bone tired, work kept her occupied, giving her little time to miss Cary.

The clinic was located in a poor section of town. Some said it was an unsafe area, but Niki had always felt comfortable here. Poor didn't necessarily mean dangerous. People had a tendency to label lots of places unsafe simply by virtue of the color of the residents' skin.

Niki walked into a packed waiting room and acknowledged the enthusiastic greetings of her patients.

"Dr. Niki, we missed you."

"Doc, you're back."

"Hey, Dr. Hamilton, wait until you see how much Tanika's grown!"

With a smile, a wave, and some reassuring words for good measure, Niki made her way toward the back room where patients were seen. She washed her hands, slipped into a starched white coat, and accepted the stack of files from Lorraine Johnson. Lorraine was another of the many volunteers who helped keep the clinic running.

The first patient Niki saw had a bad upper respiratory infection. She prescribed antibiotics and recommended liquids and almost complete bed rest. Even though the child's parents thanked her profusely, she knew it would never happen. Working-class people of any age seldom had time to pamper themselves. She was grateful for their offer of support, though. It seemed everyone and his brother knew she'd been vilified by the media.

In what seemed a short space of time and a sea of faces, two hours went by. It was pitch-black out and Niki was grateful for Phillip's offer to walk her to her car. He'd arrived hours before she had. Now she looked forward to a long, soothing bubble bath when she got home.

Akbar waited for her, his wiry body pressed against the Range Rover. He held court with a gang of youths who looked like they were up to no good.

"I suggest you get into your vehicle and head out," Phillip whispered. "These home boys aren't to be trusted. I'll wait to make sure your car starts."

Phillip had never been particularly fond of Akbar. He'd labeled him a small-time hood. The feeling was apparently mutual—definitely no love lost between the two.

Akbar had vocalized his feelings on more than one occasion. "That Dr. Jordan ain't real," he'd said. "He just ain't real." For the most part the two simply ignored each other.

"Doc, you got a moment?" Akbar peeled himself off her car and came toward them. The crowd he was talking to parted, eyeing them warily.

"You're exhausted," Phillip whispered. "You don't have time for this. He's probably after your jewelry, anyway."

"Phillip!" Niki hissed, outraged. He of all people shouldn't stereotype. Besides, she wore little jewelry, just the same watch that had been her parents' present to her when she graduated from medical school. It wasn't expensive.

Still glaring at the crowd he so often referred to as hoodlums, Phillip pressed the button of his remote. The car lights flashed and he let himself into his Lexus. Niki was left facing Akbar. She noticed that Phillip kept the car windows up.

"What was it you wanted to tell me?" she asked.

Akbar's jaw jutted in the direction of where Phillip still sat. "You need to watch that one. Homie's a player."

"Come on, Akbar. Just because you two don't get along, that's not a good reason to put Phillip down."

It wasn't the first time he had made derogatory comments about Phillip, nor would it be the last.

"Look," Akbar said, his thumb gesturing to the neighborhood gang still hovering in the background. "Your doctor friend's been talking to Quaalude. Rumor has it they're tight."

"Who's Quaalude?"

Akbar's big white teeth shone in the lamplight. "Quaalude's a dealer. Everybody in the hood knows him. Whatever you want, Quaalude can get. It's been said your Medicine Man's his supplier. In return, Quaalude does him certain favors."

"That's ridiculous. Phillip's straight as an arrow. What would he have to gain from supplying your friend Quaalude with drugs? And what kind of favors could your friend Quaalude be doing for him?"

Akbar moved in closer until Niki could smell an inexpensive cologne and the fish dinner he'd apparently had. "You'd be surprised. There ain't nothin' Quaalude wouldn't do. Remember that, and be careful now. The doctor may want to put it to you, but trust me, he ain't no friend."

For a brief moment, listening to his speech patterns had brought back memories. Niki wondered if it was Akbar she should be worried about. Had Akbar been making phone calls and sending her notes? What would be his motive?

Tamping down on the unsettling feeling that had surfaced, Niki climbed into the Range Rover. Akbar had seemed sincere enough, but how well did she really know him? Ever since his little brother had been brought into the clinic with a gunshot wound, he'd looked out for her. Niki had accompanied the child by ambulance to the hospital. She'd stayed with him until he was out of danger, and spent the weeks after holding his mother's hand. The question was, did she trust Akbar?

When he motioned for her to roll down the window,

Niki complied. "I ain't lying, Doc. What I tell you's the truth."

Niki nodded, then put the window back up. She put the vehicle in gear, and glided past Phillip, who was still waiting for her to pull out. It would be a long and most likely restless night at home. Every squeak of the floorboard and every night sound would scare her. And even with police patrolling the neighborhood, there was no guarantee whoever it was wouldn't be back. Tomorrow she would buy that dog. Had to.

Until then, she had every intention of calling Cary. Heaven help him if he was unlucky enough to pick up his phone.

Entering a silent house, Niki quickly turned on the lights. Anna Jenkins had obviously been cleaning, and the inside sparkled. Niki made a mental note to go on a shopping spree tomorrow and replace the items the vandals had ruined. Since she was starting the evening shift, she would have plenty of time. First things first. She needed an answering machine, a headboard, and a mattress. A couple of potted plants would make the place look more homey and lived in. She'd also explore the possibility of installing an alarm. It would make her feel safer, and she'd finally be able to sleep in peace. Then she would consider buying that dog.

Niki quickly changed out of her clothes. Dressed in sweats and socks, she wandered into the kitchen to retrieve the leftovers that were still edible. She'd made a Caesar salad the evening before, and the remainder, plus a crusty slice of bread, would serve as her dinner. She poured bottled water and, taking her plate with her, hoisted herself onto a stool at the kitchen counter. After munching on a few mouthfuls of salad, she pushed her plate away. She was much too exhausted to eat.

Now or never, she decided. Time to call Cary and give him a piece of her mind. Never mind that she missed him and that she refused to acknowledge he'd broken her heart. She wouldn't do tears. And she was too proud to beg him to come back after the way he'd treated her.

Niki dialed Cary's work number. After several rings, his answering machine picked up. She hung up, deciding not to leave a message. She had his home number somewhere. She found her address book and dialed again. This time the sound of his voice on the answering machine gave her goose bumps. Where could he be? Her anger at him turned to worry. Though all signs indicated he had simply packed up and left, what if he'd been abducted or detained and simply couldn't get to a phone?

A wild thought. There'd been no sign of a break-in or even a struggle. Everything had been neat and orderly when she'd arrived home four days ago. Maybe his friend Aaron knew where he was. It was worth a call, if only to reassure herself Cary wasn't hurt.

A call to directory assistance provided her with the number for Aaron's pharmacy. He'd once told her his business stayed open twenty-four hours. Niki dialed the number before she could get cold feet. A clerk picked up.

"Smith's."

She identified herself as a doctor and requested Aaron.

"I'm sorry," the woman answering said, "Mr. Smith's not here tonight. You can try back tomorrow. He's usually in at eight."

"I really do need to speak with Mr. Smith tonight."

"It's an emergency, then?"

"Yes, an emergency."

Still some hesitation on the clerk's part. "OK, let me see if I can conference you in with him."

She felt incredibly guilty while she was waiting. She'd

intentionally misled the clerk, making her believe she was a doctor with an emergency. When it came down to it, she was, but she wasn't about to ask the kind of question Aaron Smith anticipated.

The phone rang for an interminable number of minutes. Eventually a deep voice answered. Aaron, thank God.

"Yes?"

The clerk introduced her. "Doctor, what did you say your name was again?"

"Hamilton. Niki." Niki prayed Aaron would make the association. As close as Cary and Aaron were, surely he would have told him she wasn't the matchmaker he thought, but a doctor.

"Hamilton," Aaron repeated. "I don't know a doctor— oh, yeah, Niki, Cary's lady. What's up, girl?"

Reassured Niki hadn't misrepresented herself, the clerk hung up.

Niki and Aaron exchanged the customary health inquiries before Niki explained the purpose of her call.

"I thought Cary was back with you," Aaron said.

"I take it you've seen him?"

"A couple of days ago, and only for a short while."

The bastard! Still, she couldn't help asking, "Was he all right?" She already knew the answer.

"Given everything he'd been through, he was fine. My boy seldom goes through changes."

She would put him through changes! The anger Niki had sublimated surfaced. Cary was obviously well enough to make his way back to New Jersey. He was fine enough to see Aaron and speak with him, but didn't care enough about her to give her a call. Not that it would make a difference now. Nothing he could say or do would make a difference.

No point in prolonging the conversation. She'd gotten enough information. Cary Thomas was now a closed chapter in her life. Niki hung up with a heavy heart. She gathered her dirty dish and made her way over to the sink. It wasn't worth running the dishwasher for one solitary plate and a set of utensils. Maybe she was better off living alone, accountable only for herself and her own actions After a three-month marriage to a man easily distracted by the next-door maid, she hadn't thought she'd let herself hurt again.

After Niki was through washing the cutlery and the dish, she decided a nice long soak in the tub might help her relax. She ran the hot water, added bubble bath, and waited for the tub to fill up. The medical journal she pretended to read didn't hold her attention.

To block out thoughts of Cary, she replayed the conversation with Akbar. Did it merit consideration? Should she give it credence? Phillip's job was to save lives, not ruin them. She'd known him for years. He wouldn't hurt a fly.

Stripping off her clothes, Niki climbed into the now full tub, luxuriating in the steaming bath water. She turned on the radio, kept on an overhead shelf, closed her eyes, and drifted. After a while, Cary's face filled her vision. His tender touch trailed across her skin. Loving words caressed her ear—words that were overdue. Words she'd waited too long to hear.

Niki wanted to sink into the warmth and simply forget—how he'd made her feel, forget that she must have said or done something awful to make him run away. She was hurting and could do nothing to fix that hurt.

She was practically asleep when she thought she heard a car door slam. A neighborhood dog barked, and she assumed it was someone arriving home late. The romantic ballad on the radio soothed her. No vandal in his right mind would enter a house before midnight, not unless he wanted to be caught. Was that a key being inserted in her front door? Nonsense.

Niki closed her eyes and let the scented water take her way. Willing herself to relax, she drifted with the music. Her subconscious registered footsteps coming her way. She bolted upright, remnants of bubbles clinging to her nude body, the hair she'd soaked a tight cap against her head.

The doorknob jiggled. Niki opened her mouth to scream.

"Honey, I'm back," Cary announced, entering. "Did you miss me?"

"You bastard." Niki began to cry. Her whole body trembled.

Still fully clothed, Cary climbed into the tub beside her and gathered her close. "What's wrong, honey? I'm here. I never plan on leaving your side. Not ever. Not unless you want me to."

Niki pounded his chest. "You walked out on me. You promised not to leave me unprotected, yet you left me without a word." She gulped air, but the tears kept coming. Her nose filled up.

"I did no such thing," Cary argued. "I left you a note. I tried calling. You were never home. My note was on a brown paper bag."

A brown paper bag. Why did she remember a brown paper bag? She'd made her sandwich dinner on that bag, gotten it greasy, and tossed it away.

"I'm sorry, honey," Cary repeated. "I'm sorry I had to leave you. I'll tell you about it when we're in bed." He sank down into the tub with her, holding her tight against him, cradling her, whispering sweet nothings into her ear that coming from another man would sound silly.

"You've got a lot of explaining to do," Niki said, when her tears finally stopped.

She wanted to believe him—needed him to convince her he wasn't just a player.

Chapter 22

"You've got to understand my position, babe." Cary stroked the length of Niki's naked body. "That child was my life until I met you. He was kidnapped by his own mother, and I didn't have a clue where he was."

Niki had listened quietly until now. "You must have been worried sick," she said.

"To put it mildly."

Their lovemaking had taken place half in and half out of the bathtub. Now they reclined on her bed. Cary's fingers circled her nipples, stopping to tease now and then. She sighed and nestled closer to him. She was slowly coming around.

"You've got to believe me," Cary pleaded. "I wouldn't just walk out on you without leaving a note. I called you at least three times. But when I found out Elsa had taken my child into the city, I did what any responsible father would do. I took action. That didn't leave me a heck of a lot of time to keep in touch with you."

Niki's fingers kneaded his back muscles. "You're pretty tense."

She sounded slightly more forgiving. He dared to hope.

"What's your schedule look like tomorrow?" Cary asked, quickly changing the topic.

"I'm working the night shift. Why?"

His arms wrapped around her midriff, pulling her closer. "I thought we might go out and buy that dog."

"It was on my list of things to do," Niki said, yawning.

Cary pretended to be outraged. "You were going to go out and buy a dog without me?"

"*You* were nowhere to be found."

"Touché. So what are we going to get? Shepherd? Rottweiler? Collie?" he asked.

"Pit bull, maybe. They're certainly scary to look at."

"You're kidding. They're nice dogs if trained properly, but the poor animals have gotten bad press."

Smothering another yawn, Niki rolled away from him. "I'm going to try and get some shut-eye. Good night."

"Good night, love." Spoon fashion, Cary fitted himself up against her. "Sleep tight."

The next morning, having showered and eaten breakfast, they set off to take care of the list of things that needed doing. Included on that list was buying Niki's dog. The first hour or two they spent trotting through stores. Cary bought Niki her answering machine and a few hanging plants. She selected a headboard and scheduled it for delivery later that week. That task completed, they decided a visit to the humane society was in order.

The pound was located on the outskirts of town in a less congested area. As they entered a low brick building, the pungent scent of dog and cat lay heavy in the air. Niki heard the high-pitched sounds of animals vying for attention. Initially, Cary had suggested they contact a breeder, but Niki had convinced him strays and abandoned animals had a certain appeal. There were plenty of animals needing homes at the shelters.

"It's so sad," Niki said, shaking her head. "Times like these I wish I had a farm. I'd take them all in."

He squeezed her hand. "I know what you mean. Brett keeps after me to get him a dog. Somehow I never got around to it. Maybe after he gets back from visiting my sister."

An attendant led them down row after row of metallic cages. Furry heads poked out, some growling, others letting out a plaintive wail, all anxious to ingratiate themselves. No end to the lineup of dogs, it seemed.

Niki squatted down, cooing at a dog that made a big production of rattling its cage.

"A Great Dane," Cary said, supplying the breed. "Big, lovable, but not what we're looking for. They've got a limited life span."

"What *are* we looking for?" Niki asked, again taking his hand.

He went through a list, naming many of the kinds of dogs he'd rattled off earlier.

"Then find me a rottweiler," Niki ordered.

"At your service, madam." He smiled, clicked his heels, and started up the line again. The attendant followed.

A high-pitched keening came from a cage that showed no sign of habitation.

"We just took in Pepé this morning," the employee explained. "He appears a little depressed."

Cary bent over to see what kind of dog was inside. A

black head rose from between two paws to inspect him, liquid eyes looking him over suspiciously.

"Pepé," Cary called. "Come here, big boy."

Languidly, the dog rose and trotted over obediently. His big black head and tan markings denoted his rottweiler breed. Wanting to pet him, Cary stuck his fingers through the spaces in the cage.

"Don't," the attendant warned.

"Why not?" Niki asked. "Come here, Pepé. Come here, baby. Can we take him for a walk?"

"Sure."

Across from Pepé, a standard poodle woofed to get their attention. Niki turned to compliment the poodle briefly. "You're pretty, too. What's your name?"

"Don't even think of it," Cary admonished. "You need a watchdog, not a show dog. How old is Pepé?"

The attendant pointed to a plate attached to the cage that provided all the statistics. "A year and a half."

"Perfect."

On returning from their walk, the rottweiler flopped his large body down, tongue lolling, and let out a high-pitched whine, dog talk for *please take me*. That sealed the deal. After filling out forms and signing oodles of papers, they left, leash in hand.

The rest of the day was devoted to Pepé. The dog quickly acclimated to the house and property and made the couch home. Too soon, it was time for Niki to go off to work. Cary wanted to drive her, but she declined.

"You stay home and take care of Pepé," she instructed. "By the time you wake up, I'll be back."

Much as Cary wanted her home with him, he understood she had a profession, one she'd neglected for the last six weeks. Still, there had to be some way for them to be together. He could not allow Niki Hamilton to get away.

* * *

A flurry of activity greeted Niki when she entered the hospital. The doctor she was relieving seemed more than happy to turn things over. He briefed her quickly and raced for the door. Niki swallowed the bile that had suddenly risen in her throat. Must be the stress. Where had this light-headedness come from?

She took deep breaths and concentrated. There had been an awful car accident, leaving the driver dead and three little children in critical condition. Add to that a slew of patients needing to be seen. Time to pull herself together. She couldn't afford to be sick.

She forgot about her own discomfort as she tended those most critical and made rounds. Hours later, she was finally able to enter her small office. She flopped onto her chair and typed in her password. Presto, she was in. The technician must have been by and fixed her computer.

The clock on the wall indicated it was close to midnight. A night crew should be on in the technical support center. Niki picked up the phone and dialed. A distracted voice answered.

"Tech Support Center."

Niki identified herself.

"Yes, Dr. Hamilton, what can we do for you?"

"Can you tell me who came by to fix my computer?"

"Is there a problem?"

She hastened to reassure him. "No. Everything works perfectly. I was able to get in."

She heard the relief in the technician's voice when he responded. "Let me check the work order."

Paper rustled and there was a rumble of conversation in the background. After a while he said, "Pete Marshall, but he's not here. He was on the day shift."

"What was the problem?"

There was a long pause while the technician referred to his papers again. "Pete thought maybe you forgot your password. You know how it works. If you keep typing the wrong password, the computer automatically locks you out the third time around."

Niki thanked the technician and hung up. Someone had definitely tried to access her computer. Was there a legitimate reason for doing so, or was someone out to sabotage her? Glenn had known her whereabouts all along. It would have taken one call to get the information anyone needed.

This business with Zachary Adams's records still bothered her. If the boy had been a diabetic, she would have remembered. Most certainly she would have recommended a special diet. And she would never prescribe aspirin to a patient with liver problems. It increased the likelihood of internal bleeding. She might just as well pronounce him dead.

Using her mouse, Niki clicked on Zachary Adams's folder. Her eyes grew misty, as they tended to when she remembered any deceased patient. She took her time scrolling through the file, noting the dates Zachary had been seen by her. He was a sweet little boy who'd fought an awful battle and lost.

Niki scrolled through document after document trying to decipher her notes. Considering the child's medical history, no competent doctor would ever prescribe aspirin. Nowhere in her notes did it indicate she did. Nor did it say the child was a diabetic. She reread the file just to be sure.

A knock on her door got her attention. She looked up to see Bill Morris hovering. He waited to be invited in.

"Come in, Bill. Isn't it a bit late for you?"

Bill smiled sheepishly. "I had some catching up to do. But I thought I'd take a break and say welcome back in person. I tried calling you in New Jersey, but you were never there. We missed you. Everything OK?"

Niki simply nodded at him. Since when was he so gracious or so interested in her well being? She kept her eyes fixed on the monitor.

"Well, I see you're busy," Bill said, pointing to her computer. "Amazing that you remembered your password. When I'm out more than three days I usually forget."

Warning bells went off in Niki's head. Was this an innocent comment, or did he know something?

"Remembering my password's never been a problem," Niki responded. "Even so, I arrived back to find myself locked out. Basically unable to access my computer. I think someone tried to get in."

Bill tsked. "You're not implying someone was attempting to sabotage you?" He raised a skeptical eyebrow. "Most likely one of the staff needed to use your office. You know how short on space we are. Finding a computer was an added bonus."

Bill had a good point. But she still couldn't shake her uneasiness. How to explain the fact that her copies of Zachary Adams's file did not indicate he had diabetes, nor had there been any mention of aspirin prescribed?

"Was there something else you wanted?" Niki asked, suddenly wanting Bill gone. The man's saccharine tones grated on her. He'd always tended to get on her nerves.

"Actually, I came by to ask you to supper."

Her mind went on instant alert again. Bill asking her to supper? Unheard of.

"Will Glenn be joining us?"

"I wasn't planning on inviting him."

"Oh?"

"This is the perfect opportunity for a brother to get to know a sister better," Bill explained, actually leering at her.

"After all these years?"

The phone next to her jingled. Niki reached over to answer.

"Glad I finally caught up with you, hon." Cary's velvet tones caressed her ear. "Pepé and I miss you."

"I miss you, too," Niki said. "You have no idea how much."

"Ahem." In the background, Bill cleared his throat. Niki looked up to see him edging from the room. He pointed his index finger at her. "Supper tomorrow, remember."

Niki ignored him and focused on her conversation again. "How's my sweetie Pepé?"

"Pepé? What about me? I thought I was your sweetie." He sounded outraged.

It felt good to hear his voice, to cement the connection between them. It was reassuring to know he was there for her, and that when she returned home he would be waiting. How long that would last, she didn't know. For now had to be good enough.

After a few more minutes, they ended the conversation. Niki was just about to shut the computer down and return to her rounds when the phone rang again. Thinking it might be Cary again, she picked up.

"Yo, Doc," the person on the other end greeted. Her heart rate accelerated and her breath came in short little bursts. Was there no escaping this nightmare?

Niki couldn't say a word. She knew she should hang up, but her hand refused to cooperate.

"Hey, Doc, you there?"

"Yes, I'm here," she said finally. The speech patterns were urban. Street. "Who's this?"

"It's your bro, Akbar."

"Akbar," Niki said, exhaling. How on earth had he managed to find her here? This was a private line. "Is something wrong, Akbar?"

"You goin' be working at the clinic tomorrow night?"

"I should be," Niki said carefully. She volunteered two to three evenings a week, depending on her schedule. Mondays, Wednesdays, and sometimes Fridays.

"Good, I goin' wait for you. I'm goin' prove to you Akbar's no liar."

"That's not necessary," Niki said, wondering where this was leading.

"Ah, but I got a rep to maintain. I goin' show you what's goin' down between Quaalude and your doctor friend. Rumor on the street says Quaalude's running short of supplies. Your West Indian doctor goin' meet him behind the supermarket for a drop."

It took Niki a while to process the information. "Phillip and your friend Quaalude are meeting to do what?"

"Get one thing straight, Doc, Quaalude's no friend. You need to come with me and see what the peoples are talking about. Soon as you're done at the clinic, you and me will drive over."

For a fleeting moment, Niki considered Akbar might have his own agenda. Nice as he'd been to her, he and his crowd operated under a different code of ethics. He'd made it clear from the get-go there was no love lost between him and Phillip. He felt Phillip had sold out.

Niki also remembered Phillip's warnings, his feelings that the entire group were up to no good, that they were thieves. Could Akbar have his own reasons for wanting to get her alone? Was this a setup? What was to stop Akbar from taking her to the supermarket parking lot, then mugging and robbing her?

Niki decided her imagination needed to be reined in. Akbar had always been respectful of her—respectful and grateful to the point of being ingratiating. Ever since his little brother had been shot and Niki had gone out of her way to save him, he'd sworn his undying loyalty.

She owed it to herself to see if this was merely the babbling of a highly imaginative young man, or if she'd been wearing rose-colored glasses about Phillip. To regain control of her life, she would have to take a chance. She needed to see this thing through.

Chapter 23

"I don't like this one bit," Cary said, drumming his fingers against the kitchen table. The dinner he'd prepared had turned out better than he'd anticipated. Now they lingered over their wine.

Niki set down her wine glass. She was wearing those disfiguring horn-rimmed glasses again. "What about it don't you like?"

"Everything. Something smells big time. How long have you known this Akbar? Do you trust him?"

Niki relayed the story of how she'd met Akbar, explaining that the teenager was loyal to a fault. He spent hours watching her car and had never once accepted a dime for it.

"I'm still not convinced he's trustworthy," Cary said, rising to clear the dishes. "He could easily have an ulterior motive." He tossed out the leftover salad and fettuccine.

Niki got up to help him with the dishes. "So you're suggesting that I not go with him to this supermarket parking lot?" she said while stacking dirty plates in the dishwasher.

"No, I'm saying you don't go alone. I couldn't forgive myself if something happened to you."

She shut the door on the dishwasher and pushed the wash button. "Akbar's not going to be very receptive to some stranger arriving with me. He's not very trusting."

"How about if I follow you in my car?"

"All right. I'm usually done at the clinic by nine. How about I give you directions on how to get there?"

After wandering off, Niki returned with a piece of paper. She scribbled on it. Cary put the directions safely away, and the two worked to clean up the kitchen.

"When will you be going home?" Niki asked when the kitchen was once again neat. Her face was devoid of expression. She didn't even blink.

Cary plucked the silly glasses from her face. "We need to talk about that."

"I'm listening."

How could she simply stand there, cool as could be, speaking in that damned British accent, while inwardly his heart was breaking. This impending separation was not something he looked forward to. It might kill him.

"We'll talk in the bedroom," he said, tugging on her hand and bringing her inside with him. He waited until they were both sitting on the bed before positioning her between the V of his legs. Wrapping both arms around her waist, he said quietly, "I can't leave my business forever, so what do we do?"

She sighed. "I knew that all along. There's not much we can do."

"We can stay in touch, return to our separate lives, see how it goes."

"That might do for a start."

He wished she didn't sound so matter-of-fact, so emotionless. Was that all *they* meant to each other?

"We might drift apart," he said, trying not to let his hurt show.

Niki sighed again, a hopeless sound. "We might. But I can't expect you to give up your life or business and move here."

"Would you consider giving up your life and business and moving to the Jersey shore?" he asked, holding his breath.

It wasn't exactly a proposal, but it indicated some level of commitment on his part.

"I couldn't do that. My job is here."

He'd known it was too much to ask. They'd reached an impasse. Niki had a practice in San Francisco, and he had a business and son waiting back in New Jersey. That was all there was to it. For now it seemed an impossible situation.

Back in her office, Niki removed her stethoscope and plunked it down. She took off her glasses and laid them on the desk next to it. Rubbing weary eyes, she rotated her shoulders. It had been touch and go for a moment, but the trauma team, through superhuman effort, had somehow managed to resuscitate the eight-year-old girl who'd almost drowned. The child lay in critical but stable condition.

She sorted through a number of messages, putting them in piles of priority. Michael Edwards, the officer assigned to her case, had called. He wanted her to call back as soon as she could. Maybe later when she felt better.

She'd been dizzy all afternoon. Dizzy and nauseous. It was to be expected, she supposed, running around on an empty stomach. Everything seemed to get to her lately—the sight of blood, the stench of vomit, the odor of antiseptic, even the smell of hospital food. Given all she'd been through these last couple of months, something had to give.

Niki managed to raise her head and gulp in the stale hospital air. Water might help, food possibly. There was a small refrigerator off to the side where she kept juices, water, and snacks. She'd just squatted down to retrieve bottled water and a ziplock bag of carrot sticks when someone cleared his throat behind her. She turned to see Phillip standing in the doorway. It was the first time in a long while that their shifts had coincided.

"You look awful," he said, confirming the way she felt.

"I feel awful." She swigged the water right out of the bottle.

"Have you eaten?"

Niki shrugged. "When there's an emergency, who has time to eat?" Rising, she rested her butt against the desk and faced him. Phillip had always been sweet to her. Sweet and concerned about her well being.

He came closer. "I have a few minutes. Why don't we go to the cafeteria and get you a bite to eat?"

"She's going to have to say no," a voice from behind them said. "Dr. Hamilton and I have plans."

They both turned to see Bill Morris standing in the doorway. Niki suppressed the urge to snap at him. How dare he simply show up and not call? They hadn't made firm plans. Still, it was an awkward situation.

"I see," Phillip said, his Caribbean accent very pronounced. "I would not want to intrude, then." He addressed his next comments to Niki. "You're not well. Skip the clinic. I'll cover for you."

"We'll see," she said to his retreating back. "Touch base with me later."

"You're not well?" Bill said, eyeing her up and down.

"I'm fine," Niki lied, collecting her purse and following him from the room.

When they were seated in Die Hards, Bill leaned across the table. His mustache wiggled, making him look like an animated cartoon character.

"Has Glenn talked to you about resigning?"

"What?" Niki knew incredulity registered on her face, but his words were so unexpected.

He bit into the huge hamburger he'd ordered and chewed slowly. Niki sat quietly digesting what he had just said. The bowl of chicken broth she'd finished had settled her stomach a bit—that plus constant sips of ginger ale.

"It figures he wouldn't talk to you about resigning," Bill said, his eyes never leaving her face. "Why don't you simply save him the embarrassment of asking you? San Francisco General has gotten horrible press since this Eldridge business. Compounding that, there've been so many complaints registered with the medical board." He took another bite of burger, this time chewing rapidly. "It'll take years to investigate and come to a conclusion. Even so, it's not good for business. Certainly not good for the hospital."

His agenda was clear. Get rid of her. But why? Because they had butted heads before? Because as contracts administrator, she'd upon occasion asked him to intervene with the HMO? Niki felt her cheeks go warm and knew that within seconds her face and throat would get splotchy. She rose, gathered her purse, and tossed down a few crisp bills.

"I'm not sure why you're the messenger, Bill. Let Glenn do his own dirty work."

Before he could say another word, she strode from the room.

Niki was greeted by another emergency when she returned to the hospital. She ran for the remainder of her shift, but she found a minute to make a quick call to Cary, just to confirm he knew how to get to the clinic. It wasn't until right before she was scheduled to leave she was able to find Glenn. He was meeting with another doctor and asked her to wait. She managed to smile, wave, and signal to him to call her.

Two hours later, she was still knee-deep in patients at the clinic. Her eyes were beginning to cross, and that queasy feeling had surfaced again. She'd barely had time to acknowledge the frown Phillip threw her when their paths crossed. In fifteen more minutes, she was due to meet Akbar.

Half an hour later, Niki found Akbar lounged against her Range Rover. He greeted her with a "Hey, Doc, you're late."

"Sorry, it couldn't be helped. Have you been waiting long?"

He shrugged.

There was no sign of Cary or the rented Sable. She'd suggested so as not to alert Akbar, he park down the block. He was to wait until the Rover pulled out before following. Niki opened the doors, climbed into the driver's seat, and motioned to Akbar to get in.

"Nice ride, Doc," he said, stroking the leather interior. "Expensive ride. Doctors live large."

It wasn't anything he hadn't said before, yet his comments left her uneasy. What if Phillip and Cary were right? What if he wanted to lure her off to rob and—who knows?—beat her? She glanced into the rearview mirror, hoping to see Cary's rented vehicle pull out. It was nowhere to be seen.

Squelching her unease, she followed Akbar's grunted directions.

"See that Stop and Shop? You need to make a right there, Doc. Now a left."

The area grew seedier and seedier. Streetlights illuminated dingy warehouses and ramshackle buildings. Homeless people, their eyes vacant, trailed cardboard boxes behind them.

"Now turn down that block, Doc."

Niki's gaze shifted to the rearview mirror again. Headlights indicated there was a car behind her. She couldn't tell its make.

"How much longer?" she asked Akbar.

He shifted uneasily. "Another block or two."

For one quick moment, Niki wondered if he was going to hold a knife to her throat or a gun to her temple. Nonsense. Why would Akbar wait all this time to mug her?

Because the opportunity presented itself, her brain screamed.

"Watch out, Doc."

Niki swerved, narrowly missing some pitiful souls staggering across the street.

"Take a left and pull in there," Akbar announced as an illuminated sign blinked DEFAZIO's.

Given the hour, the supermarket's parking lot was fairly full. Following Akbar's direction, Niki cruised to the back of the poorly lit lot, where a half a dozen vehicles were parked, two of them Lexuses. Another car trailed them. A quick glance back revealed the make to be a Toyota Camry. Where was Cary?

"What do we do now?" Niki asked Akbar.

"Cut the lights. Sit. Wait. Listen to music. They should be here."

Akbar bowed his head and played with the dials. His crazy-looking braids pointed in every direction. His movements made her uneasy. Were these delaying tactics? Signals to someone hiding out there?

He found a station eventually. Harsh rap music blasted through the interior. He bobbed his head in time to the guttural lyrics and tapped his sneakered foot. Niki began to regret she'd agreed to come to such a remote location. She barely knew the man.

Minutes went by. Cars slid in and out of spaces. No sign of Cary, Phillip, or Quaalude. Fifteen minutes, then half an hour. Still nothing. Deejays changed; so did the music. Old Motown took the place of rap.

"I think we should go," Niki said, about to start up the car.

"Nah, Doc. Patience. Look over there in that last row."

A Mark VIII slid into the spot next to one of the Lexuses. A giant of a man emerged, a doo-rag wrapped around his head. The ends of his scarf flapped in the night breeze. In the weak lamplight, Niki could barely see his face, but a gold earring winked at her. He approached the Lexus and rapped on the driver's window. Almost instantly the glass slid down.

Phillip stuck his head out of the Lexus. The two exchanged words. Packages were handed over. After a quick salute, the man called Quaalude slipped back into his car and zoomed from the parking lot.

"See, Doc," Akbar said, "your medicine man's bad news."

She didn't answer. She was still processing what had just taken place. Phillip often treated pretty rough types at the clinic, but she'd never known him to befriend one. While the exchange of packages could mean anything, she needed time to think.

The driver of a car three rows down flicked his headlights on and placed his vehicle in reverse. Niki recognized the Sable. She exhaled the breath she didn't realize she was holding. Cary had been there all along.

"There's nothing more to be accomplished here," she said to Akbar.

He nodded. "See, I didn't waste your time, Doc."

Tomorrow she would call Michael Edwards.

Chapter 24

"So what's your take on this thing?" Cary asked, the moment he and Niki sat across from each other at the kitchen table.

Dinner tonight was pizza he'd picked up on the way home.

Niki munched on a crusty slice and fed the rest to Pepé. The dog whined for more. Niki ignored him.

"I don't know. It could be innocent. I can't imagine Phillip risking his reputation."

"Then why the subterfuge?"

"You mean why drive to a dim parking lot on the other side of town and meet a reputed dealer?"

"Exactly. If it were purely on the up-and-up, why not just have the man meet him at the clinic? Your Phillip's a respected doctor, or at least that's what you said. Why play cloak and dagger with some neighborhood thug?"

"My Phillip?" Niki raised an eyebrow at him. "Since when did he become *my* Phillip?'

Cary narrowed his eyes. "You spend an awful lot of time with him, or at least you used to. You also mentioned dating him and finding out you made better friends."

"That's true. Sounds to me like you're jealous."

"I admit it."

Niki rose to hug him. She kissed the nape of his neck. "You, my dear, have nothing to worry about. I have no interest in Phillip, nor he in me. He's extremely well respected in the community. He volunteers at the clinic, and, like you, devotes time to adult literacy programs. He's even funding a Phillip Jordan scholarship for promising medical students."

"The Lexus I understand, but do doctors have that much disposable income that they're able to fund a scholarship?"

"Hmmmm . . . I never gave that much thought. I assume he's well invested."

"Sounds a little full of himself to me."

"He can be, but that doesn't make him a bad person. Hey, did you check the answering machine?" It was clear Niki wanted to change the topic.

Cary turned to see the red light blinking. He rose, headed over, and depressed the rewind button. A male-female tag team inquired about Niki's well-being.

"Devin and Charlie," Niki confirmed.

Next Brett's voice came over loud and clear.

"Hey, Dad. Dad, are you there?"

"Too late to call him back," Cary stated matter-of-factly. "I'll touch base first thing tomorrow." Much as he loved being with Niki, he missed his kid.

Then Michael Edwards came on the tape. "I really do need to speak to you, Dr. Hamilton. Call me first thing tomorrow."

"I wonder what that's about?" Cary said, scooping her out of the chair and worrying the top button of her oxford shirt with his teeth.

Pepè, who'd stretched out on the floor next to them, snorted.

"Sounds like it might be important," Niki said. "Perhaps they caught my vandal." She looked hopeful. "Maybe this whole thing is over—the calls, nasty letters, the worrying."

"We can only hope." Cary worked another button free and he blew against her skin.

"Stop it, you pervert." She playfully clouted the top of his head.

"Ouch." He nipped at her skin, his tongue laving the hollow of her neck, and moved downward. "You smell like antiseptic."

"What a romantic you are." Her breathing had increased.

"Smells delightful to me," he said, undoing the rest of her buttons and cupping her lace-covered breasts in his hands.

"Feels delightful to me." She squirmed, settling herself firmly in his hands.

"Then I may continue?" He could hear his own ragged breathing, feel himself responding.

He rapidly stripped off her bra and took the shirt with it. His mouth settled around her nipples, nipping, teasing. Niki pressed herself up against the length of him. Cary pushed the knee-length skirt she wore up around her hips and leaned her against the table. There was a clatter of plates as dishes shifted. He took a moment to sheath himself before tugging her black lace panties aside and fitted himself against her. Niki gasped and closed her eyes.

Sliding the panties further aside, he pushed against her softness, seeking her warmth. Niki clutched the sides of the table, bracing against it. All throbbing sensation, he found her opening and inched his way in. He could smell her, hear her, feel her. His slow strokes built in intensity. He drove in harder while she urged him on. Satisfaction was only partially what he was after—satisfaction and release. He wanted to elicit a promise from her, some assurance that what they'd found wasn't some transitory thing.

"I love you, baby," Cary admitted, going first. It was a relief to get the words out, panted as they were. At least he'd committed.

"And I love you," she managed. "Not just for today, but forever and ever."

He'd gotten what he wanted. Now the ball was in his court.

"You'll need to make some time for us," Michael Edwards said when Niki got him on the phone first thing in the morning. "Coleman and I need to talk to you."

Niki wondered what could be urgent enough to merit a visit from the two officers assigned to her case.

"Sure," she said, knowing she wasn't due at the hospital until late afternoon.

She hung up the phone and repeated to Cary what the officer had said. He nodded distractedly. "Give me that," he said, gesturing to the receiver. "Sounds to me like there's been a new development."

Cary dialed Brett's number. First and foremost, he remained the loving and involved father. It was one of the things that had attracted her to him. She listened to the brief, one-sided conversation. After the usual inquiries about health, she heard him say, "I'll probably be home next week. I'll be there in time for your game."

While she hadn't expected him to stay forever, hearing him say he was leaving still hurt. She called on her medical experience, managed to keep her face neutral, and tamped down the sadness engulfing her. She'd become too dependent on him. Dependent and needy. She needed to change that quickly.

Even so, she couldn't help wondering what it might be like to have his child. A ridiculous thought. She was far too old. Too set in her ways. In a few months, she would be forty-three. Women her age were grandmothers. What could she be thinking?

"How about breakfast?" Cary tempted, after he'd ended the call. He got out the frying pan and placed eggs and the fixings for an omelette on the kitchen counter.

Niki shook her head. "Maybe just tea and toast." The light-headedness had returned, and her stomach churned.

"You OK, hon?"

Niki hastened to assure him she was. If this slightly off-kilter feeling continued, she'd have Phillip take a look at her. It would give them an opportunity to talk. Maybe find out what was really going on.

She and Cary had just finished eating when the doorbell rang.

"Officers Edwards and Coleman," two loud voices announced.

Cary went off to answer the door and returned with the two undercover policemen. Niki ushered them into the living room.

When both men were seated on her couch with mugs of coffee, Niki cleared her throat. "You wanted to see me?"

"Ah, yes," Kenneth Coleman, the larger of the two said. He easily tipped the scale at two hundred and fifty and had a large shining dome instead of hair. He emptied the contents of a manila envelope onto her coffee table. A gold earring spilled out. "Recognize this?"

Niki scrutinized the earring carefully. It was a sizable hoop and seemed vaguely familiar.

"Ah, ah. Don't touch," Michael Edwards cautioned, when she would have reached over to pick it up.

"It's not mine." Niki said, studying the earring. She never wore hoops.

"You're sure?" This came from Coleman.

"Positive."

Cary had taken a seat on the arm of the sofa and had his arm round her. "What's this about?" he asked the officers.

"The earring was found in Dr. Hamilton's backyard. So far we have an earring and a button."

She knew she'd seen that gold hoop before. Someone was wearing it.

"Think, Dr. Hamilton," Edwards coaxed. "Does it belong to a friend?"

But Niki couldn't think. Her brain had shut down. She was already gearing herself up to do combat with Glenn. She would confront him and find out if she was being asked to resign and, if so, on what grounds. He owed her an answer.

A few hours later, Niki stormed into Glenn's office. His half-moon glasses on the end of his nose, he sat poring over a large sheaf of papers. He looked up and smiled at her. "What can I do for you, Niki?"

She thudded her palms on the desk separating them and glared at him. The water glass next to Glenn's elbow rattled. "What is this nonsense about having Bill do your dirty work?"

"Whoa! I haven't a clue what you're talking about."
Glenn got to his feet.

"Don't give me that."

"Really, I don't."

Niki explained what had transpired between her and
Bill, finishing with, "So if, as Bill indicates, I am going to
be asked to resign, the administration better have a
damned good reason."

Glenn gazed at her as if she'd lost her mind. "Come
on, Niki, you know I would never let that happen. You're
a good doctor. One of our best. Besides, we have no conclu-
sive evidence you've done something wrong. It will take
the board years to rule."

Niki faced him head on. "That's all well and good, but
meanwhile someone's working diligently to discredit me.
You know my files have been creatively edited, but did you
know someone even tried accessing my computer? Thank
goodness they didn't know the password."

"Who would that be?" Glenn asked, moving closer.

"You tell me."

"You don't think—this is a serious accusation." Glenn
touched her arm.

"Remember the Adams boy's file? You mentioned Wite-
Out had been used to change some things."

"I remember."

"My copy of that file indicates the child was never a
diabetic. I would never have prescribed aspirin for anyone
with liver problems. It only increases the likelihood of
bleeding."

Glenn stroked his chin while pacing the room. "So
you're telling me you think this is sabotage."

"I don't know what else to call it."

"Several doctors requested use of your office in your
absence. I saw no reason to deny them. When I began

getting requests from the medical board, I gave the key to your filing cabinet to one of our nurses and asked her to retrieve the records."

"Which nurse?"

"I don't remember."

Was he being deliberately evasive? How could he not remember who he'd asked to retrieve highly confidential files? It would have to be a person he trusted.

"I assume Zachary Adams's records were among them. Where did you keep those files?"

Glenn tapped the smooth wooden surface of his desk. "Right here. I keep my door locked."

Niki cocked her head to the side and eyed him skeptically. "Even when you go to the bathroom?"

"Well, no. In that case, I'm usually not gone long."

"My point exactly. So anyone could walk into your office, make off with a file, and return it at a later date?"

"I suppose." Glenn didn't look happy.

Memories of the gold hoop surfaced again. She'd seen someone wearing one. Who?

Niki started to leave the room then turned back. "Glenn," she said, "if I were you, I wouldn't even think about firing me. I won't walk away without a fight."

"I never said anything about firing you. I'll speak to Bill."

"Do that," Niki said, looking him straight in the eye. "This whole thing isn't about me, anyway. This is about managed care denying a specific course of treatment because they ruled it experimental and expensive. Never mind that the treatment has met with success in other countries." She laughed derisively. "Our caring HMOs here in the United States decided it didn't merit consideration. Three kids died because of the almighty buck, and

Bill sits fat and happy in his office negotiating contracts that are advantageous to the hospital but not to the patient."

"You're getting overwrought," Glenn said, coming toward her.

"Am I? My reputation's being raked over the coals. My life's turned into a living hell. Some sick person is after me. I get crank calls, threatening letters. My house has been broken into." She ticked off the list on her fingers. "Don't I have reason to be overwrought?"

Turning on her heel, she slammed the door in his face.

Niki returned home to find Cary packing his bags. Pepé woofed a greeting as she stood in the doorway assessing things. She'd calmed down remarkably since her encounter with Glenn.

"I thought you weren't leaving until next week," she said, watching him fold shirts and slacks.

"Ideally I would have liked to, but I'm having problems with the business. I need to get back and smooth things over. My clients are pitching a fit. Projects are running behind. A college kid, good as he is at running Carett, isn't used to handling such problems."

Niki remembered that he'd left Mason, a college intern, in charge of his business. She felt guilty.

"How long do we have?" was all she managed as a lump invaded her throat.

"Not long. I'm leaving tomorrow." Cary opened his arms. "Come here. You have to know I wouldn't leave you unless it was important."

But he *was* leaving her, and there wasn't a damned thing she could do to stop him. Choking back tears, she fitted herself into his arms. She would miss the feeling of those arms around her. She would miss depending on him. She would miss that warm body in bed next to her. Pepé was a poor substitute.

"Hey," Cary said, "stop that."

Despite her resolve, she was crying openly now. More than anything, she didn't want him to go.

Chapter 25

Niki twisted and turned, seeking a more comfortable position.

In the dim light of the parking lot, the man's dark skin glistened with sweat. His face, partially hidden by shadows, was not unattractive, though the scarf wrapped around his head Arab style made him look silly. A doo-rag, she'd once heard it called. What did he want with her?

As he came closer, his face came clearly into focus. Quaalude. An earring hung from one lobe. Not just any old earring. A gold hoop.

Niki jolted awake, dripping sweat. She brought a shaking hand to her chest, hoping to still her rapid breathing. Cary snored softly beside her. She swung both legs off the bed and padded to the kitchen to get a glass of water. Pepé followed.

She remembered the glint of gold in Quaalude's earlobe that night, remembered the doo-rag, and knew with certainty he was the one after her.

Of course, she could be overreacting. Plenty of people wore earrings these days. Earrings had gone unisex, and men wore two just as easily as women.

What if Akbar was right? What if Phillip was Quaalude's supplier, and in return the thug did whatever he asked? But why target her? What had she done to Phillip to warrant such vicious behavior?

Niki gulped her water and contemplated the situation. At a more reasonable hour, she would have called Officers Edwards and Coleman and shared her suspicions with them. She replayed the events. Threatening letters, nasty phone calls, her home being broken into and ransacked. A medical record changed. Pretty awful things.

She thought about Bill. She'd never liked the contracts administrator. There was something shady about him. But why would he try to discredit her? And what were his motives for telling her she was on the verge of being fired? Glenn had denied any knowledge of it.

Then there was Glenn. She wasn't entirely stupid. She knew his feelings for her were far more than platonic. *He,* more than anyone else, had access to her medical files. *He* would have had ample opportunity to change anything he saw fit. Could he have considered himself a man scorned? Was he getting even? Tomorrow she would take a closer look at Zachary Adams's records and see if she could figure out the handwriting where the records had been changed.

Niki wondered if she should add Todd Eldridge's parents to her paltry list of suspects. They must be distraught in their grief. But there were so many other ways for the Eldridges to go about discrediting her. They could have sued her personally, even started a smear campaign.

Instead, they'd filed suit against the hospital, indirectly naming her in the process. She'd found them to be reasonable people; these were unreasonable acts.

Niki must have fallen asleep at the kitchen table. The next thing she remembered was being shaken awake.

"Come to bed, honey," Cary urged. "Come to bed."

She wanted to tell him about her dream, share her suspicions with him, but it would hold until tomorrow. It was late, and she was suddenly very tired.

"You need sleep," Cary said with some finality. "I'm going to make sure you get it."

It felt like she would never get a full night's sleep ever again—not with him leaving her, not with some sick person out there gunning for her. Niki leaned her head against his shoulder and allowed him to lead her back into the bedroom. Pepé trailed them, nuzzling the back of her legs. Tomorrow was time enough to try to put the pieces together. Right now she would try to sleep.

The next morning, Niki shared her dream with Cary, and her suspicions that Quaalude could be the person who'd broken into her house. Cary was scheduled on a red-eye flight leaving later that night. He immediately got Officer Kenneth Coleman on the phone.

"Niki needs to talk you," he began without preamble, handing her the receiver.

Cary listened as Niki relayed what had transpired between Phillip Jordan and Quaalude. He felt torn. On one hand, he needed to get back to his business—back to his son. On the other, he hated abandoning Niki. They'd come so far in their relationship, and now he had to get home. Commuting made sense, but more often than not those relationships didn't work out. Eventually one or the other would decide it was too much effort and call it quits. He couldn't let that happen.

"I'll wait to hear from you," Niki said. "Beep me when you're through speaking with Quaalude."

"Fill me in," Cary demanded the moment she hung up.

"Edwards and Coleman are off to question Quaalude. Apparently he's got quite the record. He's been picked up a number of times for breaking and entering. He supposedly makes most of his money dealing, but he's never been caught red-handed, and they haven't been able to bring him in."

"This could be our man, then."

"Sounds like it."

"So it's sit, wait, and hope."

"Mmm-hmmm."

"Meanwhile, we need to figure out what we're doing today," Cary said, changing the subject. Niki wasn't scheduled to go into work until later that evening. He wanted to make today special. This might very well be the last time they were together.

"I'd like to stay home," Niki said, surprising him.

"Home. Not a bad idea." He hugged her. "You and me together. No outside interruptions."

"Well, there is some gardening I need to do, and I'd like to pop out to the nursery and buy plants."

Cary tweaked her nose playfully. "Translation: You want me at home to help you with the dirty work. I'm to uproot plants and bushes while you sit and drink lemonade."

"I'm a very capable woman," Niki said, standing on tiptoe to kiss his lips. "I can get my hands equally as dirty as you. But what I do need you to do is transform my scrap of backyard into an Eden. Design me a paradise. A place of tranquillity, something that will always remind me of you."

It was a wonderful idea, but it sounded as if she wanted to erect a memorial. Mentally she was preparing herself to leave him, and there wasn't a damned thing he could do. It was Niki's way of telling him it was over, of saying their relationship had meant a lot to her, but now it was time to move on. It tore him up inside. His stomach actually burned.

"I would love to," Cary said, biting back the bile. "The tools of my trade are back in New Jersey, so I'll have to do it the old-fashioned way, with pen and paper."

"I'll get you some," Niki said, disappearing.

Together they worked all day on her slip of backyard. Cary washed down the tiny deck and polished the teak outdoor furniture. They'd shopped for a shady umbrella and huge terra cotta pots with flowering plants and trailing ferns. They'd even bought a fountain. Cary erected the umbrella and strategically positioned the flower pots, angling them into every nook and cranny of the picturesque backyard. All the while, water trickled from the fountain, creating a soothing melody. Tranquil background music.

When he was done, Cary brushed off his hands. He came to stand over Niki, who was still busily digging holes and planting impatiens. "I'm starving," he said. Her cream-colored legs in cutoff denims ran for miles. Cary squatted down beside her and flicked a speck of mud off her cheek. "What are you going to feed a starving man?"

"This." She slapped down her trowel and slipped off her T-shirt. She was braless. Turning toward him, she offered her breasts.

The tug in Cary's groin was instantaneous. He accepted a nipple in his mouth and nibbled gently. They were now both kneeling. He manipulated her other nipple with his hand. Niki tugged on the elastic waistband of his shorts, pulling them down around his thighs, then pressed herself up against him and guided his hand to the top button of her denims.

"Make love to me," she ordered.

There was nothing he would like to do more. The warm midafternoon sun beat down on his back as he shed his shirt. He inhaled the rich, warm smell of newly turned soil which clung to both of them. The tinkling fountain provided rhythmic background music. Shades of Sade. Different from Barry White, but captivating in its own way. Eight-foot-high walls kept them secluded. The arched doorway leading into the backyard had been padlocked closed, a recommendation made by the cops after Niki had mistaken them for burglars. There was no one to see them.

They stripped off the last of their clothes, and Niki lay back on the grass, opening up her arms to him, no further conversation needed. Cary covered her body with his, laving her neck with hot kisses, letting his hands trail up and down her sides, pressing himself into her. He wanted to disappear inside her until she cried out, wanted to feel he would never emerge again. That they were one.

Niki bucked her hips against him, urging him on. He removed a condom from his wallet, slid it on, and entered her effortlessly, reveling in her moist warmth. She wrapped her legs around him, pleading with him to go deeper. Encouraged by the squeeze of her thighs, he took the plunge. Sensations took over. Every outdoor smell heightened: her awesome scent, her caring touch, the warm sun on his back, the trickling water. What a heady experience. It was like nothing he'd ever felt before.

All of it came to a head in a dynamic explosion. With a final thrust he let go, taking Niki with him, hurling them over the edge.

"Oh, God, baby," Cary gasped. "How can I ever let you go?"

In his heart of hearts, he already knew he couldn't.

By the time Niki was getting ready for work, she still hadn't heard from the cops. She'd called Edwards and Coleman several times and ended up leaving messages. It must be taking them forever to find Quaalude. Determined not to think about it, she jumped into the shower.

When she was done, she discovered Cary had taken his suitcase and garment bag to the car. Niki rifled through her closet, looking for a clean oxford shirt and a knee-skimming skirt. Despite the fact her clothing still remained, the empty space where Cary's things had been equaled the emptiness in her heart. His scent lingered in the one remaining jacket. He'd planned on traveling in it, she supposed. Could she pack her emotions away in the same manner he'd packed his things? God help her, she couldn't. She already missed him.

Niki buried her head in his navy double-breasted jacket and sobbed silently. She inhaled the heady scent of him, his familiar spicy cologne. The light-headedness returned, but she was determined to ignore it. Dr. Hamilton, in command of her emotions, had been reduced to this.

"Are you OK, hon?" Cary's deep, rich voice came from behind her. His arms encircled her waist, pressing her up against him. "Why are you crying?"

"No reason."

"Liar."

Niki squeezed her eyes shut, calling on everything she had in her to stop this flow of emotions. It was imperative she pull herself together, control the nausea. Patients needed to be seen, and she had a long night ahead. She planned to get to the hospital early so she could leave around nine, take an extended break and head for the airport to see Cary safely on his plane then return.

"It's not over," Cary said, rocking her back and forth. "Believe me, it's not over. I'll never let that happen."

"How could it not be over? We live on opposite coasts."

"We'll work it out somehow," he said, kissing the top of her head.

Summoning a smile, Niki turned toward him. "Always the eternal optimist."

"That's me." He brushed her remaining tears away with his thumb. "Seriously, how often do two people find what we have? You and I share a similar background. We know what it's like to be biracial." He silenced her with a touch of his fingers to her lips. "Yes, I know I look white. Your parents were the mixed couple, mine were two generations removed. It hasn't been easy for either of us, but we persevered. Made something of ourselves. On top of that, we enjoy each other. Enjoy being together. We talk. Our lovemaking is out of this world. I'm not prepared to throw that away."

Neither was she. Deep down in her gut, and as much as she had denied it, she'd known it from the very beginning. Cary Thomas was like a breath of fresh air—exactly what she needed to feel human again.

"You're going to be late." Cary released her and tapped the face of his watch.

She threw him a watery smile, grabbed her shirt and skirt, and began getting dressed.

An hour later, feeling somewhat better, Niki sat in her office studiously reviewing her medical files. Glenn had made copies of what he needed and returned the originals to her. She found Zachary Adams's file and flipped through it, finding the document she needed. Someone had carefully used the same color ink to make changes and had done a masterful job of attempting to recreate her writing.

Niki zeroed in on the words *aspirin* and *diabetic,* noting how the person had looped *i*'s and *t*'s. She still had roughly forty minutes before her shift began. Perhaps she could catch Glenn, or even Bill, and get a writing sample.

Niki headed off for Glenn's office. His door was open, but he was nowhere to be found. She used that opportunity to walk in and scrutinize the stacks of paper on his desk. She found a notepad off to the side where he'd scribbled a message. A fountain pen lay uncapped next to it. Niki picked up the pad, examining it closely, looking to see how Glenn wrote his *i*'s and *t*'s. Without loops. She heaved a sigh of relief.

She raced from his office and headed for Bill's. The contracts administrator's door was closed. He'd left for the evening. She made a U-turn and headed back to her office when another idea began to percolate. During her absence, Phillip had covered for her at the clinic. He would have been responsible for updating her files. She wasn't due at the clinic until tomorrow, but she'd looked at the schedule when she'd checked in, and he was here tonight. Maybe she could get a sample of his writing.

Niki skidded to a stop, almost bumping into Phillip. He was at her door. "Just the man I hoped to see," she greeted.

He appeared delighted to be welcomed with such enthusiasm. He was such a handsome man, and a caring one at that. Niki often wondered why he had never remarried. They'd tried dating way back when, but she hadn't been physically attracted and had suggested they remain friends. Still, she'd trusted him once as she'd trusted few. She wanted to give him the benefit of the doubt.

"Is there something I can do for you, Nik?" His sultry Caribbean tones washed over her like a warm breeze.

"As a matter of fact, there is. I need you to play doctor."

He looked amused, one eyebrow raised quizzically as he regarded her. "*You* need a doctor?"

"I haven't been feeling well."

"Hmmmm. For how long?"

"A week. Maybe two."

"Let's take a look."

Niki unlocked her office and preceded him in. She told him about the nausea and light-headedness, about sometimes feeling clammy and faint.

"When do these symptoms come on?" Phillip asked as she unbuttoned her lab coat and the top buttons of her blouse. He placed his stethoscope against her chest, listening.

"Different times of day. I've attributed it to stress, to not eating at the proper times, to everything that's been going on."

"Any chance you're pregnant?" Phillip asked, his face expressionless.

"Impossible."

But it wasn't. She remembered the night she and Cary had made mad, passionate love under the boardwalk. Perhaps the condom had been faulty. They weren't designed to last forever, and their lovemaking had gone on for hours and hours it seemed. Niki suddenly felt clammy and sick again.

Phillip tightened the cuff on the sphygmomanometer and began checking her blood pressure. Next he used one of her syringes to draw blood and captured it in a vial. He scribbled something on the clipboard he set down. Niki leaned forward, trying to read it.

"You know the routine," Phillip said, evenly. "Rush the

blood to the lab along with your urine sample. If they know it's you, you'll get a quick answer.''

Silently cursing her stupidity, Niki thanked him. She'd found out what she wanted to know, and not just about her health. She didn't like it one bit.

Phillip all of a sudden seemed in a hurry to leave. They'd never gotten around to discussing why he'd come looking for her in the first place.

"Was there something you wanted?" she asked as he was halfway out the door.

"It isn't urgent. It can wait. Take care of yourself. Go home. I'll cover for you.''

Niki glanced at the wall clock. It was a magnanimous offer, but much as she didn't feel like working, she couldn't take him up on it. In a few brief seconds her little world had been turned upside down. The beeper clipped to her waistband vibrated as she shooed Phillip out the door. She depressed the button, memorized the number, and dialed.

A policewoman answered. Niki asked to speak with Michael Edwards. He was apparently expecting her call, and she was immediately put through.

"Dr. Hamilton." Coleman's deep baritone invaded her ear. "We've got Jimmy Johnson in custody.''

"Who?''

"James Johnson, better known as Quaalude. It took some time finding him, but we did it. He had a very interesting tale to tell. The story's been substantiated by a couple of his cronies. My colleagues are on their way to bring Dr. Jordan in.''

Niki's heart pounded. It felt like it would fly out of her chest. "Are you telling me Phillip's responsible for all that I've been put through?''

"Seems that way. Quaalude's allegations are pretty serious. He's looking to plea bargain, anything so we don't put him away and throw away the key. If his allegations pan out, Dr. Jordan's career as a doctor has ended. He'll be locked up for quite some time.''

Niki hung up and raced for the bathroom. This time the nausea was real and had little to do with a possible pregnancy.

Chapter 26

Niki emerged from the bathroom several minutes later. The nausea was under control, but in its place lay hollowness. The overall numbness she attributed to shock. Too much had happened this evening for her to digest. Just the thought of being pregnant had knocked her for a loop. To top that off, Phillip was about to be brought in for questioning. It certainly sounded as though he'd deliberately set out to hurt her.

Niki couldn't stand being in the hospital for another minute. She couldn't start rounds when Phillip was about to be picked up. Eventually the news would spread like wildfire and everyone would be staring at her, speculating. She'd find another doctor to fill in, needed to.

Pleading illness, Niki was able to get one of the interns to cover. Knowing she could not possibly cope with a medical emergency—she had her own—she turned her beeper down and tossed it in her bag. Unheard of and out of character, but necessary. She was sick of it all. Sick of playing doctor—at least for tonight.

Spotting a handful of reporters still keeping vigilance out front, she used the back door to exit the property. Cary would not have left for the airport yet, she hoped. Numbed from the shock of the evening's events, she drove slowly, almost lethargically, but the moment she pulled into her driveway and saw the dark house, she knew Cary had already left. Niki slid down in the driver's seat and rested her head against the steering wheel.

"Can nothing go right?"

Little in her life ever had. She'd promised Cary she'd meet him at the airport around nine. They'd planned on having a bite to eat and saying a proper good-bye. Already she'd used valuable time getting over here, but if she hurried, maybe she could catch him in the boarding lounge.

The drive to the airport took an hour and twenty-five minutes. An accident had traffic backed up, and she thumped the steering wheel, uttering oaths that would make a sailor flinch. When she was able to get out of the congestion, there was little time left. Niki parked the car in short-term parking and flew through the terminal, following the UNITED AIRLINES signs.

She had to see Cary. He, more than anyone, understood what she'd been put through. She was still undecided whether she would mention the possible pregnancy.

Niki ignored the PASSENGERS ONLY sign, acted confidently, and tried sauntering through the security checkpoint. She was greeted by a loud beep and was further aggravated when the female security guard insisted on patting her down. After several annoying minutes of being frisked, she was able to reclaim her purse and move on.

It was going on ten o'clock by then. Niki flew through the terminal, stopping briefly to check the monitors and see what Cary's departure gate was. His flight was delayed, thank God. Even so, all that racing around had made her feet hurt, and the gate was clear across the concourse.

Niki came to a skidding stop in front of a lounge packed with passengers. Travelers stood in long lines waiting to be checked in. She scanned the area, looking for Cary. Not seeing him, she entered, sidestepping bulging backpacks and odd-sized hand luggage. He must be waiting for her at one of the many restaurants she had passed.

"Looking for someone?" Cary's rich voice came from behind her.

Niki turned and hurled herself into his arms. The tears she'd held back flowed steadily.

"Hush, baby, hush," Cary said, hugging her closely. "This isn't the end."

She twined her arms around his neck and kissed his face all over. Several passengers stared at them openly, some shaking their heads. What a spectacle they must be making.

"I was worried when you didn't show up," Cary admitted. "First I called the hospital. Then I tried beeping you. What took you so long?" He gathered his garment bag and took her hand. "We have at least another half hour before boarding. I'm a member of the Red Carpet Club. We'll order a drink, sit and talk."

Niki explained about muting the beeper and tossing it into her purse. She told him about her journey home and about being further delayed by an accident.

"And that's it?" He shot her a skeptical look. "You're usually not the weepy type. What's really going on?" Placing his free arm around her waist, he led her into the club.

They found an area less populated than the rest. The only disturbance was the soft drone of a TV. Most passengers nursed drinks; others dozed. Mindful that she might be pregnant, Niki declined the glass of wine Cary ordered and opted for club soda.

"It's not like you plan going back to work," he said.

"That's true."

"Suppose you tell me everything that happened tonight. It's clear you're shaken up. I suspect that has nothing to do with my leaving."

He was right on the money with her, another reason she loved him. Niki told him about returning Coleman's call, and about Quaalude's having been picked up, about how he'd supposedly ratted Phillip out, and now Phillip was being brought in for questioning.

"I knew that man was a snake," Cary muttered, slamming his balled fist into his curled palm. "Think about it, Niki. He's had your telephone and beeper number from the beginning. He's had access to your medical files and could easily change anything he wanted to. He was supposed to check on your apartment. He had your key. He probably hired Quaalude to do his dirty work, sending you hate mail, making those calls. That would explain the quality of those letters. The misspellings. He would have hired him to do the breaking and entering. That's why the earring was found in your backyard."

"But why? What would be his motive?"

In answer to her question, the talk show on television was abruptly interrupted.

"A prominent San Francisco doctor has been arrested tonight for allegedly supplying a dealer with drugs," a popular newscaster reported. "Those close to Dr. Phillip Jordon describe him as an upstanding citizen . . ."

A photo of Phillip being led away in handcuffs filled the screen. Cary raced over to turn the volume up, while Niki remained unable to move. Phillip had been her friend from the first day he'd joined the hospital staff. Why would he do this to her?

The reporter continued. "While in the middle of his rounds at San Francisco General, Dr. Jordan was picked up by police officers and is currently being held at the Golden Gate precinct. Earlier today, Jimmy Johnson, alias Quaalude, a notorious drug lord, was arrested on charges of breaking and entering. Johnson had an extensive history of arrests for larceny and fraud. Police say it did not take much for Johnson to immediately finger Jordan. Sources close to the investigation speculate Dr. Jordan had a drug habit and might be in cahoots with other prominent hospital officials. There's talk of kickbacks and corruption within the administration. More arrests are allegedly slated for tomorrow. Dr. Jordan's lawyer insists he's innocent."

The camera panned to the streets of San Francisco. Patients Niki recognized as being from the clinic vied to get on TV. They told tales of witnessing transactions between Quaalude and Phillip, of Quaalude's bragging about how he could get his hands on any kind of drug, mentioning he'd been paid handsomely to break into another doctor's home, of Phillip being called the Medicine Man.

Finally, pictures of Phillip's two impressive homes flashed across the screen. They came complete with tennis courts and guest cottages. His speedboat and two-seater plane added to the image of a man living large. Speculation followed as to how he had been able to afford all of it.

Niki hadn't known about the plane or the sprawling second home in the Caribbean. She listened, mesmerized by what the reporter had to say, realizing she hadn't known Phillip at all.

"This still doesn't explain why he did what he did to me," she said to Cary.

"You once dated him, didn't you?" His fingers kneaded

the tense muscles of her back. She would kill for a glass of wine, but couldn't have one.

"Yes. But it didn't work out. We went back to being friends. He seemed OK with that."

"Have you considered your hospital administrator, Jacoby something?"

"Glenn."

"Your contracts administrator and Phillip might be in this together. Phillip may have been deeply resentful of you; maybe he felt that your relationship with Glenn put him out of the running for the highfalutin position of Chief of Staff Pediatrics. You were the more popular physician. You achieved some modicum of success. You were depicted as championing the underdog. You'd gotten all the press. You were the devoted doctor who put patients first and stood up to HMOs. If these guys were getting kickbacks, your sense of integrity and fair play stood in their way. Also remember the advocacy groups loved you.

"As Phillip got deeper into drugs, his life began to fall apart. He was desperate for money. He had a high standard of living to maintain. A habit. His only hope was to discredit you. I'll bet you anything he and that Bill person encouraged the Eldridges to sue."

"They wouldn't dare."

'I wouldn't put anything past those men."

Niki couldn't believe she'd been this naive. Phillip had always been ambitious. She'd never thought of ambition as a bad trait in a person. But Bill was equally as ambitious, while Glenn had always come across as weak and easily led.

Cary got up and picked up his garment bag. "Time to go. At least it's over with. You can sleep peacefully now." He offered her his hand.

She should feel relieved. For the first time in a long

time, she would be safe in her own home. Instead, she thought about how awful it would be to sleep alone. She'd put in years of hard work studying to become a doctor, but no amount of books had prepared her for this. Had all the years been worth it? In the end, what did she have to show for it? An empty town house. A tranquillity garden seemed poor consolation.

Overnight, her priorities had somehow shifted. She'd always loved medicine, but deep down she'd come to love Cary more. Tomorrow she would find out conclusively whether she was carrying his child. She'd already made up her mind that if the results were positive, she would carry his baby to term, regardless of whether he chose to play a role or not. It was no fun being a single parent, but she did have an advantage. She had the desire and the money to raise a child right.

An announcement got their attention. "Flight seventy-eight to Newark now boarding at gate number eight." Cary's flight.

"I've got to go," he said, already moving toward the exit and bringing her with him. "Let's plan on your visiting the next time you're off."

Niki could only nod. A lump the size of a jumbo jet invaded her throat. She allowed him to lead her to the departure gate. Passengers were trickling on board. Now or never. *Should I tell him? There's nothing concrete to tell. But what if he walks out of my life, never to be heard from again? He wouldn't do that. But what if he does?*

She took a deep breath. Cary's arm tightened around her waist, bringing her closer. "It's been awful for you, but it's over, finally. Tomorrow we'll find out more. I love you, baby."

"So you say." She could barely talk.

"I love you so much I'm willing to close my business

and uproot my son. If being with you means moving to San Francisco, then that's what we'll do. We were meant to be together."

A declaration like that couldn't go unanswered. The lump was reduced to the size of a four-seater plane.

"Passengers holding seats twenty-five and higher may now board the aircraft," the announcer boomed.

Countdown time. Cary would have to board soon.

"So what do you say?" He had command of her chin, tilting her head back, forcing her to look at him.

"I say . . . I say . . . I may be having your baby."

"What!" Cary swung her off her feet, yelling for all to hear. "You're having my baby?"

The people on queue applauded.

"It's possible," Niki said, more quietly now.

"Then there'll be no argument from you. I'm moving to San Francisco and we're getting married."

"It took a shotgun to do this."

"Hardly a shotgun."

Tears stung the back of her lids as he kissed her soundly. When she came up for a breath she blinked at him. "If anyone should move, I should. Once I'm officially cleared of wrongdoing I'm on a plane. You've got hospitals in New Jersey, don't you?"

"A ton of them. What about your career? Your home? You shouldn't be expected to give all that up."

"I don't consider it giving anything up, not when my best friends live in New Jersey."

"Who might those be? Kim?"

"Actually I meant my two favorite men, Brett and Cary."

"In that order?"

"Mmmm."

"Final boarding call for flight seventy-eight to Newark," the announcer brayed.

"I want to marry you, girl," Cary shouted as the microphone went silent.

"Yes," Niki managed, wrapping her hands around his neck. "Yes."

The two remaining passenger service agents giggled. "You go, girl," one said.

"I love you, babe. I can't live without you," Cary swore. "Our Brett needs a little sister or brother." He kissed her hard.

"When did you know?" Niki managed.

"The moment you opened your mouth and said hello. I loved that sultry British accent. I loved you."

"You're going to miss your flight," one of the gate agents said, tapping Cary on the shoulder.

"What flight?"

"What flight?" Niki repeated, leaning in for another heart-stopping kiss.

Dear Reader:

A Reason To Love is the sequel to my debut novel *Remembrance*. Many of you may remember beautiful Onika (Niki) Hamilton, described as a half-British, half-African combination of good looks and amazing brain. If you don't, this may be the perfect opportunity to pick up a copy of *Remembrance* and become acquainted with the four Mount Merrimack classmates.

Niki's story niggled at me, demanding to be told. Despite a succession of personal challenges, *A Reason To Love* was finally born. Perhaps you will tell me if I have done a convincing job of showing you that love can be found in the most unexpected places.

I enjoy hearing from readers. Please feel free to e-mail me at mkinggamble@aol.com or visit my new Web site at http://romantictales.com/MarciaKing-Gamble/index.html. Be sure to sign my guest book. You may also write me at:

P.O. Box 25143
Tamarac, FL 33320

Please include a stamped, self addressed envelope.

My sincere thanks for your support and for letting me know how much you enjoy my stories. You enable me to continue to do the thing I enjoy most—write.

May you be blessed,
Marcia King-Gamble

ABOUT THE AUTHOR

Marcia was born on the island of St. Vincent in the West Indies. At age fifteen she relocated to the United States and has since lived in New York, New Jersey and Seattle. Currently, she resides in Florida. Marcia is a graduate of Elmira College and holds a degree in psychology and theater.

A world traveler, Marcia has spent time in the Far East and in exotic parts like Saudi Arabia and Istanbul. She successfully juggles a second career and is an executive with a major cruise line.

Two of Marcia's books, *Eden's Dream* and *Illusions of Love*, were voted Top Picks of the month by *Romantic Times*. She has completed five novels and two novellas.

Do You Have the Entire Collection of MARCIA KING-GAMBLE?